A CHILD OF PROMISE

BY MARSHALL THOMPSON

Order this book online at www.trafford.com
or email orders@trafford.com

Most Trafford titles are also available at major online book retailers.

Printed in the United States of America.

ISBN: 978-1-4120-4241-3 (sc)
ISBN: 978-1-4251-9656-1 (e)

Trafford rev. 07/27/2012

www.trafford.com

North America & international
toll-free: 1 888 232 4444 (USA & Canada)
phone: 250 383 6864 • fax: 812 355 4082

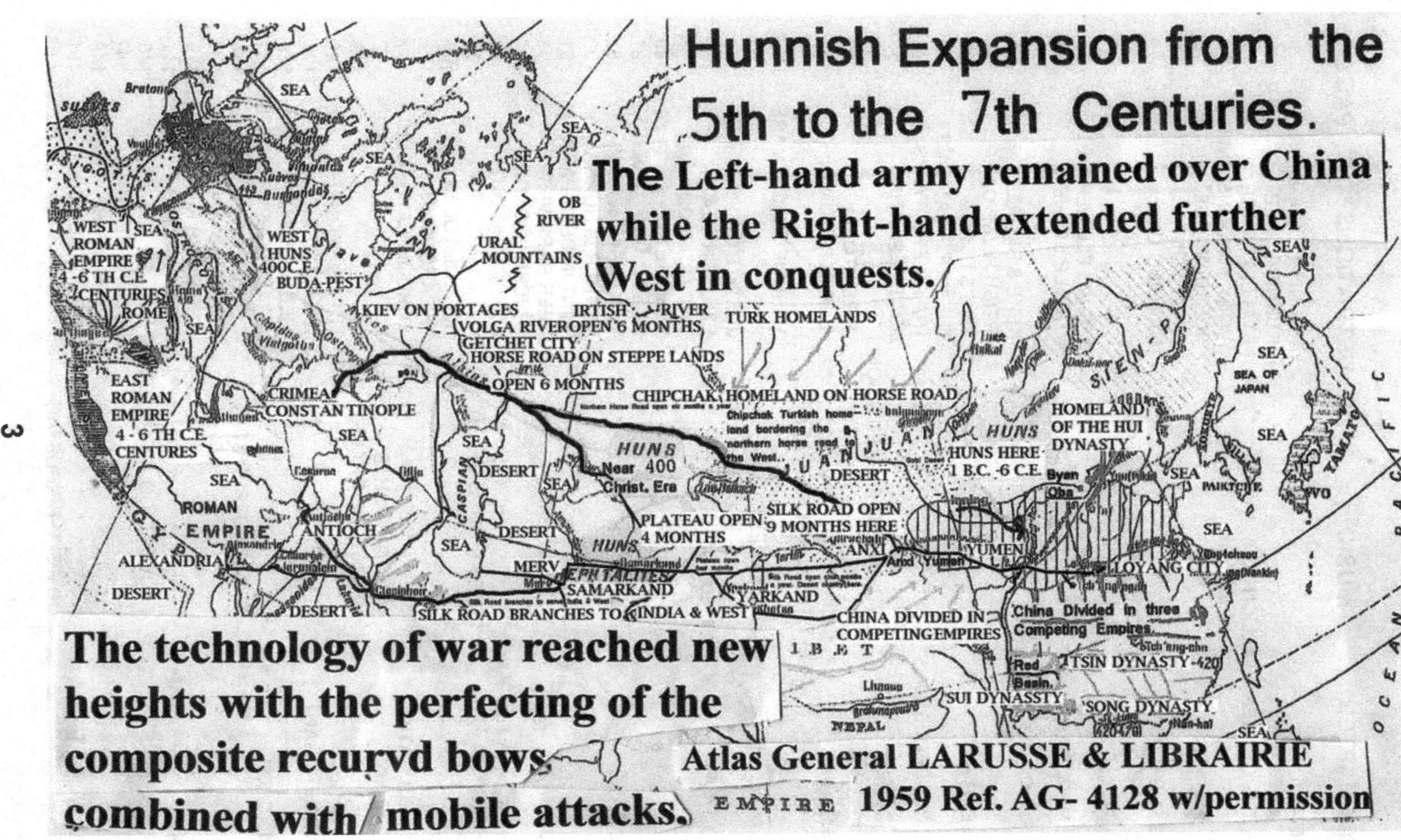
Hunnish Expansion from the
5th to the 7th Centuries.
The Left-hand army remained over China
while the Right-hand extended further
West in conquests.
The technology of war reached new
heights with the perfecting of the
composite recurvd bows
combined with mobile attacks.
Atlas General LARUSSE & LIBRAIRIE
1959 Ref. AG- 4128 w/permission
WEST ROMAN EMPIRE 4 -6 TH C.E. CENTURIES
ROME
WEST HUNS 400C.E.
BUDA-PEST
OB RIVER
URAL MOUNTAINS
KIEV ON PORTAGES
VOLGA RIVER
IRTISH RIVER OPEN 6 MONTHS
GETCHET CITY
HORSE ROAD ON STEPPE LANDS
OPEN 6 MONTHS
TURK HOMELANDS
EAST ROMAN EMPIRE 4 - 6 TH C.E. CENTURES
CRIMEA
CONSTANTINOPLE
CHIPCHAK HOMELAND ON HORSE ROAD
Chipchak Turkish homeland bordering the northern horse road to the West.
HUNS
Near 400 Christ. Era
HOMELAND OF THE HUI DYNASTY
HUNS HERE 1 B.C. -6 C.E.
DESERT
CASPIAN
ROMAN EMPIRE
ANTIOCH
ALEXANDRIA
PLATEAU OPEN 4 MONTHS
SILK ROAD OPEN 9 MONTHS HERE
ANXI
YUMEN
LOYANG CITY
MERV
EPHTALITES
SAMARKAND
YARKAND
SILK ROAD BRANCHES TO INDIA & WEST
CHINA DIVIDED IN COMPETING EMPIRES
China Divided in three Competing Empires.
TSIN DYNASTY -420
SUI DYNASSTY
SONG DYNASTY
NEPAL
SEA OF JAPAN
YAMATO
WO
PACIFIC OCEAN
SEA

TABLE OF CONTENTS

> - - - - - - >   > - - - - - - >   > - - - - - - >

DEDICATION

I owe a debt of tribute to Charles Lamb, author of The March of the Barbarians and also The March of Moscow. To him, I owe my early interest in Central Asia.

Many friends have read, corrected, advised, and helped shape this work. Especially: Joy Stuart Martel, Suzanne McGillivary, Margaret Ryan, Lois Campbell and others. Eileen Dauphinee contributed five illustrations. A few were taken from miniatures and the rest are my creation. The music too, apart from a few borrowings is largely my attempt to arrive at original possibilities. To all of my helpers I owe a debt of gratitude.

My thanks to the many workers of Trafford Publishing for the help and encouragement both practical and technical to learn the difficult task of preparing the manuscript to make a printing master.

There are throughout the countries of Russia, Iran, Moldavia, Ukraine, Kazakhstan, Uzbekistan, Sinkiang Province and in the Caucuses Mountains historical sites, graveyards and church ruins as well as remnants of tribal people that demonstrate a wide spread historical Christian presence in spite of nationalist and religious pressures to be something else. To them I dedicate this effort to make their faithfulness known.

Especially to Hazel Fay Vincent Thompson, my wife, who frequently had to do without a husband who was otherwise occupied; my love and thanks.

To Yesu Cristus, I owe my life and inspiration to research and write the epic of this tribe.

MARSHALL B. THOMPSON JR.

HISTORIC FOCUS

The historic period includes the end of the fourth and start of the fifth centuries. The world was threatened by technological advances that would shift the power, safety, locations and the future of its inhabitants.

The self-designated Left Hand Hordes of Huns are poised around the loop of the Yellow River of China. The Right Hand Hordes of Western Huns, holding the Ukraine and the Hungarian Plains, press into Europe. Poised above India, the White Huns are taking lands in what became Afghan country. Behind them, Turkish tribes and others gobble up the leftover pieces of land and goods. Bulgars, Tartars, Avars, Chipchaks, Uygurs, Kazars and nameless others press on their yielding world. Life at that time held delights and horrors difficult for us to know or share, yet we easily understand their tensions and triumphs. This is your chance to share a new look at a world of long ago. Technology and tactics had again changed the world and the balance of power. How long would their victories last?

The book is designed for reading pleasure as well as instruction in ways far different from those of the modern world. The life and vision of a versatile, Arctic people culturally adapting to their changing physical, social and technical environments with astonishing success should inspire us to attempt the same. Equilibrium and level-headed choices in the midst of radical changes are admirable and seem to be connected with vision for a good life for all. 'Where there is no vision the people perish.' An ancient insight of the wise should inspire us to open our minds to that possibility for all people. The source of that vision will be conceived differently, according to varied traditions, but surely those varieties of ideas cannot work deliberate harm to a neighbor. This is precisely where the rub and scratch of daily life comes. This is where success or failure of the vision is fulfilled.

Read and enjoy fiction placed in historic situations.

Marshall B. Thompson Jr.

NOTE: The foreign words have been modified for English speakers. You will not find them in their dictionaries as spelled here. The letter G is always hard, as in gift. Most other differences have been modified into English spelling and phonetics. MT

AUTHOR'S REMARKS

I hope that the printing of this book of fiction placed in situations of historic importance will supply an escape from the pressures of our technical world. It is relaxing yet stimulating to face the seemingly easier choices of other, more distant days when different external problems occupied the human mind. The perennial, internal human desires fuel the drama to help us identify with the characters' feelings and reactions. To avoid tedium in an age of space-warping speed, I have narrowed considerably the ratio of time/distance in the travels.

Writing this adventure story was a joy and a labor of love, but like many loves it had it's high and low points. The characters developed with the events and their basic heart values. The book was started in 1991 and has suffered periodic neglect from then till now. Although it was finished in about four years with its music, I lacked courage and cash to publish. The pictures, largely my own work, took longer.

I have taken liberties in order to help the reader. I have used modern geographical names. I have used ethnic names that came into being at a more modern date in order to identify possible descendant peoples. In special cases, where a particular custom is unknown or still controversial, I have used an older or clear neighboring practice, and sometimes I choose to take sides in such disagreements. Political and social attitudes of the novel's characters and their statements are not always those of the author. They must answer for them. M.T.

RUNNING FREE

PEOPLE, PLACES & PLOTS IN CHAPTER 1

Cha vush: means sergeant, he is a leader, a man of forty.
Day'day: an ancient warrior and traditionalist.
Er'kan: Leader of a Chipchak band, grazers living in yurts.
Gooch: a leader of marauders that attack caravans.
Ke'ke: a Goth, enslaved and being carried to the East.
On'basha: corporal Kansu, a warrior and tribe member.
On'der: a young trader from the oasis city of E'peck Kent.
Vash'tie: a girl of the Alani, a Christian slave trained in Persia.
Yuz'basha: a young lieutenant of the Chipchak tribe.

GLOSSARY HELP: (English phonetics with accent markings)
bar'ish: peace; good will; tranquility.
bey: is used as sir or mister in direct address after a name.
boo' roo-ya gel': come here; to this place; come to me.
E'-peck Kent: Silk City; a city dedicated to trade with China.
ev'it: agreement; yes; alright.
gel: come; approach.
Tan'ra: the benevolent creator; who is unpredictable.
Tan'ra o-voo-lure': Praise God; Thank God; praises be.
tesh-eck-koor': thank you; thanks.
ya-ya soos': now hush; quiet down; silence; shush.
yurt: a felted, willow framed tent, whose roof is made in the shape of a walnut half-shell.

1 THE GOLDEN STALLION

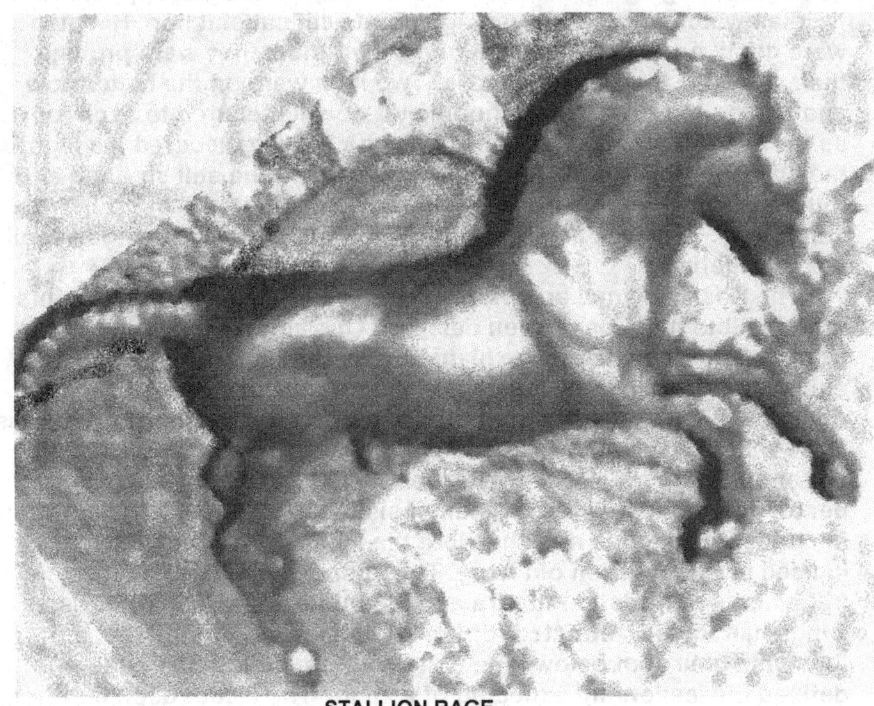

STALLION RAGE

A powerful straw-colored stallion running at full gallop was the first indication of trouble. His tawny hide shone suddenly gold as he turned the bend in the road and the noon summer sun glinted from his back. A golden horse, running with only a halter round his neck to indicate that he had ever been subservient to man, appeared. Pride, strength, and freedom, showed in the arch of the neck and the high-held tail, blowing in the wind of his speed.

The guard on Sentinel Rock, Chavush, waved one signal flag and immediately another. The message was "running; intercept."

Yuzbasha, the lieutenant, ordered the men to mount, which they did speedily; they had spent the morning waiting. The promise of action and excitement sped them up the road beyond the sentinel. They could hear the hooves of a great horse.

"It's a stallion. Spread out and net him," shouted a second guard at closer range. A few men brought out partridge nets. The men spread as the stallion, shining yellow, rounded a rock. Several men lunged for the halter while others threw their nets. The stallion neighed and reared, throwing off those nets and pawing and kicking at the men who tried to touch him. He wheeled and would have made off, when an old man came down a side trail with a noose on the end of a long pole. This he neatly placed over the stallion's head and tightened the noose. Rearing again, the stallion stridently voiced his opposition.

Erkan watched from his vantage point with satisfaction. His men were good, and, though not all of his own tribe, they were proving their worth by their effectiveness. Two men were on the halter now and two on the rope while a hobble was being secured to each foot as the stallion plunged and pawed the air. Having secured his legs, they brought the golden fury to the ground, but he still strained and fought, panting out his challenge. The men gathered around admiringly. This was a horse in a million, worth more than they would see in a lifetime.

The Khan frowned and bit his lip. The caravan was to arrive this morning, but must have been delayed. This animal must have come from that source, the only explanation for the halter. He wanted this animal for his own, but was being paid for the escort and protection of the caravan. The messenger had assured him that the caravan was large with slaves and goods and would pay well. He was a man of honor and was proud of always keeping his word. His small black beard, graying temples and clean, if simple vestments, lent dignity to his pride. Around his neck he wore the medallion of his office, an incised swan, cut from old ivory. The source, mammoth's tusks, lay frozen in permafrost on tundra and mountains. The king of birds, wings half folded, retracted for landing and neck outstretched towards some spot below. The written words around the edge defined the leadership expected of a khan. 'The leader decides when and where to descend, for the good of all, in order to feed his flock.' Khan Erkan of the Chipchaks, protector of caravans, fully made up his mind and began to give orders.

"Onbasha, take one man with you to the yurts. There is a mare of mine in heat, a dapple gray, tied behind my yurt. Bring her here. Keep this one tied, but let them nuzzle before leading her away toward the yurts. Then untie his legs and the two men who stay here with him and the two with the mare will ride with them. The mare will be coy and flee towards the herd. Let him take her if he can, but don't take him into camp. Leave our restricted lovers in the birch grove in the hills above the yurts."

The assigned men grinned at the astuteness of the Khan and nodded vigorously as their friends joked about being assigned to a wedding party. They would be home with their wives before the others, strongly inspired. A few joking threats were made about sticking to their own yurt and not looking at others. Most of it was said in fun. One of the four, the old one – Day-day -- spoke up,

"*Bey*, Sir," he said, "I have such a mare as well."

"Excellent," replied Erkan, "but I will have the colt. We will arrange the details later; proceed as planned."

The weakened troop moved off to find the caravan. Normally, they waited well inside the borders of their recognized territory, but with what had just occurred and the possibility of interruption of their plans, they moved on.

Out of sight of Sentinel Rock, below a hill in a large wood, they found two dead men with arrows in their bodies, part of the caravan's security guards. Each caravan had its own guards from the point of departure as well as the guards of the escorting tribe, who were paid for the right of transit. Without home security guards, the temptation to treachery might have overcome the tribesmen. Erkan stroked his gray-touched goatee and surveyed the possible courses of action.

"Strip them, but keep each man's goods separate. We may have to return them to relatives or owners. Spread out and give a shout when you have a trail." He wondered if it was an ambush or treachery.

This was a rich haul. He would profit by whatever had happened. Being located at the north passes on the long but faster steppe road to China, there was much less traffic than southern desert routes and less profit for the tribes just south of the Altai Mountains. Here, there was less opportunity to obtain the coveted artifacts of Rome and China; India and Persia. But today, Tanra – God -- had smiled upon him. As rescuer, salvager or posse; he had already come out ahead.

Yuzbasha signaled near the woods where more bodies were found. Suddenly, from the woods stepped a young, expensively dressed oasis merchant, holding a large jade handled knife.

"*Bar'ish*," he called. "Peace, the caravan was attacked by Persian marauders. Are you the Chipchak guard who were hired? We need your help."

"*Eh'vit*," Yuzbasha replied, "Yes, we waited and decided to seek you out."

"*Tan'ra ya ovulur*, God be praised, you came," the man replied.

IVORY SWAN INSIGNIA (PAGE10)

"There are wounded among us. Please help us. The robbers are still about, fighting behind the stream and woods. I'm Onder of *E'peck Kent.*" He turned a bit and staggered as an arrow buried itself in the left back shoulder blade where someone had shot for the heart, but gotten bone instead. As he slowly slumped toward the ground, a woman screamed and two young girls rushed out to drag him to cover. The whistle of arrows sounded. Launched simultaneously they thudded, striking home. The arrivals were under attack.

The ambush was from a small ridge to the right of the wood, farther from the Chipchaks, so few men were touched on the first volley. Persians favored the heavier, closer weapons: sword and dagger; lance and shield. Fanatically brave in battle, the southerners, fire-worshipers, would sweep all before them in a charge.

The Chipchak band, ululating the war cry, urged their horses back the way they had come. Out of bow range, they turned and swept toward the back of the ridge. Every man armed his short, recurved, bone-reinforced bow. Splitting into two groups, a few on the wood side of the grassy dry ridge and the rest behind it, they poured down on the attackers.

Those on the wood side, led by Yuzbasha, were purposely a bit later than the group led by Erkan, who was to root them out of the entrenched position. If any ran for the woods, they would be caught by the second group.

The band's tactics were based on rapid fire, rushing attacks. In their opinion only fools stood and fought as did the southern people with their vast armies in trials of strength that spoke more of wealth and resources than bravery and intelligence.

The Persians were caught in a file, huddled behind their ridge. Their backs were exposed to the incoming band. To run was to be cut down as if they were animals in a hunt.

Hurriedly, they turned, massed together, their shields before them, to confront the attack. But in spite of heavy body armor, the steady stream of arrows halved their numbers. Those few bandits, scattered too far away from the main body, never reached their horses or the woods. Many of the horses and captured pack animals were swept up by the Chipchaks in their charge, for the Persians could not use the bow, mount a horse, and protect themselves with the shield at the same time.

Fortunately for the marauders, the Chipchak attackers were fewer than the shield ring, which dug itself in on the ridge, the men crouching behind their defenses. The Chipchaks made a second pass at a greater distance and then called off any further action because their arrow supply was getting dangerously low. The situation had turned into a stalemate.

Yuzbasha did not make a second sweep back up the ridge with Erkan. He and his few men entered the woods waving and shouting,

"*Bar'ish*, peace, we must withdraw quickly; everyone alive, come to us." A few merchants ran hesitantly from cover. Again the leader shouted "We are your guards and helpers; your goods and lives are safe with us. *Gel* - come, quickly."

More drivers, guards, merchants and women started to appear and a babble of languages conveyed the message and called friends and helpers from hiding to action. Some pack animals were collected and driven from the side of the woods farthest from the ridge.

While a few of his men started to strip the dead, Yuzbasha set the remaining few in line to stand between the line of struggling merchants and the ridge to watch for a charge. If the Persians recovered enough to make a foot charge behind shields, the band could not stand and the slower of the men and pack animals would be taken.

The sight of even part of the caravan's escape had rallied the marauder's commander. He was shouting now, at his men,

"Will you have it all or only a small part? I, Gooch, promised you riches, but you must fight for it. These tribesmen will not stand; they will run away as fast as they came."

Persian was a language of trade and commerce of the Central Asian cities and therefore, understood by many of the tribes. So, no one was in doubt as to what the commander wished as he tried to rally these bandits from many tribes and cities, whipping them into a frenzy of greed and anger.

Erkan rode up to Yuzbasha and stationed his men also between the retreating merchants and the ridge.

"They will massacre the wounded, so get them to horse," he ordered. The extra horses taken from the Persians were mounted up and sent ahead of the loaded merchant beasts. At that moment the extended Persian shield wall came over the ridge. It was a tactic learned from the Greeks of Alexander's days. There should have been a line of archers behind to put the enemy under flights of arrows and to discourage counterattack on the flanks. However, the marauders had been too reduced for anything so elaborate; they were angry men feeling cheated of their hard-won prey. Behind them a small group of wounded bandits sat on the ridge and lobbed a few arrows from wooden bows at the line of horses.

The horse line skittered, but waited. A few more Chipchaks rode up, their horses loaded with goods taken from the dead or fatally wounded. Several had gathered spent arrows and distributed them to their tribesmen. They knew that there would be time for two volleys and then flight. They would aim for exposed feet, legs, arms and sides on the first flight and then any good target with the second.

Erkan waited till they were just in spear-throwing distance for he doubted they would risk their weapons. Just as he gave order to fire, however, about half the wall launched their javelins and drew their swords. With a rush they tried to close the distance, shouting defiance. The arrows cut gaps in the charging line of men.

The nervous horses plunged ahead and the second arrow was sped from fleeing horseback. Several horsemen were hit, caught and skewered. The Persian losses were heavy. The wounded sprinkled the battleground.

Yuzbasha's small line fled toward the wood and circled back over the field just covered by the shield wall and caught a number of marauders with their backs exposed. With that, they left the scene of conflict, calmly collecting spent arrows as they went.

The Persians had no strength to follow, but managed to catch a number of merchant stragglers, still in the woods, too busy collecting their wealth and animals to escape capture. Most of the marauder band, however, stayed on the field of battle lest the Chipchak's return.

The Chipchaks had no intention of returning to the field until they consolidated their gains. They had removed most of their slightly wounded, and took what spoils had fallen to them and ran.

A rear guard formed after the pack animals, and a messenger was sent ahead to the yurts to prepare the clan. Reinforcements, mostly old men and boys, would come in case they were followed. Persians were known to be tenacious and vengeful. The gains were too large to put at risk.

The scattering of merchants shepherded their goods and animals. Wounded were carried or mounted and helped along the way. Their complaints and curses were loud. They seemed to show no gratitude for the salvation of their lives and part of their goods. They grumbled continually about wasted money for protection that arrived too late, but they lowered their voices when a clansman rode near.

The two girls supported the young oasis merchant between them, struggling with his weight, the arrow shaft broken short, but still in the shoulder. The girls were young, one scarcely sixteen. She was blue-eyed with wild, blond hair, but hearty and stout. The other slender girl had shining brown eyes and black hair braided neatly, perhaps twenty years old. They struggled some, but managed to help him, though loaded with some bundles on their backs. No one offered to help them as all struggled to put distance between themselves and the brigands.

When it seemed safe, the pace changed and the Chipchak urged the remnant into a tighter herd. Yuzbasha passed the two girls and stopped to look more closely. Their clothes were worn, but seemed to be of good stout make. They were in the style of the Volga River Huns. Their dialect also, was Hunnish. Yuzbasha found he could not take his eyes off the tall one. He was abrupt and angry.

"We have far to go; you are too slow. If he can't walk, you must find a horse." He rode off before they could answer, but stopped after a few lengths to stare at the ground. He did not know how to make amends, but he wanted to go back. As he turned his horse, he found himself looking into the eyes of the tall, black-haired girl. She held a salvaged bridle and bit toward him in her hands as if she intended to put it on him as she spoke in the softest of voices,

"I am ready, where is the horse?" The weight of the youth dragged the blond down as he fell. Yuzbasha was both mystified and irritated at the same time. Chipchak women were dutiful when it came to authority and commands, but this tall one seemed to challenge him to put up or shut up. He blinked his eyes away from her and swept the column of struggling humanity. One of his mounted men was leading a plunging, kicking black mare taken from the Persians. His eyes gleamed with delight. "*Boo roo ya gel,*" he commanded, "come here." As the man obeyed, Yuzbasha motioned him to, "mount behind me." The man did so without touching ground. Yuzbasha handed the reins of both horses to the girl who took them and sidestepped to the black's side. Its head went up and ears back as she put a hand on the mare's neck.

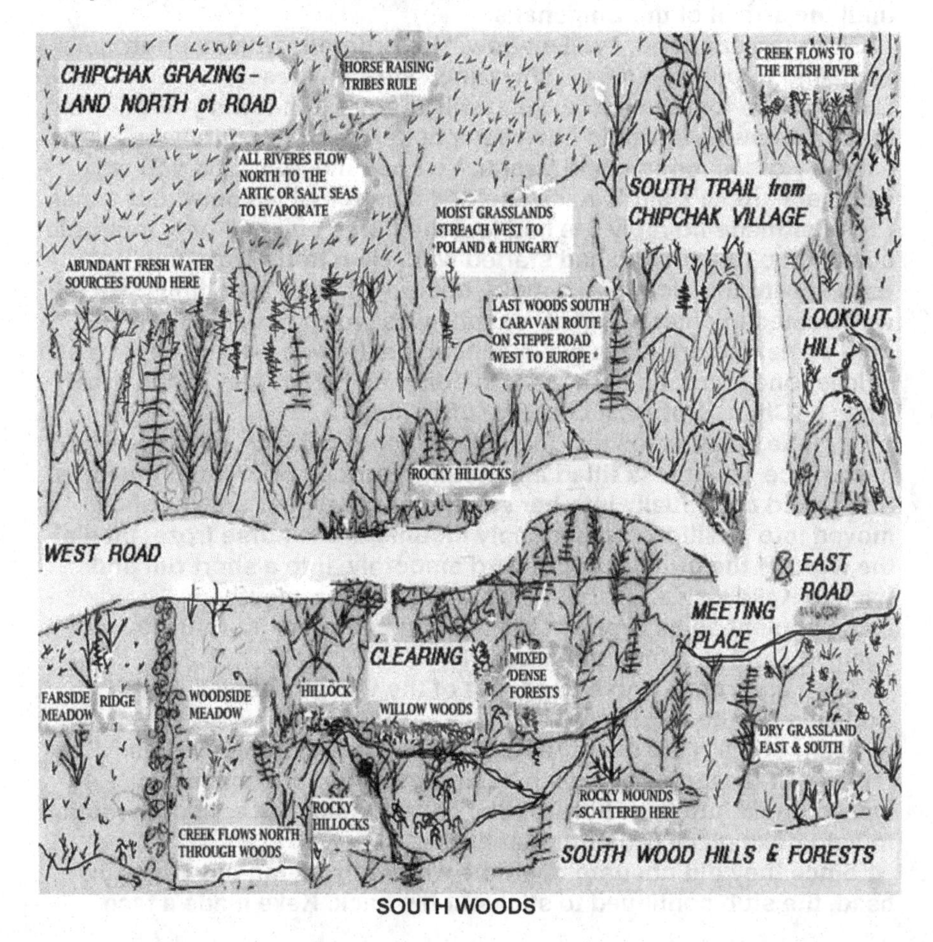

SOUTH WOODS

"*Ya, ya, soos*," she whispered, "*Ya, ya, soos*: quiet, don't be afraid!" The black plunged her powerful head up and down and quivered. Then she stood quiet. "Keke, *gel*," She called, "Keke, come," to her waiting friend. The blond ran quickly to take the reins from her friend's hands and led the tribesman's horse away to the side of the wounded man. Her lip curled as she looked at Onder.

"I do this for Vashtie, because she says we should show mercy. I think we would be better off if we left you behind and be free of you." He turned his face up and gave her a disapproving frown.

"One rarely hears of mercy among the pagan Goths; you may learn something useful if you listen to Vashtie." He sighed. His world now lay in disarray; all his plans in shatters. He moistened his dry lips. Perhaps it would have been better not to survive the Persian attack. He had led the defense and retreat into the woods after the brigands had enveloped the head of the caravan and when the remaining guards had retreated, he had rallied the caravan to hold until the arrival of the Chipchaks.

"Give me your hand; I will sit now." He ordered. With an effort he managed to pull up and sit, shivering with weakness.

"You have lost the horse; what will you do? What will you offer the Emperor now? We would have been better off not to purchase all the extras: Horses, goods, and Vashti. You had me. What did you want with her?" Keke's shrill voice scolded him, full of jealousy and anger.

Onder made no reply. He had lost the horse and had only four gold coins left of the fifty he had started with. He bitterly regretted his escape with the blond Keke, bold, outspoken, and avaricious; yet so well trained in entertainment. Vashtie was worth more than the ten gold coins, the price of a slave concubine. Now, he would have to sell at least one, perhaps both girls, to continue his journey to the great Khan of China. But what could he offer him?

Vashtie adjusted all the gear on the nervous black, making sure each piece of harness fitted and nothing rubbed or irritated the mare. She talked continually into her ear and soothed her. Slowly, she moved into position and suddenly mounted. The horse froze, then at the word of the girl moved forward smoothly, into a short run and back to Keke's side. Yuzbasha watched in open-mouthed astonishment as he dropped his man on to another surplus horse, again without touching the ground.

"You are from a horse band, not of the village people!" he exclaimed as he rode up.

"I am of the Alani near the Kafkas, the Caucasus Mountains." She replied, "My people have been destroyed by the Huns and incorporated into their horde." She dismounted with a smooth motion to help Keke place Onder on the horse.

Since they did not dare open the wound by taking out the arrow head, the stub continued to stick out his back. Keke made a face when ordered on behind him, but she obeyed Vashtie and held him up round the waist. The Goths at the western edge of the sea of grass could ride as well as anyone. She joined the column going up the hill. Yuzbasha drew near as Vashtie loaded more bundles on the black.

"You can stay at our yurt till your brother recovers. Mother is the medicine woman." He offered in dignified embarrassment. "I will stay with Chavush, our sergeant."

It was the girl's time to blush, "*Tesh eck koor*, thanks, he is my master, not my brother. I am not free," she confessed. The Chipchak war horn sounded behind them just as she rode away.

"Back, hurry!" Yuzbasha ordered. "Erkan bey called for help!"

FIRST CONTACT (PAGE 12)

PEOPLE, PLACES & PLOTS IN CHAPTER 2

Cha vush': the sergeant encounters satisfying duties.
Er'kan: the Khan finds his victory profitable.
Ke'ke: means one who stutters, but she sings and dances.
Mer'yen: medicine woman, mother of Yuzbasha and Maya.
Ma'ya: child of the medicine woman. She is busy helping.
On'der: caught in rebellion and disaster, he nurses his wounds and plans a way to win out.
Op'tal: means fool, an entertainer, and bear-master.
Pesh': flutist, juggler, a performer from India,
Se vim': the wife of Erkan, childless, barren and past thirty.
Vashtie: has a sick master and the wayward Keke to care for.
Yuz'basha: the lieutenant finds a source of fascination.

GLOSSARY HELP:

***ay'ran*: a drink made of thin yogurt and water.**
***bah-tan'iye*: a wool blanket or useful bed spread.**
***bosh'ooze-two-nay'*: I'm under your orders; I'll obey; immediately, sir.**
***goon eye-dune'*: a bright day; good day; hello; glad to see you.**
***i-yup'*: shameless; how disgusting; what a scandal; shameful!**
***iz-ah-niz'lee*: with your permission; I need to get on this.**
***sin'e beck-lair'um*: for you I wait; I always wait for you.**
***tom-mom'*: okay; It's alright; I agree.**
***yorgan*: a quilt stuffed with down or fluffed wool.**

DANCING GIRL

With fierce screams and war cries, Erkan and the rear guard launched a lightening attack that Yuzbasha and others reinforced as a second wave. A merchant had just emerged from hiding in the woods with his four pack animals loaded and fell into the hands of the Persians. Erkan tried to win captive packhorses back from the mounted marauder band, who were at the point of departure from the battlefield. The first wave got two mules and Yuzbasha another, but an arrow killed the animal; the tribe lost the pack, and the raiders retreated with a defensive show of success. The tribesmen retained the merchant and enough goods to feel victorious; both called a halt to further exchanges. Each group made for its camp as fast as possible.

The yurts were a welcome sight to the fatigued and wounded band of merchants and tribesmen. Word of their need and condition had preceded them. Food was cooking in every pot, and whole carcasses were being roasted at several large pits. The guests were welcomed and brought into the guests' yurts, where the afternoon winds would not chill them. There they rested, ate and warmed themselves, and each had a chance to relate his own struggles, narrow escapes and heroisms.

The wounded were tended by the local medicine woman, Meryen, and her plump little daughter, Maya. They were fed lighter foods and soup. Onder lay on his side, a *kilim* beneath him and a *yor'gan* over him. Heated rocks were placed near but not touching his body, as the medicine woman gave him willow bark tea and afterwards, would cut into his back to remove the arrow.

There was much oozing blood, and the wound was puffy and angry red around the edges. Having fortified him with all the alcoholic liquids and poppy possible, she started working the arrowhead out of the bone. Each movement of the shaft sent waves of pain through his body. It was considered a mark of bravery not to cry out, but groans escaped him. The arrowhead was deeply imbedded, and he fell into a stupor before it was out. The wound was then cleaned with willow tea, and some of the ragged edges of discolored flesh cut away, and the bleeding started again. Folds of felt were wrapped smoking around a smooth, white limestone rock that had been heated in the fire. It was not hot enough to break up the rock, but enough that the heat penetrate the felt and arrive at the bleeding surface of the opening. The wad was the size of the deep hole in the man's back. As the oozing blood soaked the felt, there was a moment of steam and smell. Onder suppressed a scream, writhed and mercifully fainted.

> - - - - - - >

The girl, Vashtie, sat by Onder and dozed as the first light entered through the open door in the yurt. In her hand she held her talisman, a bracelet of white pierced stones with a T attached at the tie. It was a gift from a wandering holy hermit she encountered at a wood on the Kuban River. She, again, vividly remembered the details. She was only twelve, and in shock, having been led all night tied on her horse. Her skin was chapped with tears and dirt on her face. Her clothes were blood-stained, in disarray. She could remember nothing but the sound of shrieks and cries of pain; her father's arrow-filled dead body lay before the house and the anguished cries of her mother inside the house as the men raped and killed her. The sound of her own cries had faded as she fainted from the pain.

As they stopped near the water, an old, gray-haired man with a serene, strong face came towards her. He opened his hands to show himself without weapons and walked to the side of her horse. He took the white-stone bracelet from his belt and extended it to her.

"Take this, child; it will protect you from evil." He urged her compassionately, "Have faith in my Master, the Cristus Yesu, and pray. God will hear you and build you up. He promises you a sure house, though shadowed by enemies, if you will it."

The Hun raiders frowned, angry, but ashamed. They had a superstitious dread of the anchorites, men who lived alone and ate God knows what to stay alive. They boldly served an invisible One of tangible power. The old one walked away and was lost without trace or trail in the woods.

After this they allowed her to dismount, wash face and clothes and change; then to ride on without being tied, only her horse was led. They did not molest her again. They took her down the Terik River to the Caspian seashore and sold her at market to a rich Persian family of Dagistan. There she learned the ways of the Zoroastrians, the worshipers of fire, the purity of Ormazda, but she kept the bracelet and the words of the hermit, and waited, while she grew.

Followers of Yesu were persecuted in the Sassanid Empire, but Vashtie's quick eye caught the signs of those who were different, and she met a few of her faith who would teach her the portions commonly memorized by the faithful. She would stop briefly at one stall or another in the market, and she would walk home murmuring to herself another story, another portion of the life of the One who sustained her. She was shy as a child, but learned rapidly, obedient and warm to masters and fellow slaves.

She wiped the feverish face of Onder and sighed. She was far from the irrigated gardens of her second home. She had been well taught by her mistress in the arts and crafts of the rich Persian culture. She was now passing the age of marriage, but as a servant there was no hurry. Her mistress protected her until the bey, master, had suddenly died, clutching his chest. There were debts; the estate was sold, and the wife went to her son's house with only one servant, an old trusted friend.

Vashtie was sold at the slave market to a richly dressed young Tokhari merchant. Onder already owned a magnificent golden stallion, and a girl from the West. He had laughingly called them: her and the golden-haired little girl - an investment!

"Neither of you is really very pretty or I would have had to pay more than ten gold pieces each. The saying in my country is: round, moon-faced girls to the West; long, oval-faced girls to the East. I am going East so you will bring me an increase of wealth. I might even keep you for myself," he teased. So, they had become a part of the traffic in the exotic luxury trade of women, silk, and horses.

She could not love Onder, who although of her faith, was wrapped in gain and trade, with little interest in what his family professed. She wiped his face again and breathed a prayer for his life. He had talked much of his home and the cities of Central Asia, with their rich trade in China, India, Persia and distant Rome. He, teasing, described the rich lives they would lead in some great man's harem. These plans left her cold and empty; she craved love and freedom.

She wondered how long his recovery would take, how they would fill the time. She pressed the beads into her palm and kissed the T cross. How true that life is filled with agony that must be met. `Yesu show me how.' She sighed again. She raised her eyes to discover Yuzbasha watching her with unwavering attention.

"*Goon eye'dune*, good morning." he smiled. He continued, "Mother is awake now and will watch your master. Come, take a ride down to the river to refresh yourself; then you can eat and rest."

She refused to bathe in his presence and entered the river to her knees where she washed and combed her hair. Keke, who joined them there, had no such inhibitions. After entering with her clothes on, she took them off and washed them in the deep water, her golden hair and shoulders shining in the sun. She threw them to Vashtie to spread on the bushes to dry. Then she begin to swim and frolic; until Vashtie was ashamed of her and started scolding.

"Keke, you are not a little child now; you are attracting a crowd. Stop it this second!" Keke disproved the statement by sticking out her tongue at Vashtie, which caused a shocked, "oh," from the growing audience, and then an "ooh," when she launched herself from the bottom of the stream and came out to her waist then jackknifed to the bottom again. The men chuckled while the women looked at each other and whispered, "*I'yup*, shameless."

Erkan had joined the crowd for the full display and felt shaken by desire. No, she was not a little child. He watched intently as Vashtie ran to get a *bataniye* behind which the unrepentant Keke put on her wet things again. Keke, wet clothes clinging to her form, shrugged her shoulders and walked away from the riverbank.

At the edge of the river across from the village of yurts, there was a new guests' area, still near the river, where the baggage of the merchants, their animals and temporary yurts and hunting tents had been set up. Here the outlanders who were not seriously injured were placed by order of the Khan. It was to this place that Keke directed herself. Vashtie, visibly worried, followed her, trailed by Yuzbasha.

From the alien's village came the sound of music and the mooing sound of a bear. Two swarthy, southern men were playing flute and tambourine while a stout brown bear, standing upright, swayed in time to the music. A large ring in the bear's nose and a stout stick in the hand of the drummer were proof that the performer was not completely tame. Behind the two stood, dejectedly, a scrawny tan donkey, still bearing the travel burden of the day. With him an equally scrawny brown horse, now free of the double burden of the journey, cropped the summer grass.

Around the performers a group of merchants and children from the yurts gathered. Some began to clap time to the music, while some of the children imitated the bear. The music was from their homeland, and the flute slid from note to note effortlessly. Every one joined in.

If you seek for warmth and pleasure;
Come, come to Hindustan.
If you long for love and leisure;
Come, come to Hindustan.

There you'll find great treasure:
All there in Hindustan.
There's wisdom without measure;
All there in Hindustan.

Jewels, spices, fabrics ooh!
You will find your heart's dream:
Cities, beaches, mountains too!
There you'll be content.

COME TO HINDUSTAN

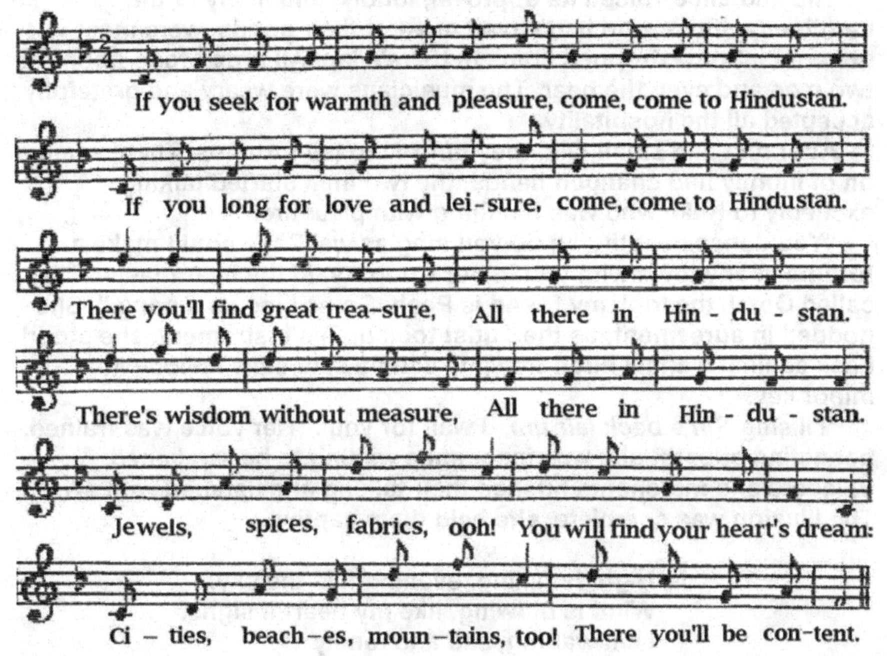

The flutist now danced before the bear. A new verse was added as the melody changed only to start again at its end. The whole song was repeated again and again. The flute's voice fluttered and trilled as the drum tried to follow the departures. Worried expressions relaxed as the three performers played to an appreciative audience, even the wounded nodded in time to the lilting tune. More people came from the yurts. Others crossed the river.

Keke arrived in time to take advantage of the full audience. Taking everything in at a glance, she immediately started to dance opposite the bear, whirling so her moist hair would stand clear of her head, then with head bent whirling her hair in a circle while her arms and hands described a flying motion. Then she took five steps right, swung her hair, then five left with the same motion. After tiring of that, she did handstands and somersaults from that position always swishing her bright beacon hair. She wore Hunnish baggy pants, but had sewn tight cuffs on the bottoms. She proceeded to do a slow, high, kick step lifting a knee up to her chin, and in a swooping turn as that one leg crossed over the other, spun her around in a half-twist. With each step she threw her hair.

At this point one of the performers, the flutist, enthusiastically started to juggle three palm-sized stones. He added another one, two and finally three, sending them high overhead. The children stood open-mouthed watching, as he gathered all six in again. Then he did a repeat with sticks of wood, twirling them in the air. Finally, he did it with three shining knives.

The audience voiced its approval, loudly, and many of the merchants, those who had saved most of their goods, were most generous. Some dropped coins in Keke's lap. All urged food upon the two men and even the bear. The musicians were weary and gratefully accepted all the hospitality.

After rest and small talk, they offered to tell fortunes. Then, when a bit of money had changed hands, the two men started talking excitedly to Keke who was blushing with pleasure.

"You dance beautifully; do you sing as well? We could make a fortune in any town with you in our troop." said the bear master. "I'm called Optal, the fool, my friend is Pesh. Come sing us a song." She nodded in agreement; as the flutist took up his instrument, she stood back against a small birch tree and sang a sad, slow melody in a minor key.

"I'll sing *Sin e beck lair um*, `I wait for you'." Her voice was trained, her acting superb; she was innocence waiting to be awakened. Villagers and merchants hushed their talking and listened with awe. The illusion was complete, she held them captive.

1. Night is falling, evening fills the sky.
   Wind is blowing, like my heart it sighs.
   I am waiting, sad and lonely.
   Come, my love waits for you only.

2. Light is breaking, morning fills the sky.
   Birds are winging, hear their joyful cries.
   I have waited happy hearted;
   Filled my love, but you've departed.

3. Noonday burning, in the bright blue sky.
   Sun is glowing, grass is growing high.
   I am yearning, let my heart burn.
   Come, my love waits for your soon return.

She paused, and shoulders quivering, danced among the watchers then returned to vary the tune slightly on the last verse. She timed her gestures to the music:

4. So my life goes; years are passing by.
Still my love grows; will until I die.
I am thinking of you, sweetheart.
Come, my love knows we can never part.

I WAIT FOR YOU

Vashtie took charge when the song finished. She was afraid of what might follow. Several rich men were moving forward to engage Keke in conversation. She grabbed her arm and hustled her unwillingly from the scene of her triumph.

"What are you doing?" Keke protested, "I want to stay. Those men want to talk to me. I want to sing more."

"Onder calls for you," her friend said. "We are needed. You will come and sing for him." Behind them all, the mounted Khan, frowning, spoke to his attendant,

"Chavush, I want those men out of the camp three hours before dark. Make them camp over two hours ride away from the merchants. Send a secret guard to watch their camp. Let them come again, if they will, for our guests need diversion from their hurts and worries, but only by day."

Chavush nodded, "*Bash ooze two nay*, understood sir. They are far too clever. They'll want to camp at the woods and scavenger the battlefield for goods and the animal's meat." He had doubts about letting such wealth escape from the tribe.

"*Tom-mom*, okay, but be careful about these guests. They mustn't indulge in long walks or rides, especially toward the hill meadows where the new golden bird roosts. I want no word of his presence to spread among these outsiders. They must remain on this side of the river. I understand more ready mares have been added to his herd; he enjoys his new duties?" The men exchanged knowing smiles.

"After months with the caravan, he finds his life's fulfillment in the tender grass of the high ground and the beauties in his harem." Chavush grinned wolfishly, "I envy the golden one. Variety adds spice." He departed with the words, "*Is a niz'lee*, with your permission."

As the Khan rode reluctantly back to his central yurt where his childless wife waited to remind him of his duties, he stared absent-mindedly around. He saw nothing but gold circles of bright moving hair. `I wait for you', echoed in his ears.

> - - - - - - >

The autumn was glorious. Vashtie had become accustomed to ride circuit with Yuzbasha over the tribal area. On a hill overlooking a lake, they laid out bread and meat on a thin square of material. Yuzbasha cut the portions for each of them with a small, serviceable knife of strange design. The handle looked like the elongated neck of a growling wolf head. The canine teeth were of ivory and the eyes of obsidian. As they sat to eat, she picked up the knife and looked at it in fascination.

"Where did you get such an interesting knife? I have never seen this design before," she mused. "See, each hair on his neck stands out and can be seen. Who made it?"

He smilled, "My grandfather gave it to me in my tenth year. Before he died, he told me it came from his grandfather who got it from his. It must skip a generation to be lucky. It is from the ancient people. The metal is not like any other. It fell from the sky, so has special power to harm or to do good. It can bring fire from a rock. Watch," he commanded. He took up the flint rock in the bundle and placed the tender beneath it. He struck the rock with the back edge of the knife and a shower of sparks fell down lighting the moss and fragments. Blowing softly he fed the flame. "See you don't need hot coals to start a fire. See the back of the blade is worn round from its use by the ancestors." While she watched open mouthed, he put out the little flame with a blow of his hand, smiling in triumph.

"Don't," she protested, pushing his hands away. "My master in Dagistan worshiped fire. We fed a perpetual flame."

He shrugged, sheathed and put it in the bundle with the flints and tender. "Fire is a measured blessing of Tanra. It must be controlled."

A leather bag of ayran, yogurt mixed with water, lay beside it. She had brought cups of wood to avoid drinking from the same bag, which in her tribe hinted at marriage.

"You didn't have to bring cups," he said laughing. "Drinking from the same bag doesn't commit you to anything among Chipchaks." He became more serious, "In fact you are, by riding away from the camp with me most days, already committed in the eyes of the people."

He reached for her hand, but she withdrew it. Slowly, quietly she said, "It is written: `Slaves, obey your masters, for this is pleasing to the Lord.' I must await Onder's decisions on the affairs of my life."

A look of anger and frustration crossed the face of Yuzbasha, and he burst out, "I could have you at any time!"

She looked at him steadily, sadly she shook her head, "Would you lose my love and respect?" He bit his lip and looked down while she continued, "I would not want Onder or others to hear of anything but good treatment on your part."

He looked irresolute and jealous, Onder was getting around now, gaining strength, Yuzbasha was afraid of a future he could not control. "You say your God answers the petitions of those who serve him," he began. "Do you then always get what you want?"

Her answer came quickly, "No, but He will give you what is best for you and His purposes."

"I trust my own purposes more; I don't understand His," Yuzbasha complained. "Besides, why does He torment us with desires that can't be fulfilled, except by breaking the very rules you say He has made?"

"He promises that with patience and trust He will fulfill our deepest needs. He gives companionship in trial and trouble and comforts our hearts. If we break His laws, we frustrate the very fulfillment of our desires."

"I like living for the present: what you hold in your hand is preferable to promises. No matter how reliable the one who declares it." Yuzbasha shook his head, grimaced impatiently.

"If you were told that you would be the Khan of the tribe some day, wouldn't you submit to discipline to accomplish it?" She retorted angrily, "If you want to become a great merchant, don't you submit to a master to learn the trade? How much more to become a child of God."

"If you truly loved me, you would give me some token of that love. No one need ever know what passes between us," he demanded insistently. "Before he takes you away." He sat sulking, his face down, drawn and bitter.

Tears came to her eyes, "One thing I am free to promise you." She laid one finger under his chin and raised his face to hers. "Home is where the heart is, my people say." She continued, after standing, "My heart continues in the yurt of Meryen, medicine woman of the Chipchak and her son, wherever I may be." She jumped to the back of her mount and cantered away. He stood long, staring after her. Then he suddenly vaulted into the saddle and rode like the wind after her, his face bright with a smile.

STEPPE FLOWERS

PEOPLE, PLACES & PLOTS IN CHAPTER 3

Cha vush': the sergeant begrudges the loss of goods or the golden horse for any reason.
Er'kan: the chief decides where his greatest profits lie.
The Hun: from a tribe of conquerors, the murdered man is unknown.
Ke'ke: finds freedom glorious, escaping danger.
On'der: demands his rights as master to decide all.
Man'ga: a tribesman, born in the Chipchak homeland.
Kan'su: a Chipchak from another tribe farther east.
Se-vim': the wife of Erkan, childless, and desperate.
Vash'tie: caught between two lovers, and three duties.
Yuz'basha: means lieutenant, his duty and feelings differ.

GLOSSARY HELP:
de'li sev'ghee: crazy love.
em'dot: help; rescue me; attention!
e'peck: silk, the main commodity of trade east to west.
gel'len: a bride, the newcomer to the house.
getch'mish ol'sun: may it soon pass; get well soon.
goul-lay goul-lay': go happily; go smiling; don't be sad.
ill-lair-ree-yea': forward; to the front.
who-jews': charge; at the enemy; get 'em; let's go!

MURDER SCENE

Onder had wakened early and lay contemplating the past and future, as he had on countless occasions the last four months. He had wished to show his wisdom, ability and independence when he began this trading venture. The only wise thing he had done was to acquire Vashtie. She was worth ten times the price. But thinking of her, his mind went to Yuzbasha. It was obvious that they loved each other. He felt a strong surge of jealousy. She was his, but he had to hold his temper and get away with her and the horse. Where was the horse? He had his suspicions but no proofs. Everything hinged on that golden stallion.

He wished he could compensate his family for his past mistakes, but that was impossible at this juncture. He had to deal with a severe uncle; since his father's death, all funds and promotions were in his hands. Uncle was not a man to trifle with, and his rage would be hard to bear. He had been brave enough during the fight with the marauders, but facing uncle was another matter.

He remembered the story of his family. While traveling west where the Tokhari traded with the Syriac speaking peoples of upper Mesopotamia, they found willing partners who trade as far as India and central Asia. Among them were people who knew their language. While his grandfather and father were there on the trading venture, the older man fell sick and was hospitalized in one of the church hospitals. There they heard the 'good news' about Yesu's sacrifice,

of pardon and freedom from sin and condemnation. They had time to think and ask many questions. Onder had been a baby at the time, home, in their oasis town, and did not remember the family before they attended the small church building on the edge of the town. That was the church his grandfather helped establish, in spite of many misunderstandings and troubles. Gradually, the town had grown to include the church, and the building had been embellished by the prosperity of the majority of its members.

Onder, as a boy, had learned the required material and memorized the portions of psalms and gospel appropriate for the children. The life and teachings of Yesu had filled his young years. His favorite had been the story of the lost boy in the far country. Now, he reflected, he was that boy, sheep and coin of the stories, in need of being found. He was willing, even eager to be reclaimed.

> - - - - - - >

The season was late now; the feel of snow was always in the air. The last of the guests had gone south to the towns of the Tarim Basin to winter or travel as weather permitted. Onder stood thin and gaunt before the yurt where he had spent so much time in recovery. His ever active mind had analyzed his situation, and he had the energy to dispatch many letters to his oasis town, *E'peck Kent*, Silk City, near the Tarim Basin. He would need two of his four gold coins to reach his desired haven. He could not dispense with his jade dagger; it was the guarantee of his inheritance, the proof of his identity and being. He pressed two Greek gold coins into the hand of Meryen, the medicine woman; saying "I regret that I have no more to offer."

"*Getch mish olsun*," she replied, "Get well." As she looked at him, she felt a strange premonition of disaster.

The girls picked up their bundles, after an affectionate farewell from their hostess and Maya, and attached them to the horses. Yuzbasha rode over, ready to guide them toward the silk road as far as the southern border of tribal territory. He entered the yurt and consulted with his mother before remounting. Erkan, with eyes only for the pert, blond Keke, explained the provision he had arranged for them. The Ulungur tribe was to give them passage southeast to the towns that skirted the *Tanra Dah*, called the *Tien Shan*, Heavenly Mountains, by the children of Han, the Chinese.

As if it were an afterthought, Erkan said, "Onder bey, what would you give if we could find the golden stallion for you?" Onder's eyes lit up, but he kept a straight face and replied, "Whatever your heart desired, great Khan." Keke froze in her saddle and looked appealingly at Vashtie.

"I have had news of a sighting in the mountains," Erkan continued. "If he is delivered to you, you will fulfill my request?"

"Yes, immediately, my Lord!" came the eager answer.

Erkan frowned, "We will see," and dismissed them. "*Goul lay, goul lay*, go happily, go merrily." The other tribesmen took up the cry, and they rode out of camp. Yuzbasha rode beside Vashtie, between her black and Onder's roan. Keke had dashed ahead. On the road neither Vashtie nor Yuzbasha could find words. Keke, full of relief, chatted and sang all the way. Onder was thoughtful, but found laughter and joking suitable to the moment.

Keke put a thin roll of felt under her nose like a mustache and imitated the exaggerated gestures of the Hunnish soldiers, then the fear of Eastern Europe.

"I was scarcely eight when I was captured. My captain talked like this: *Who jews*, charge!" She whirled a stick round her head like a sword - causing her horse to shy and rear - "*Ill lair ree yea*, forward," and she left them in a cloud of dust. They were weak with laughter as she exaggerated the accent and made the jokes broad and ludicrous.

"I spent three years with the Huns at the Don River. Then they sold me to the Greeks of *Krym*, Crimea. There, in the land of grapes and fruit, I learned my profession."

Yuzbasha looked confused, "Which is ...?" He said.

Keke made a sour face, "Pleasing men, playing and singing songs, dancing and taking care of myself." Then she smiled again and whirled her hair. "I passed my first three years in misery; the second period of three training years happily enough. The Byzantines like their women to be intellectual and know the classics and fashions well," she continued, "but they sold me for the East because of this." She held out her blond hair at full length, almost the length of her arm. "Also, because I'm better at comedy than seduction." She batted her eyelashes and tried to sing a soft love song moving her head from side to side oriental fashion and putting them in stitches again. "I carry the tools of my trade," she said, and held up a packet, "as well as my protection," and she patted her holster and arrow sheath.

Both Onder and Vashtie looked away, the one annoyed the other embarrassed, while Yuzbasha looked confused, and remembered her dealing with the women at every kill for special parts of the animal.

"I'll be rich and famous even if I'm not as talented as those bitches sent to Constantine's city." She looked grimly at Onder, "and nobody had better keep me from my purpose." The young golden-haired girl looked small and comical as she tried to look threatening.

"I have talents, learned with the Huns, that you will not want to know about." She laughed, "But today I'm free, I'm escaping captivity. I'm crazy, I believe in God and His goodness. He'll make me famous." She broke into a gallop, then stopped and started singing at the crest of the next hill; *Deli Sev'ghee*, `Crazy love,' at the top of her voice.

STEPPE FLOWERS

1. Oh how joyful he makes me.
   How delightfully free.
   My heart sings with this love, crazily.
   When his hands touch my face,
   In a tender embrace.
   My heart leaps with his love, crazily.
   Mine is a crazy love.

2. Oh how humble it makes me,
   And how proud I can be.
   His love changed all my life, instantly.
   What a shock of surprise,
   When he looks in my eyes.
   This love transformed my life, wonderfully.
   Mine is a crazy love.

3. Oh how often I've wondered,
   Who could ever love me?
   This love entered my life, tenderly.
   What a wondrous reward,
   When he smiles his regard.
   I love him so. He loves me, so sweetly.
   Mine is a crazy love.

CRAZY LOVE

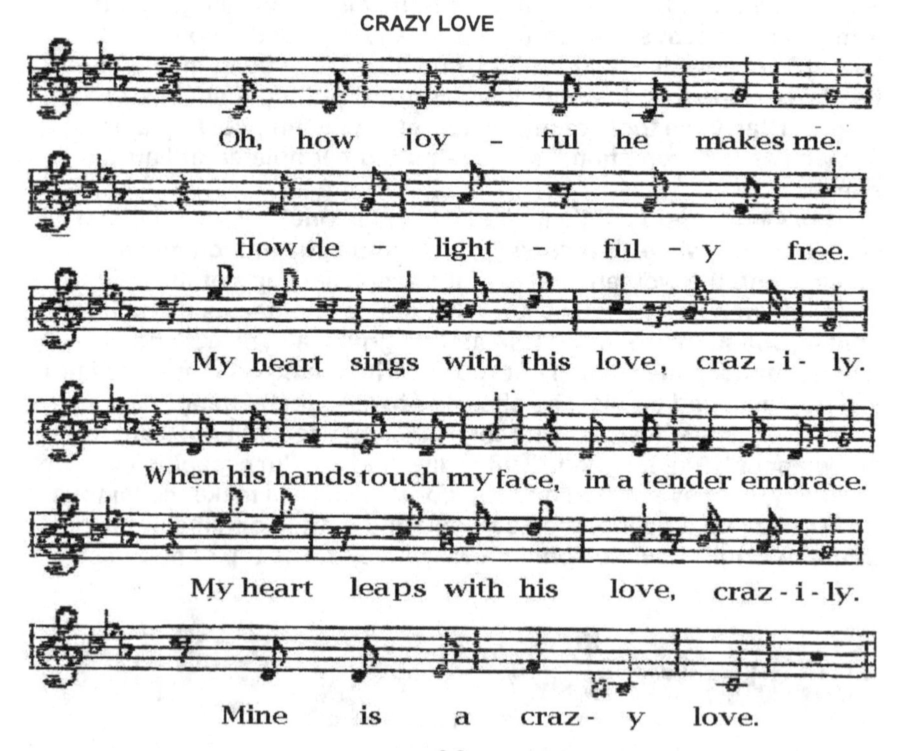

After they passed the Sentinel Rock, the last guard post, Onder dropped behind the others on a pretext, and moved toward a stream in the small woods parallel to the road. It was the place where the ambush of the caravan had occurred. The girls shivered and pressed on. Yuzbasha drew up, delaying impatiently for Onder. He wanted to talk. "I'm waiting for someone," Onder loudly insisted. "Camp near the rocks, and I'll join you within the hour." As they left, at the ridge where the renegades fell, Yuzbasha noticed a cloud of dust behind them, coming down the trail. Yuzbasha grew suspicious.

"I'll ride back and investigate," he said. "Someone is following us. Make camp here and wait." He tossed down a bundle with flint, striker, wad and other material for fire. Keke dismounted and retrieved the bundle. The girls lingered as Yuzbasha rode back, but they noticed that he entered the woods rather than continue on the back trail.

"I like camping on the hill here rather than continuing to the border," Keke stated in a decisive way and was unloading the horses before Vashtie could get down. There was a spring that ran down the hill into the woods, and there were conifer trees near it. Camp was set up and food being readied when they heard the sound of angry voices from the wood. They stared at each other in apprehension.

"You haven't enough money!"

"I love her; I'll get you enough."

"Not now, before we travel."

"You're going to sell them in the town."

"That's my business. If I get the stallion, I may not have to sell anything."

"So you leave Keke to Erkan and take mine away."

"There's a price for everything."

"My mother saved your life; isn't that worth something?"

"I gave her two gold coins; I hadn't much more."

"Take them back then, with a curse. I throw them in your face!"

"Stop, you fool!"

"You stop me, slave merchant, seller of women's bodies!"

"Get out of here, you barbarian."

There was a shout of pain and a cry of anger at the same moment; then, a clatter of hooves as Yuzbasha came charging out of the woods, and up the hill. He rode out, past them, and without stopping, galloped off, away from the Sentinel Rock.

The women stood silently. Then Keke said, "We need some wood for a fire," and disappeared into the trees. The quiet was absolute, as if all nature were listening for something. Then, there was a sound again on the road and dust just beyond the wood.

Dread swept Vashtie like a wind storm. "Oh my Lord, no!" She breathed, and ran down the hill beside the little stream.

> - - - - - - >

Keke was feeding wood from her pile to a small fire when Vashtie reappeared.

"You didn't find much," she complained as she looked at the one stout little log held like a club in Vashtie's right hand. Vashtie dropped the wood stick, walked to the stream and washed her hands carefully. They laid out some food and waited.

In the distance there was the sound of hooves. A band was coming fast. Then they heard the sound of horses from the border, and Yuzbasha swept into sight with Chavush and two other guards. He reined up beside the girls.

"There is news of a band of Hunnish raiders down the road; we must be careful."

Just at that moment Erkan was seen on a steady gray mare leading the great yellow stallion into the woods where Onder waited. Yuzbasha seemed reluctant to return to the scene of their angry encounter earlier, so he dismounted at the fire while Chavush and the men continued to where another band had just ridden up from Sentinel Rock. They waited on the road beside the wood. The news of the Huns spread quickly; they milled about, the opportunity of a hunt stimulating them.

The blast of the horn brought everyone up short. The band responded instantly to the appeal and entered the woods in a rush. Behind, the others started for the woods.

Erkan on foot was stretched to his full length and jerked about, as he held the halter of the rearing, excited stallion.

"*Em'dot*, help," he cried, "quickly... Huns, they run... Robbed the dead! I wounded one."

Several men grabbed the halter and tried to lead the frenzied, yellow beast back to the road. Almost under his feet lay Erkan's horn, strung bow and quiver of scattered arrows.

Others rode straight through the woods to the rough country beyond. Chavush led another group out to the road and back to the east border to cut them off.

In the woods lay two dead bodies. One, near the Khan was that of Onder, an old black feathered Hun medicine arrow in his chest between the right arm and the collar bone - a flesh wound. However, over his heart was a gaping knife wound. His face looked sad but serene. About 15 yards away, face down with two Chipchak arrows in his back lay a large, fleshy Hun.

As the men with the stallion reached the road, Keke and Vashtie came up to them and stood before the horse, and Vashtie began her quiet talking. The stallion stopped shying, and, trembling, let her touch his head. Erkan remained in the woods.

Two men returning to the scene scanned the confusion of tracks. Manga touched the Hun midriff with the toe of his boot. Then, he felt the man's biceps and felt the index finger for callus. On the hand there was blood and a shallow wound. He looked quizzically at his companion who raised one shoulder slightly.

"Merchant or warrior?" asked Kansu, "Maybe down on his luck?"

They looked inquisitively toward their Khan, but Erkan did not deign to answer. He was staring at the lion-like horse and the golden-haired girl beside it.

"Where did the donkey go?" Manga asked, indicating a set of prints and spoor near the center of the clearing.

"And Onder's horse?" Kansu concluded, as he ventured into the brush where the Khan's guards had plunged, and brought back an arrow, which he returned to Erkan. "One back out of three." he said, nodding at the quiver, which had been picked up and belted on the Khan's side. He looked up at the tree tops. "You must have shot high; they're lost, no sign of blood there." Erkan shrugged his shoulders and continued his contemplation. The two men exchanged glances. Kansu, a recruit from another tribe, whispered in an undertone: "Our Khan is a double winner. Is this a gift from the spirits or a stroke of strategy?" The tribesman looked away as if contemplating a high jumble of rock between the stream and the wood. Tall hillocks were scattered through the woods.

"It can't come to anything," the recruit continued in an undertone, "Our Khan has a dried-up stick!" His companion, Manga, tried to pretend he had not heard.

A number of tracks and trails were followed and the countryside scoured by the tribesmen, but no trace of the East Hun band was found near the east border. They buried the dead men hastily, as one would an intruder. Neither girl objected, but Vashtie prayed at the place, near the woods where the other travelers had been laid to rest. The marauders had been left to the beasts and weather.

The troop returned to the yurts with the golden stallion. Within the week Yuzbasha was married to Vashtie, and the next month she announced that she was pregnant. Keke, however was a greater problem. No single man in the camp dared ask for her.

KEKE'S SPORT (36)

Tribal custom demanded that an older wife consent to and sometimes choose a second wife for her husband. Tasks had to be shared and a '*gellen*,' new wife, would be required to do most of the work, but Erkan's wife, Sevim, would have no part of the `foreign whore'. Keke's unwilling work was in the medicine yurt. Her resentment showed in the face of Vashtie's happiness. Her only joy was the hunt. Her training among the Huns gave her 'star status' as huntress.

In the yurt of Erkan, there was great tension. The wife, Sevim, did everything to turn him back to herself. When, after two months she found herself pregnant, she relented and permitted the Khan his wishes. The event was accepted with a small celebration by the community, and the sulky, pouting Keke distracted the Khan with her entertainment and professionalism and her constant wheedling for jewelry and gold.

The change of status by marriage charged and reversed the relation between Keke and Vashtie. A second wife of a chief was still of higher rank than a lieutenant's wife. The rebellious Keke could not be mothered anymore. A pregnant Vashtie found much in common with the wife of the Khan, who was in need of comfort and companionship during an extremely hard pregnancy.
Vashtie's needs were different: physically healthy she suffered hostility from the wife of Chavush and others who speculated as to the real parenthood of the expected child. She needed the acceptance and sponsorship of the head woman, because there was the constant danger of an encounter with a spiteful Keke.

The women of the camp were in awe however; the pitied, yet scorned barren-one was with child. They watched joy and confidence grow with the transformation, yet pain was also evident. Those two great shapers of character were both present daily. She was the sponsor, Vashtie was the teacher. Life, internal and external, was in constant change for them both. But the child of promise was that of Sevim. What would it be? What significance would the child have for the tribe? They nagged their men about it, so that they, too, took notice of the unusual turn of events.

Keke had her own yurt where the Khan preferred to stay as the first wife's pregnancy became a trial to all. Keke would not have been accepted in the tribe because of her foreignness, except for the protection of the Khan. She could not share her past with others, but she did have several flattering women who kept her up on the gossip, and supplied her whims. They helped collect the mushrooms, herbs and animal parts she requested and processed; although some were considered dangerous. She held intimate parties where her mixtures were smoked or ingested to produce euphoria. Because she was isolated, lonesome and irritable, she began to treat the tribesmen with contempt. Her only delight was to ride with Erkan on the hunt.

This provided the brief excitement that her life lacked. At the high moment of death, her arrows never missed.

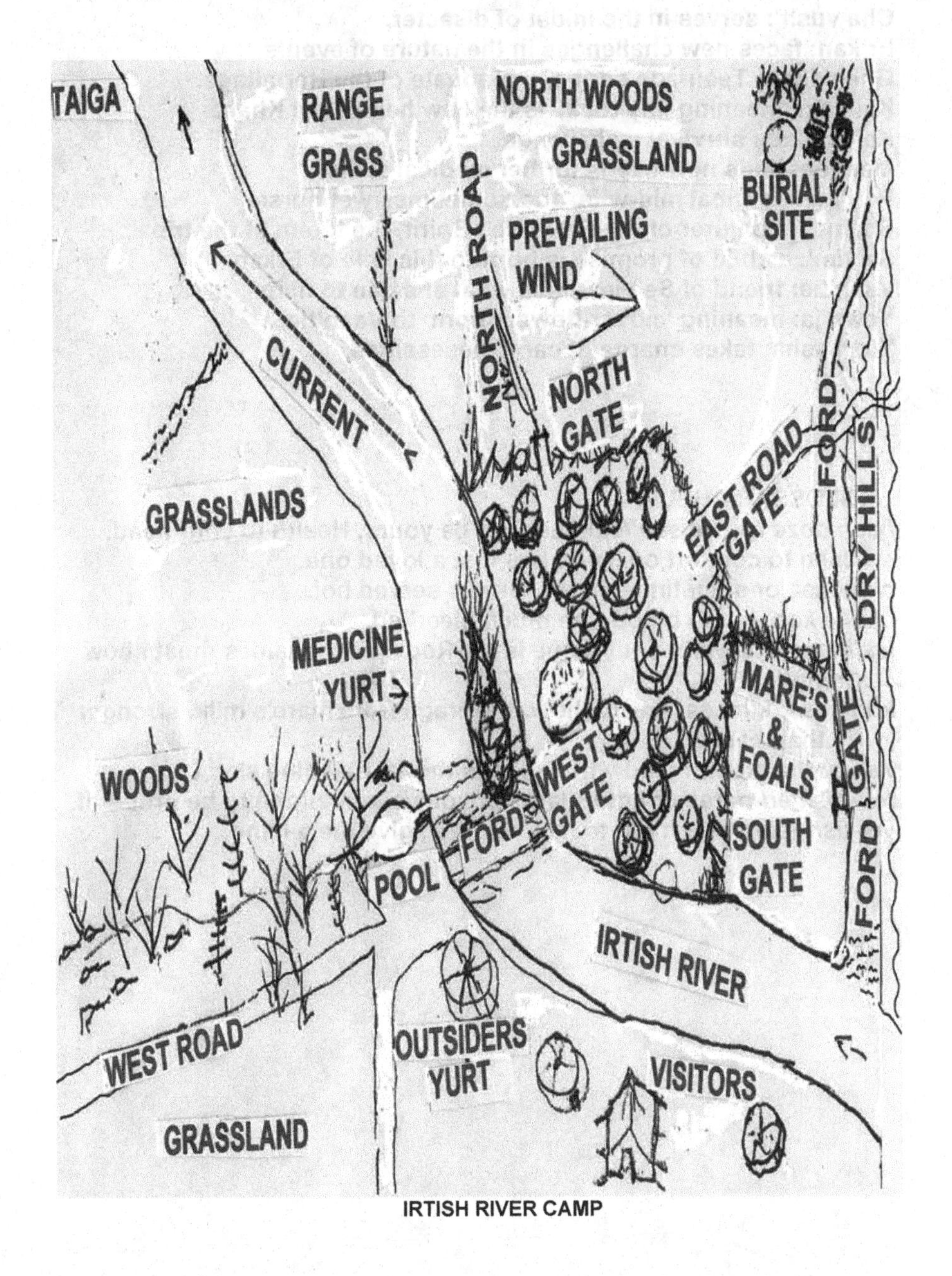

IRTISH RIVER CAMP

PEOPLE, PLACES & PLOTS IN CHAPTER 4

Cha vush': serves in the midst of disaster.
Er'kan: faces new challenges in the nature of events.
Ghen'chair: Teen-age scribe, a graduate of the Hermitage.
Kai'yam: meaning 'my rock,' is the new heir of the Khan.
Ke'ke: finds survival a challenge.
Mer'yen: finds new needs for her medical skills.
Peri'han: is tribal mid-wife, and sometimes wet nurse.
Shaman: conjurer of the Gray Wolf Spirit, the totem of the tribe.
Se vim': a child of promise is born to this wife of Erkan.
Vash'tie: friend of Se vim' does what she can to help.
Yown'ja: meaning 'clover-flower', born to Vash'tie.
Yuz'basha: takes charge of camp necessities.

GLOSSARY HELP:

bash'ooze too ne saa'luck: healing be yours, Health to your head. Used to comfort one who has lost a loved one.
chay: tea or sometimes herbal drinks served hot.
choke kon: much blood, too much bleeding.
iss'mean Kai'yam: your name is My Rock; boy's names must show strength.
koo'miss: kumiss, an alcoholic beverage from mare's milk, stronger than beer.
Tanra: the creator God who inhabits the eternal blue sky.
teb-reek'ed-dare': congratulations; you've something to be proud of.
yet-tish-tear': reach out to me; help me; give me a hand.

MEN'S LODGE

The flash of light split through the afternoon gloom, shaking the yurts and crashing into a tree near the river. The explosion of the tree and the following smashing boom of the thunder sent the dogs whining with terror past the secured hide doors of the yurts and behind the storage chests or furnishings.

Their piteous whining was more than matched by that of the screams of anguish coming from the largest dwelling placed in the center of a protective ring of yurts. There inside, the circle of women paused to shudder and to watch with awe the event that would shape the future of all the tribe. The happy miracle anticipated at conception seemed destined not to be completed in birth.

Sevim, the khan's wife, lay limp and pale, her face wet with the sweat of labor. Her black hair, gray at the temples, lay in damp disarray about her head. She was breathing in long, shuddering sighs and occasionally writhing and screaming as her body tore with the pressure of the coming child. Meryen, the medicine woman shook her head sadly,

"Choke kon," she murmured, "too much blood. Yet-tish-tear, Help me," she said to her assistant, Perihan, "Pull, it's coming."

A second bolt of lightening fell near by, and the dogs began to howl from yurt to yurt. The sound traveled to the largest yurt in the first circle around the Khan's central home, where the women gathered. Here, with a seven-yak-tail standard waving in the storm, the Khan's second, Yuzbasha, served all the tribe's elders with *chay*, tea from faraway China, served by the older boys of the tribe. The atmosphere was tense, so the men were noisier and more boisterous in their action.

"This is a great day for the tribe," proclaimed one, "the powers of Tanra approve the child with wind, fire and water."

The sergeant nodded, adding, "With the power of the bear, the speed of the horse, and the persistence of the gray wolf, he will lead our tribe to greatness."

"Yes, Chavush", said another "first the Yuzbasha's girl-child this spring and now the Khan's heir today." Heads nodded in agreement, but there were side glances at one another as the dogs continued to howl. All knew that this child was late, as Yuzbasha's had been early. A strong sense of crisis existed.

Suddenly, another howl sounded next to the door of the men's yurt; it was the sound of the wolf, but with human qualities that made the hair on the men's necks rise. Suddenly, in the silent pause thus created, the door flap was thrust aside and the form of a man dressed in the skins of a wolf and wearing the head of a huge gray wolf, as a mask, entered. The shaman, the key figure in the spiritual life of the tribe, had come to connect the present with the past and future of the tribe.

Three paces inside the flap, the creature stretched full height, and with head fully raised, sent forth a howl, that again combined all the natural call of the wild with that same spiritual quality that, had caused all to hold their breath. The eyes behind the gleaming teeth of the great head took in all the audience. Then, slowly, the impressive figure bowed cringing, hands outstretched, toward the corner where a bundle of tassels hung like shining stalactites from a lodge pole. Colored tassels of blue, red, green, orange and white, the colors of life's joys and sorrows, brevity and eternity, hung in the worship center.

The figure then moved, the nose bent to an imaginary trail and a slow dance began. Right foot starting, one, pause, one, two, three paces forward, pause, one to the rear, pause, another back, then again, the same pace and rhythm, always the retreat was half the advance. In the silence the paces and breath of the animal-man became audible. At the end of the advance and retreat, the man panted for a moment, briefly, like a dog through his mouth, and as he danced he would sniff in rhythm to the paces. The resemblance to a wolf on the scent of game was remarkable.

The totem of the tribe made his first round in the center of the large yurt and paused before the Khan. The nod of the head of the shaman could hardly be called an obeisance, perhaps only an acknowledgement of the leader, for they were bitter rivals for influence and control in the tribe.

Erkan spoke; "Welcome to the great, gray wolf, standard and protector of the tribe of the Chipchaks, ruler of our ancestors under the everlasting blue sky and leader through the shining sky-fires of the long arctic night; thrice welcome, master of the reindeer, pursuer of the great, wild mountain yak, provider of food for your thankful people."

Again, the dance and drum sounds began. This time the beast seemed to seek people out, and to move to them, stare intently at their faces. The one hunted, when singled out, stared back. Some wore frightened expressions, others showed disdain or boldness. All strove to show as little yielding as possible.

Quietly, through the door another figure crept, hiding beside the men in the shadows of their bodies. The large set of antlers made this a difficult task, though they were kept low as if the creature grazed from the ground. The men present swayed their bodies, so the reindeer could pass between them. The wolf had made a second round while searching out the guilty, and as he stood a second time before the Khan, he lifted his muzzle for the third time to howl. Then, with a growl, he leaped up and around in one movement. In the hunting posture, at the same leisurely pace, he prepared to move toward the reindeer figure, which with a long drawn out moan of terror, started to dance away from the pursuer, but with a different, faster rhythm accompanied by drums.

The wolf, a half circle from the reindeer, stood sniffing the air and started purposefully forward for the chase. The deer, startled, leaped high in place and started a high, leaping step that did not advance much, but looked spectacular. The rhythm was different from that of the gray wolf: five high leaping steps and a long pause filled with a low moan, a step back, pause, two steps back and five rapid high steps forward again. A full circle was danced by each, and the wolf continued trailing. On the second round he slowly moved up to the side of the reindeer whose leaps became slower and lower. The deer hooked his horns back toward the wolf-man, but failed to make contact. The two figures now danced in tight circles round each other.

The small tambourine like finger drums, each with the rhythm of one of the beasts, had started on the first round of the chase. They were now joined on the third round by an oboe-sounding woodwind, a reed instrument. The notes were long and sustained like wind in the forest taiga or a storm on the frozen tundra. It swooped, swelled, called and faded. The meeting of death and life, renewal and oblivion, victory and defeat had arrived.

The two figures ceased circling and the drums' rhythm changed to a slow pulse beat. Slowly, the reindeer went to its knees in submission. Head down it cowered. The shaman had ceased the growling, angry sounds and was now panting as if satisfied. First, he stood full height while receiving the submission of the reindeer.

Then, he raised it to standing position, but it remained bent over, head at waist level. The wolf-man, dancing, circled to the rear of the animal, then, suddenly circling and dancing, leaped to the back of the reindeer, riding it. The reindeer carried him slowly in a full circle to near the door; where it fell, thrashed, and seemed to die.

The wolf began its rhythm again, followed by the sound of drums and now, wailing flutes, looking behind the men and in the corners for something. It seemed to be searching in vain and would periodically hold its arms up to heaven as if making petition and seeking a reply from Tanra, the creator god. As the creature completed his circuit, he held his hands out to the men of the left and then to those of the right. They also raised their hands in supplication; the oboe and flutes wept the need of the people, `Tanra, Tanra,' they wailed accompanying the voice of the men and sway of the bodies.

The form lying near the door, moved and snorted. The resurrected animal lifted high his brown head and stiff neck-mane. No longer a reindeer, the transformed animal became Tanra's new gift. The horse leaped upright and started to caper and dance. He nodded his head to the rhythm of the fast, loping dance: starting right foot, one, two, three, pause, one, two, three, pause. On the pause the lead foot would be raised and held. The animal nickered. Then, the same movement would be started backwards or with a whirl, the horse continued back to the starting point: one two three, pause, one two three, pause, kick. Only one hand drum continued loudly, the wolf beat, all the rest of the instruments joined the horse with glad, triumphant squeals.

All the men raised their hands in praise of the animal, some with cups of wood or bone skull-cups in their hands. Barley beer, was drunk to the coming of the horse, while the horse, joyful in its praise, made its circuit. After another complete turn of the circle, the horse caught up to the wolf-man. The gray wolf began to act like a happy dog romping before the horse, even barking excitedly as the wolf drum and rhythm suddenly died. In time with the horse, the great wolf-dog danced and barked excitedly like a great kangal: a herd dog. Then, the dog and horse danced round each other, and the horse permitted the creature to mount him, and, to the rhythm and the happy excitement of drum and flute, rode the circuit quickly to vanish through the doorway. The instruments slowed and gradually ceased.

The genesis of their tribe set forth in summarized form as drama and music left the men in a quiet meditative mood. Silence fell over the yurt and again the external sounds of nature bore in upon the occupants. The crises still existed, but the people were better prepared to face it.

Suddenly, at that quiet moment, while the world seemed to listen, someone fumbled with the fastening at the door flap. A moonfaced woman belonging to Chavush, shouted into the room.

“It is a man-child." and was gone; as the Khan shouted, "and the woman?"

The noise level raised in the room, and Erkan accepted all the "*teb-reek ed-der*, congratulations," shouted at him by the men who were now breaking out the stronger drink, kumiss, clear as water, made from the fermented milk of mares.

> - - - - - - - >

In the central tent, one group of women were busy washing the child in salty water and milk, while another placed a pinch of salt on his tongue, so he will not be tongue-tied. Old Meryen and her assistant, Perihan, were sponging off the mother when she spoke.

"Let me see the child." The mother's voice was clear and firm, but her face was yellowing and wax-like in the semi-dark. They held the child to her face and offered to place it in her arms, but she would not take it. Instead, she spoke to the offered child.

“You have been a rock within me," she said, "a millstone in my middle, grinding the life out of me. But you are the foundation stone my man has yearned for so long.

"Iss-mean *Kai-yam*, your name is `My Rock’," she said her voice dropping, "let another carry him." She nodded to Vashtie.

Vashtie, Yuzbasha's woman, laid a T-shaped cross between her lady’s breasts and took the child. The woman fell back, her strength ebbing away, into the arms of those who had raised her up. Old Meryen put her head on the woman's breast and put a bronze mirror to her lips, but there was no life remaining. The cries and death chant of the women provoked more howls from the dogs and the yurt of the men fell silent.

Erkan, stared thoughtfully into the hearth fire in the center of the yurt. He had lost two wives and a few children. This third one had been with him for more than 15 years, yet his heart loved her still, but none of his women had given him an heir. A girl-child brought wealth with the bride price, but she also might be robbed in a raid, and you had nothing for your pains. Yet, girls were his portion and few at that.

Sevim, his last bride had been bought from the East from merchants who said she was Abakani, a khan's daughter from the small tribes in the Sayan Mountain valleys. She had been taken on a raid, and so was not virgin, but he loved her warmth of spirit and practical care of their affairs.

The shaman had predicted a son, who was to be her only, yet great, child. The divination ceremony over pure clear water poured from cup to cup was accompanied by flute, drum and chanting. When convulsions seized the shaman, the water spirit's voice had been clear and precise. Greatness was assured to the Khan's house. A child of promise would come. He had not thought it would cost so dear.

His wife had been too ill to attend to any duties and had not attended the spirit calling ceremony. She did not obey the ancient ways, but had become a believer in the religion of the West, followers of Yesu. This new faith was brought by Syriac traders to the Tokharis in the East, in the Tarim Basin where it competed with the Buddhists, Zoroastrians, the old religions of China and the ways of the Shaman. The recent growth of the Manichean heresy, a mix of Western Gnostic Christianity and Persian dualism, split the churches.

Erkan nodded automatically to the condolences of his men, "*Bash-ooze two ne saa-luck*," and managed to look alert enough to avoid offence. The son was to be taken to the yurt of Yuzbasha's mother, Meryen, as the Khan's heir could not remain in the yurt of the dead. Also, the breast of the woman Vashtie would be full, since she had delivered three months before.

The child was brought in, and the father allowed to see the new chief-to-be. He inspected the child carefully to see that there were no defects. He tested the child's strength and grip as he hung from the two fingers of his father's hands, supporting his own weight. Erkan was well satisfied with the child and thankful. He returned the baby to the nurse, Vashtie, to care for. He sat in silence and listened to the retreating thunder of the electric storm.

How quickly things had changed. Months of preparation and, suddenly, everything was as you had hoped; and at the same moment as you had never dreamed it would be. He sighed and immediately several of his men spoke up to distract him from sorrow. One fell against him in an intended accident.

"The child is ugly." Chavush declared to all.

"He will never equal the strength of his father." Yuzbasha stated emphatically.

"The new generation will never be like the old ones, the heroes of legend." Day day's complaining, nasal voice whined, "He's mixed blood, like so many lately" He looked hard at Yuzbasha. "Recruiting men of many tribes, waters down the pure humans." Now, he looked at the Khan. They had ceased trying to protect the child from the envy of men and spirits, and had entered the arena of politics and prejudice.

Suddenly, the thunder of hooves beat on their ears, the panic-stricken neighs of horses in distress. Running from the west along the river, they were in the camp in a moment. Wildly, they tripped over food troughs and pails, barking dogs and shouting, hand-waving men, even blundering into some of the yurts.

A few of the men, rushing out of the yurt, were able to catch some horses that had bridles and ropes attached. They mounted in a leap. Others jumped but failed to find a firm seat, and were thrown aside. One of them, a figure in wolf skins and head, tried to mount a passing stallion, but the horse shied, and with the smell of wolf paused to rear once, before plunging on. The figure of the gray wolf with crushed chest and arm, writhed in agony, gurgled, convulsed and lay still.

In a moment the men had recognized the new danger, fire! The whole western sky was filled with flame and smoke. A driving wind was bringing a wall of death upon them. Made tender-dry by the long, arid summer, the tall, prairie grass that stretched away to the far west was a mass-funeral pyre; animals and birds fled its presence to no avail. Only those who were wise enough or could fly high enough, discovered salvation south of the river, where the fire had not spread.

The Chipchak band proceeded to grab the nearest valuables and wade across the interval to a small island near the north bank. Then, some men with the panic- stricken horses tried to swim the main body of the stream.

However, the current was swift and the mighty Irtysh River deep. The body of water carried them far down river towards the fire coming from the west. The water was filled with thrashing, drowning, wild creatures. The horses struggling to the bank were saved, only to be lost as they pulled away, and ran wildly into the distance.

The island was too small to contain the camp. Vashtie left the two babies with Keke and Perihan, ran back to her yurt and rescued four, large skin bottles. She emptied them on the run, returned to her place again, and blew them up. She and Perihan with the two babies strapped on their backs, and Keke following, launched themselves onto the surface of the water. Kicking vigorously, they guided their improvised floats toward the south bank. Keke hung on and screeched when the cold water hit her face. She was terrified.

The men were busy cutting brush and trees and roping them into bundles, on which they placed some of the women and children, trying to get them across to the bank in the same way. However, the bundles only held the surface and tended to sink when weight was placed on them. Only by swimming and pushing could they get across. A child was swept away, and drowned.

Some of the men had stayed to try and fight the fire. After all, the camp was not full of high grass, and there was sand on the banks, but the heat drove them repeatedly into the water. They had no time to dismantle any of the yurts and many burned, although a few had the felt only scorched. The flames and heat passed quickly, leaving smoldering piles of ash and coals in their wake. The island was not burned, although the trees were scorched and ash covered it.

The blistered men threw water on the felt and on the skeletons of the yurts to salvage some of the goods. The buried food and grain supplies were not damaged, but, nevertheless, personal losses were high.

The uninjured joined the four-legged scavengers in seeking those animals roasted by the fire, and brought the meat to the camp. Those on the other bank cut trees to make rafts to bring the camp together again.

Erkan was not in camp and none could recall seeing him after the coming of the horses. Yuzbasha and Chavush, burned and limping, automatically took command of the salvage operations. They had men douse and beat out fires in camp.

Red, gray and black were the predominant colors; and burnt roast flesh, the perfume of the evening.

> - - - - - - - >

Erkan was far away and riding fast. He had caught the halter of his black and swung up, riding bareback, letting it run with the herd. The wind, however, drove the fire faster than the speed of a horse.

To the east the river bend appeared, a large tributary flowing south-west out of the Altai Mountains to join the Irtysh leaving a high embankment about three meters above a beach at the junction of the rivers.

Sighting the juncture Erkan started waving his arms and shouting, trying to take part of the herd to the river bank. Only a few mares and colts moved to the right towards the water's edge. The others swerved left to try to follow the tributary up stream. The fire caught them before they had run fifty meters. The screams of the horses pierced the air. A few turned and tried to run back through the flame wall.

The beach between the river and embankment was narrow and the water deepened rapidly. Several of the colts were knocked into the water and swam back nickering. The mares balked not wanting to go farther. Erkan kicked and screamed curses at them, as the fire swept up to him.

High over his head the fire streamed ashes, bits of burning straw and sparks raining down on them. The mares screamed and reared, their manes and tails aflame. More fell into the water along with the sparks and coals. Erkan's horse reared, and the increase of heat from the embankment above singed his hair and caught his shirt afire. The black fell back into the water in a daze.

As suddenly as the fire had come, it ceased. Without more fuel it, as rapidly, died and was blown out. Here and there a bit of salt bush or camel thorn continued to smolder or burn, but the great heat was gone. Desolation remained.

> - - - - - - - >

High on a meadow on a west facing ridge, a teenaged lookout watched the horizon of fire advance to the river below him. If the sparks bridged over the river or coals blew across, he knew that he would have to save the golden stallion, with the mares and colts. He watched the racing man, and the tragedy of burning horses near the river junction. He hoped the man had escaped, though he saw no evidence of it. The other herdsmen had gone to the celebration. His responsibility was the stallion and harem.

Yelling, singing and beating the small hand drum he had brought, with the two great Kangals barking, young Ghen-chair started them

moving down the east side of the mountain ridge where the rain shadow of perpetual western winds broke the sea of grass into dry and patchy remnants of the grassland bounty. The desert's edge was a place where no grass fire could hope to hold unbroken sway. There safety was assured. Behind all was a blackened ruin.

THE WOLF-MAN DIES (PAGE 44)

PEOPLE, PLACES & PLOTS IN CHAPTER 5

Blume: red-headed daughter of Yuhan and Katze is learning about life on the water road.
Cha vush': the sergeant faces the new disasters bravely.
Day'day: an opponent of the Khan and a traditionalist.
Er'kan: the Khan in pain and distress, senses the needs of his people for safety.
Hans: older son of Yuhan and Katze, learning the commercial routes east for faith and wealth.
Kat'ze: the small, energetic wife of Yuhan, mother of four, is adept with boats.
Ke'ke: the Goth hopes for escape to a new future.
Mer'yen: serves effectively in her nursing duties.
On'basha: a head of ten, a Corporal with ideas of attacking others.
Se vim': provokes a confession of failure by the leader.
Peri'han: a busy healer.
Vash'tie: helps in the camp and listens to the news.
Yobert: the youngest son, helps and sings.
Yu'han: East Goth merchant using the water road west.
Yuz'basha: the lieutenant is busy with the directing of help in the disaster.

GLOSSARY HELP:

***de'li sev'gee*: crazy love.**
***git*: go, in farewells; to go happily.**
***Hristian*: the name for Christian.**
***koo'miss*: kumis, clear fermented mare's milk for special occasions.**
***nay-o-lure'*: please; let me, used when pleading for some desire or chance.**
***toot*: catch; grab hold; hold tight.**

5 CONSEQUENCES

TRAVELERS' TALES

A black horse, limping, raw and red, wearily pulled itself up the river bank. A lank figure held feebly to its tail. The river's north-bound current had brought Erkan back to his starting point, the smoldering yurts near the small island where his people had taken refuge.

Those who came forward to hold and sooth the horse noticed that the horse's head was burned, the skin peeled on the left side and the horse was blind on that side. The man too was burned on the left side and back of the head. His hair was scorched off, but his left eye seemed to function, although without eyebrow or eyelashes. He was utterly spent.

The night council met without campfire or yurt hearth, in the open on the small island. Some of the men sat with burned hand or foot in the water that flowed between the island and camp. Others moistened cloths to put on aching parts. Melted butter shone on the faces of not a few. Many ate cold, roasted flesh gathered from the fire. Others ate bites of salvaged grain or flour provided by the women. A few sat listlessly, exhausted by exertion or injury. By morning the fate of the band would be settled.

Erkan, somewhat recovered, sat brooding. He was ruined. Many riches from the battle with the Persian band of marauders were lost in the fire. The herd was disbanded and destroyed as were some of the yurts. Neighbors would hear and some would widen their frontiers. They might lose their part of the steppe silk road. Leaders rose and fell on such acts of God or caprices of spirits. The shaman's death cut off the contact of spirits.

Day-day, a scrawny, rough and ready old grandfather spoke up in a sharp querulous voice.

"We have been careless of the ways of the ancestors, and they or the spirits we no longer appease, have avenged themselves on us. We must divide the remaining herd and go to our relatives or our women's tribes to find shelter for the winter. We will salvage what we can here and move while the weather remains good. May we have better protection in the future." He glared at Erkan and continued.

"When justice is not meted to the murdered and innocent blood spilled without revenge, the world of the spirits is set in turmoil," he said, staring belligerently at the lieutenant. Yuzbasha, who was known to favor his wife's ways, spoke up with a bit of heat.

"Such things as these happened in the days of our fathers and ancestors, good and bad; we now face the same trials. This is not unjust. Tanra gives to all both good and bad things as a test. We must choose to submit and obey rather than rebel or despair. Tanra rewards men for that which they choose. As for the other matter, Tanra revenges the innocent blood; it is his promise. We will see it."

Another man, Onbasha, whose arm was bound between two bone splints spoke up. "We could raid our southwest neighbors the Kalpakla. Those fire worshipers have treasure from the road and karakul sheep."

Chavush snorted his contempt, "You will lead the raid, no doubt, with all our valiant warriors," his hand swept the line of dejected wounded men, "and you will win their treasures and women and settle on the short grass to raise sheep."

The whole assembly laughed appreciatively. At this point Erkan stood and motioned for silence.

"Men of the Chipchak band, consider our glorious past. We have been a place of refuge to other bands in their times of distress. Is their memory so short as to forget a debt or hospitality? Rations can be gathered in this way; they will not refuse us help." Heads nodded affirmatively.

"We have a few mares by the tributary and some across the river. We will gather them and add any wild ones from the south. We have the golden stallion and his mares on the ridges. He will father our new herd." Again heads nodded.

"Fall hunting still remains to be done. There is an abundance of wildlife this summer. There may yet be a late caravan on the North Road who will renew our coffers." There was a buzz of conversation and some shrugs.

"If we raid our neighbors, they will raid us. If we face disaster cheerfully, some may admire our courage and even help. To return to the past in fear is not the way of the Chipchak. However glorious our past, it is to the present and the future that we turn. The ancestors taught us the reality of all the worlds: flesh, spirit and mind. The Buddha taught that pain comes from an increase of desire. Zoroaster taught that good and evil are ever in conflict. We must weigh our motives that our hearts be pure. The Cristus teaches that God provides our salvation and freedom through Him, if we will accept His ways and the Holy Spirit's guidance." The council and people were spellbound listening.

"People of the Chipchak, we face a hard winter perhaps, but good must follow bad as sure as day follows night. Night has come, but let us now sleep and rest our wounds; tomorrow the light comes again."

On this note the camp went to bed, but Vashtie, Perihan and old Meryen worked late with the wounded. During the night the river rose because of rain in the mountains. Water, now too deep to wade, cut the island off from the north bank.

Dawn brought no relief to the band. More rain threatened, and the water did not abate. The Khan looked out on his dissolving dominion in despair through a swollen and raw face. He walked to the high point of the little island and prayed repeatedly. At first he whispered, then shouted.

"Whatever God will help me now, will be my God forever." He sat for a while in silence waiting for some quick reply, but none came. He wondered if the gods thought his band too small, wicked and insignificant to notice. The island became steadily smaller.

It was noon and the last of the wood had been used for heating the last of the day's rations. No one was satisfied.

A hearty shout sounded from the south, upstream. From there a raft bore down on the island. At the stern a large, bony man moved a tiller oar and four children, a large fat, red-haired girl and three skinny boys, paddled from the sides. A very small, bird-like, women ran forward with a rope as they steered the narrow north channel of the island.

"*Toot*, catch," she shrilled at the surprised watchers and threw with strength the rope in her hand. It was weighted by a small hollowed stone and flew into the midst of the bystanders. It was caught and looped round a tree stump. The raft wheeled over and swept to the island's side. Several large hide floats buoyed up the sides of the raft, and it slid right up over the flooded river bank to the land. The occupants of the raft jumped to land and tied up the raft securely to the bank.

"Thank God, we make it here," the woman said in the Hunnish trade language, "River grow big with flood." Their clothes were rough and poorly made of skins of the north, but their faces and accent were Gothic. The Ostrogoths had adopted the horse culture of the Ukrainian steppes but kept some of their woods and river crafts alive.

"You trade food for help?" she said, making all the appropriate gestures. "We go back, own country, long trip, need food. Katze cook for Blume unt Hans, Kinder grow strong. All born in China, learn home road. We help you leave island, big danger here. More water come."

Meanwhile the boys and the girl, Blume, ran a rope to the up-stream (south) side of the island and secured it firmly to a tree trunk. Helping several of the stronger Chipchak children and women aboard, they cast off, as the woman, Katze, remained to talk. They swung the boat, using poles and paddles, to the opposite, village side where they unloaded and secured another rope. Then they swung back with a pulley, while the little woman continued to exchange information with the tribesmen. All but the most severely wounded and the medicine woman were ferried across by these new friends. They were safe from the flood.

Two bags of grain and a pile of burned animal flesh were laid on a skin and given to the boat people. A feast was being prepared now that the people were reunited to their ruin of a camp. From the under-ground grain depot more food was brought. Every one ate well that night.

Keke talked long with the boat people in their language. They seemed to be in agreement about something. Keke looked happy and went about singing her favorite song: "*Deli Sevgi*, Crazy Love."

None of this escaped Erkan's notice. He called Keke to come with him to where the khan's yurt had been located and as she obediently sat before him, he dug up a small metal chest covered by the charred remains of the yurt. The metal lid opened to reveal silver and gold coins and beneath them a pale yellow comb of electrum, an alloy of silver and gold. He held it up before her face.

"You have been a comfort to me during the pregnancy of my wife. I would have you take her place, but I know I cannot hold you against your will. Here is the proof of my love. I found it at the woods where your master lay dead. You know the penalty of a slave murdering her master." He held it before her eyes. Then he put it into her hand, saying, "We know this is yours. It's of the Greek style. You wore another like it on the hunts." She gasped, nodded her head and clutched the comb to her breast.

"I didn't know where I lost it. I heard the quarreling, I was afraid, but curious, so I went to see."

"What did you see?" Erkan demanded.

"The dead men," she whimpered, "with the arrows in them. Lying there, staring."

"The other men, the donkey," He insisted, "What of them?"

"No others, just the donkey and Onder's horse." she mumbled, "just two dead men, Onder bey and the Hun warrior."

"He was no warrior," Erkan laughed, "only a poor merchant with a loaded donkey." He continued seriously, "beside women's tracks there were two or three very indistinct men's tracks in the woods. They robbed the bodies, stole the animals."

"I touched nothing, nothing at all." she started to cry stuttering, "I ran ba- back, to help ...they were d- dead."

"But a knife, was it in his chest? He was stabbed several times," he continued. She nodded in affirmation.

"Everything was there, clothes, knife, weapons, donkey and horse. You said Hun warriors were there."

"I lied, to hide and destroy the tracks and signs from my men," he said quietly. "When I found your comb at the grove, I feared you might bear a heavier part, so I deceived them, partially, but someone will have to bear the guilt."

"I had to know, Yuzbasha and Onder were so angry," she insisted, sobbing. "I shouldn't have g- gone... but I d- did... to look. Will I be p- punished?"

"If you touched nothing, no one need know about your being there." He touched her chin lifting her face, and said kindly, "You see how much I love you. You will stay and not go with the boatmen."

"Yes, I understand now," she said, "you truly are good, I w- will stay with you."

He let her go back to the women at work on the bank. She went to clean up the space where the new yurt would stand. He hefted the weight of the small chest in his hand and removed a very small gold coin. Burying the chest in the ground of the old yurt site from where he had removed it, he turned and walked down to where the boatmen feasted.

The Goth had a slow but understandable command of the trade language, and as he and Erkan talked, they found that each sharpened and pleased the other. Erkan asked many questions. He found the man interesting; they stimulated each other as they exchanged information. The Goth said he was making his second trip from China. He was becoming a prosperous member of his community. An older son by an early marriage had stayed with the goods in the Carpathian Mountains. The younger boys were learning the route and making contacts with key people and places.

This was their last trip, please God, and they would retire; stay home and tell about their adventures. They would go down the Irtysh River to the Tubol River and then up to the Ural Mountains where the Finnish tribes dwell. All this to avoid the Tartars. They would portage down to the Volga River, go west, up river, if prudent, or down river, south to the crossing at Gechit City. It was a prosperous commercial town of tents and yurts, and full of Jewish merchants. However, the capital of the Right Hand Horde or West Huns, formerly on the Don river portage, was reported to have moved west into the land that had remained of the East Goths. The Ukraine was being lost. That part of the return would depend on circumstances. Erkan asked him about the new faith many of the Goth were following.

"It is both easy and not easy,", the man, Yuhan, said. "Easy because it is God who acts to forgive and direct. Not easy, because you first have to learn to obey; also that any good thing you alone try to do, will prove to be damaging to others. Stranger still, that mistakes or even evil done to you, can still be used of God to the good of those damaged."

"You mean a person cannot act according to his own judgment?" Erkan asked incredulously, the oil on his burns shining under his bandaged head. "And evil will turn good?"

"It is a great humiliation to know that all your best intentions turn out badly and need forgiveness. While evil men's plans and bad events that happen will eventually be turned into a blessing for those who do God's will."

Erkan was confused, "But this God is full of love and giving as well as judgment. How can it be so hard to understand?"

"Because it pleases Him to give freely the unexpected or undeserved gifts and to frustrate the keenest plans that unbelieving men may devise for what they consider their own best interests," Yuhan stated.

He continued, "Let me illustrate this with the desires of Constantine, the Emperor of East Rome and the city named for him. He planned, in his life, to use the Christian church as glue to hold his empire together and prop up his throne, but on his establishing the church, discovered that it was fracturing into quarreling theologies. He was forced to persecute to achieve his plans. His glue has split the Empire into partisan rejection.

"Yet on his hunting trip while visiting our King and country, came an unexpected, an unasked for grant of a thousand years to the Empire he had now established from Constantine's city! The new Rome will last a thousand years."

BOAT DEPARTING (PAGE 58)

"Who told him this news?" questioned Erkan.

"A hermit of the woods," replied Yuhan. "Walked right up and picking out the emperor though all were dressed for the hunt, he just made the proclamation, `A thousand years for Christ's Glory.'"

"Kings and commanders wear a different aspect. It shouldn't have been hard to know who he was," argued Erkan. "How did he convince the King?"

"He drew him aside and told him the meditations of the king's own heart. He is said to have told of family secrets known only to those intimate with the king."

"An unsought grace of a thousand years," mused Erkan. "How great is this loving Fatherly God you profess! I have decided to follow him and the teaching of his Son."

"You do well," said Yuhan, "but beware your plans; they may not bear expected fruit. Set no goals for your own glory."

"My only plans are to prosper my people, do justice and train my heir in military skills that he may be like me and grow in greatness."

"That alone may be harder than you think," Yuhan replied, shaking his head vigorously. "Those are fleshly desires for men's glory."

"A thousand years means nothing to each generation; they have only their one life," Erkan said thoughtfully. "It might well become a burden to a people."

"The burden of greatness?" Yuhan asked.

"The burden of a promise of which each generation can have only the tiny one-life part," replied Erkan. "The longing for a larger share, and in addition, the probable misunderstanding of the thoughts and intents of their predecessors. To have great pride in a misunderstood past." They were silent and thoughtful.

Finally, Yuhan spoke, "Since you don't covet such a boon and favor, perhaps the Lord will give it to your family." He gestured open armed, "Lord, grant a grace of a thousand years of greatness for the family of the Khan, for only a truly powerful God can. It would last as long as Constantine's Empire."

"The Chipchak are a great people. They have no need of empires to prove it. The uprightness of our actions show it. Empires bind; we are free." said Erkan, getting up. The men, sitting by listening, heard the first statement by Yuhan, but missed the reply of the Khan. They took it as a prophesy.

The children and Katze came near because their provisioning and preparations were complete. The boy, Hans, took a large leaf and holding it with a small bronze Jews harp before his teeth produced a tune that was strange to their ears.

"Time for our vespers. Sing: God has sent a loving Savior," commanded the father. "I will help you." The hymn was sung with gusto by all the family.

1. God has sent a loving Savior;
He has broken Satan's hour.
Yesu hunts you, when He finds you,
You will know transforming power!

Chorus: Yesu died and rose victorious;
Yesu saves us from our sin.
He will free you from hell's power,
Give abundant life within.

2. God has seen you sad and lonely;
And He knows the yoke you bear.
Yesu took your heavy burden,
Gives a heart that's free from care.

Chorus:

3. God will pardon all that shames you;
Now, in Yesu's name you die.
You will live to give God glory,
And be changed to live on high.

chorus:

YUHAN'S CHILDREN'S SONG

"Your words touch me and bring me strength. I will believe; I must believe." The agony and exhaustion of the last days showed clearly on Erkan's marred face.

"Be firm, but don't strive. Rest in his promises and faithfulness," Yuhan replied with a concerned smile. "You are learning, when you are ready you can be baptized and be a *Hristian*."

"I'm one now. I've decided. If you leave, it may be several seasons before anyone comes. All Christians are baptized, aren't they? Have you been baptized?" He peered in the tall man's face.

"Yes, by Bishop Ulfas himself! My father said wait, but I could not. My heart burned within me to obey Yesu. Afterward, I had to travel to live, but I never regretted it. So, I found my wife and my life by trade," he smiled serenely.

"Baptize me now, I'm ready. I had pledged myself to the God who answered me. Yesu answered. Now, I believe, and I have Christians in my camp who can teach me and the tribe." He watched the effect of his words. Yuhan sat shaking his head. "The woman we spoke of is my only wife. She is from the West; I will keep your rules and have, but one wife. I will make a yurt for a worship place. *Nay o lure*, please."

"It is dark now. Who will witness it? You are injured. Will you wish to be wetted again in flood waters?"

"Water will cool my burns. My tribe is at hand; some already favor this new way. Accept us now." The Goth's face reflected uncertainty; Hope shone on Erkan's.

"Go ahead, father," urged the oldest boy, Hans. "You did already in the Yellow river village where we stayed." Yobert nodded his agreement.

"This is different. We lived with the Ma family many months, and the Suriyani traders had taught them before us. We have been here only a few hours," the big man protested weakly.

"He believes, Father, and there will not be another opportunity. He is ready," the boy insisted bravely.

"I too, believe and would obey Yesu with my Khan." The voice was that of Yuzbasha. "My wife is already baptized, and she teaches me." The big Goth shrugged and stood up, all took this for acceptance.

"I, too, would follow my Khan," Chavush's great voice boomed out. "Let me walk in the way of Yesu."

"Baptism is not a test of loyalty to one's earthly ruler, but to a heavenly one. Faith must come before obedience," objected Yuhan, facing the new solicitor.

"When I was a child, I obeyed my mother, for I knew she was wise. As a youth I obeyed my father and my Khan for the same reason. Now, there is a Higher Spirit who leads through you and my Khan. How can I do other than follow?" He held out his hands in appeal to

Yuhan and then turned toward the listening men. A murmur of assent spread among them. Several moved forward to offer themselves. "It is Tanra's will."

"Let God's will be done; I will do it," Yuhan's voice rose triumphant. They all moved toward the swirling waters of the river.

> - - - - - - >

"We will remember you in our prayers every day as we travel and as long as we live," stated Yuhan, standing wet in an equally wet circle of men.

"You have changed the future of our tribe and brought us Tanra's blessings. We will tell the story of these events in the yurts of our grandchildren."

"We will move on before morning. The flood may subside, but now we will sit by the fire and rest a bit," said Yuhan to his family and new converts. "Then, we will go. You `new-born' must rest. Meditate well on all you have promised and pray for strength to keep your vows. God will lay a foundation stone in your hearts, but you must build on it. You have promised God and God will send you His promise, His foundation stone.

"I have spoken from my heart. Go with Tanra's blessing and the friendship of Erkan: Khan of the Chipchak."

"The grace and power of our Lord be with you, friend." replied Yuhan.

"Remember our agreement that we spoke of earlier, about my wife," said Erkan. The man nodded.

"Goul lay, goul lay git, Go happily." Erkan walked away , limping toward the area where Keke was readying the bed. Then, he suddenly changed direction and walked to the yurt of his wife, Sevim, which stood intact next to his own destroyed dwelling. "How strange that the yurt had not burned," he thought. The structure held several bodies now, cleansed and wrapped for burial. It would have to be after several more days of salvage and rebuilding. They could not delay long. He stood in the dead room and an apology shaped itself on his lips, but he could not say it; it was too late.

The tribesmen plied Yuhan with other questions, while his family slept. Gradually all slept. The Khan did not sleep. His mind found several unexpected God sent grants: A golden stallion; a golden-haired wife; a golden-skin son and heir, a child of promise. These surely are the promised foundation stones. He would build on them. He knew his plans for them would bear abundant fruit and blessings for all the tribe; only good will come from this.

The boatmen left early, before first light, with food and whatever they had gained trading in the East, free and unmolested. They carried joyful memories, but no additional passengers.

FIRE STORM (PAGE 46)

PEOPLE, PLACES & PLOTS IN CHAPTER 6

Cha'vush: the sergeant does unpleasant duties to satisfy old expectations.
Day'day: is a stubborn and outspoken traditionalist.
Er'kan: whirls among a new faith, old traditions and human problems.
Kai'yam: meaning my rock, the child of promise named by Princess Sevim.
Ke'ke: the Goth finds herself slumped between new sensations and old experiences.
Se-vim': a dead princess is the source of new experiences and old traditions for the tribe.
Sha'man: still leads the way, southwest to the tribe's future destiny.
Tan'ra: the ancient creator and sky god is enlarged into a newer mold.
Vash'tie: finds strength to proclaim her faith in action.
Volf': younger brother of Keke, taken captive by the West Huns to be a horseman.
Yown'ja: red-haired baby girl of Vash'tie, despised as of foreign blood by some.
Yuz'basha: faces double responsibility for the tribe.

GLOSSARY HELP:

jan'um: my soul; my dearest; beloved; a term of affection used for any in a family.
kill'im: a woven rug that can be rolled and is portable; also used for wall hangings.

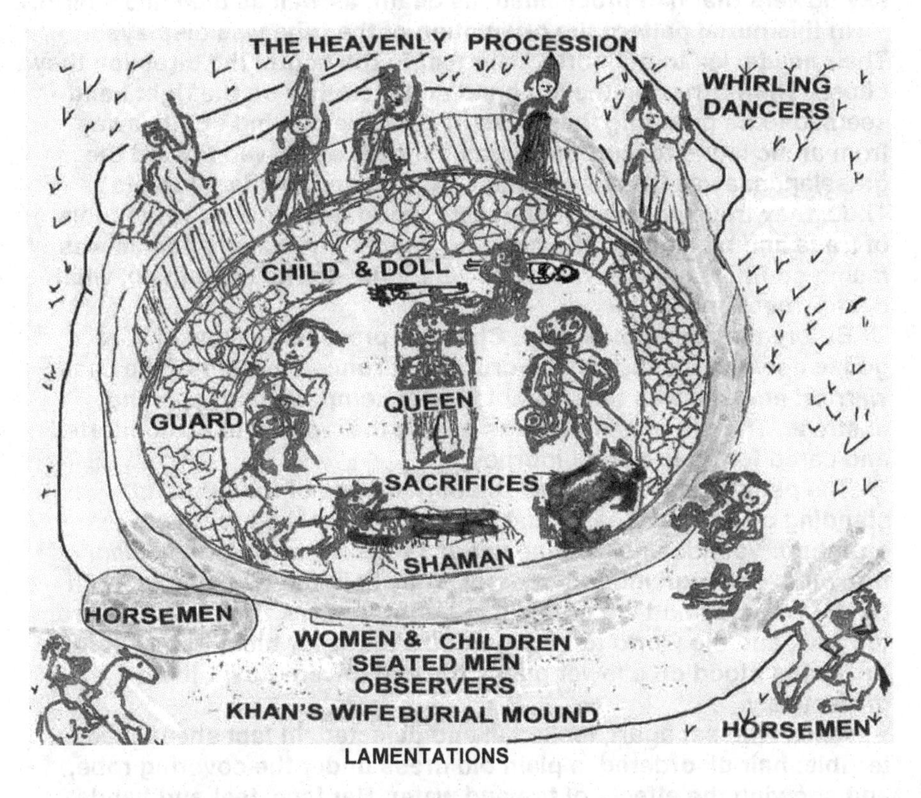

LAMENTATIONS

The burial mound was prepared somewhat hastily on the fifth day after the fire and flood. The mother of the heir was laid on a bed of reeds and skins with her favorite jewelry and robes of state. Most were of local manufacture and contained the art of the Yenesi River smiths with writhing animal figures in bronze or silver and embroidery in silk and colored threads of steppe flowers and fruits.

Princess-like she lay, dressed in her finest. The fire had failed to penetrate the heavy felt yurt. Her hair filled the wood frame in the elaborate coiffure of tradition. Her complexion was a pale, transparent, yellow blush. She seemed to sleep. Above her head lay the bodies of two old women: one burned in the fire; the other injured but able to sit drunkenly in her place of burial. One female attendant would have been enough, but the living one was in such bad condition, past the age of children, and her only son had been killed in the stampede, so she desired to join him. The son and another older man were positioned left and right, east and west, beside the central figure. Each held weapons and favorite articles, including a saddle. Under the feet of the royal lady lay the shaman dressed in wolf mask and skins, facing south away from the group. Close by his distorted face and twisted limbs lay some of his secret medicines and paints. His assistant had painted his face with the zigzag lines of the sky powers that had proclaimed his death, as well as the child's birth.

In this burial pattern the orientation of the tribe was displayed. Their heads lay to the north, their feet to the south, the direction they chose. The warrior on the left hand and the other on the right hand seemed to be guarding the flanks of a people moving south, away from arctic lands toward the warmer sun. They moved toward the grasslands, away from the reindeer tundra and the dark forests. Thus, they traveled even in the spirit world, with their favorite tools of trade and pleasures. The honored, feared and hated shaman was facing south, leading to the lands where the spirits drew them, where destiny beckoned.

Before the assembled tribe, Chavush pressed a pillow of wild goose down to the face of the drugged, drunken mother of the dead warrior; and she was thus, enabled to accompany both son and mistress. The drowned child was beside the women to be comforted and cared for on the spirit journey.

The people gathered round the buried base of the tumulus, standing on the piled earth that would serve as the top-fill of the structure. Vashtie and Perihan sagged together sitting on a *killim* thrown over a high mound of earth. They held the two infants, both tightly wrapped and cocoon-like in bright binders. Tiny infants were too frail, and the world too dangerous a place for them to be left free. Yuzbasha stood on a lower plane, but still towered over them protectively.

Keke, who sat apart, looked ill and dejected. In fact she looked terrible: hair disordered, a plain old dress under the covering robe, and showing the effects of fire and water. Her face, feet and hands were dirty. Her eyes were red and swollen. She had slept little in the last four nights. Erkan, in agony with his burns, had not permitted her to rest. She had to aid or relieve the equally exhausted medicine woman, Meryen, and help Perihan and Vashtie in the changing of bandages; the application of cool, clabbered milk in poultices; cut loose the burned cloth from wounds; apply fresh butter; grind more herbs for poultices against infections; and wash bodies, living and dead.

Keke was relieved of any opportunity to care for the new born. She was ordered not to touch the baby, the heir and child of promise. No possibility of damage to the infant, because of envy or ambition, was permitted to a second wife or concubine.

At night too, Erkan demanded Keke's attention. He craved love and affection, but must be touched with care because of the burns. He was passionate, but in agony which changed to fury, if a burn was touched. He abused her; praised her; cursed her; offered her extravagant gifts; threatened her; and demanded she tell all she knew about life, faith and customs among the Goths. His mind would not rest, and neither could she. He was near dementia, and he drove

Keke before him.

She sat dully, too exhausted to sleep. Against her will, it all came back to her in memory. She was a child again with a different name, a flower name, happily playing in her mother's kitchen or out among her father's horses. They were important people living on the Ukraine grassland beyond the Dniester River, but there were feared enemies in the East, savages of great ferocity.

She was big for her age. She had already completed her eighth year and was nearing another year, when she was captured. They had been picking berries in a small wood near a stream, when a band of roughly dressed men rode up. They pursued and swept away her mother and attendants with the horses. The children had hidden while the chase across the flatlands went on. Father had gone to the military encampment to wage war, so there was no one to rescue them. Her brother Volf, now six, had whimpered and cried softly while she comforted and shushed him.

After a long silence, with the sun lowering, they ventured out. They had not taken ten steps out on the steppe when a voice cried in their language, "Stop. don't move." They froze as two men with strung bows rode between them and the wood. They looked doubtfully at the brother, but he was large for his age and these horsemen were of small stature with stout, heavy bodies and short legs. He may have looked two years older to them. They wore small goatees and large mustaches on their brownish faces and had only a queue of hair under their pointed metal helmets. Their torsos were covered in a leather and metal breastplate, and they wore cloaks fastened round their necks and loose down the back.

It was growing cool, and the children shivered. "March, that way," the younger man ordered, pointing them south and east to where mother had said the great Dnieper River lay. After that, they walked their horses after them and spoke in a strange tongue. They passed a bag of drink among themselves, drinking by squirts without touching the spout and ate meat by taking a bite in their teeth from a big piece and putting a knife before their chin, cutting upward to sever it.

After three hours, the last two under the light of a rising moon, they arrived at a camp. She had carried her brother on her back for part of the last hour. As long as they trudged on, the men did not yell at them. They had eaten berries and food on the outing, but they were famished when camp came in sight. The men were greeted, the catch was looked over and an argument broke out over the sleeping Volf. The two guards shrugged and rode off to a tent to eat. A scruffy old man gave them a wood cup of watered down clabber to drink and a few scraps of dried meat.

They were dumped with a large band of 50 children who were being walked from one camp to another. Herds of cattle and horses too, were being driven across the plains in the same leisurely fashion. At the night camp there was always warm food and blankets of wool. By day there was only the exertion of walking and the whip for laggards.

The tear-shaped drove of children moved across the steppes at a regular, if slow, pace. None played, ran, or did more than move to one of the edges to relieve themselves. There were older children among them. They automatically took charge and tried to keep the stragglers caught up, carrying some of them. They were allowed to rest every hour for about ten minutes. The older ones carried bits of dried meat for them to suck on. Others carried ointments for blisters, cuts and thorns. In the rest time a few would lead in prayers or songs as they trudged toward the Don River.

1. Yesu, see our hard condition.
   Yesu, help your children through.
   Give us daily bread and love us.
   We will share with others, too.

2. Yesu, see our nightly vigils.
   Hear the prayers we make to you.
   Shield your children from the devil.
   Let our hearts belong to you.

3. Dry our tears and heal our soreness.
   You felt thorns and lashings too.
   On a cross you died to save us.
   Let us live and die for you.

CAPTIVES' PLEA

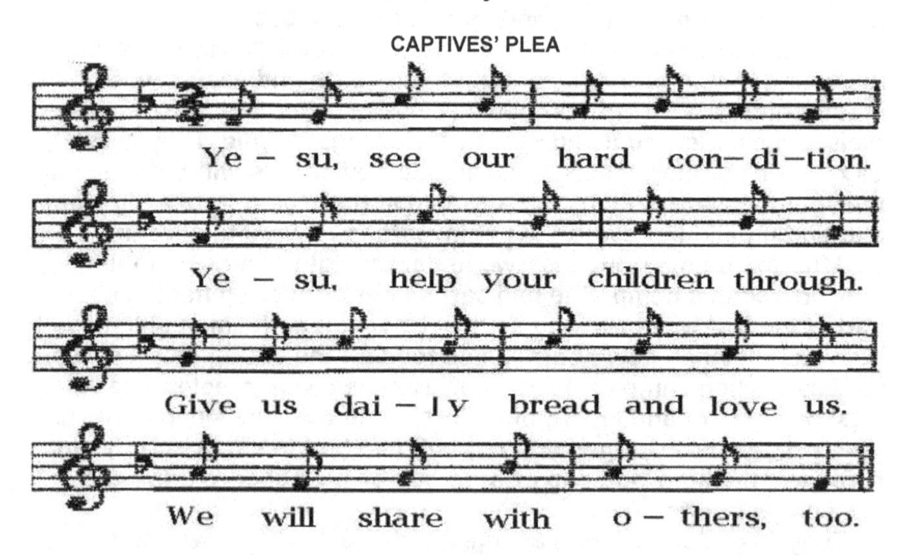

Keke knew the hymns for her mother had faithfully taught her, but she was starting to doubt God's care for her. She did not like being driven with the whips and shouts, always being hungry with so little

food. She grew tired of caring for the little ones, many of whom died, and sharing food with her brother who failed through exhaustion to get his part. She became very anxious to please the guards. She did not want to die.

The march lasted from an hour after sunrise to an hour before its setting. The strong developed more strength, and the weak grew weaker and died or were left behind. If a child, or a group tried to escape, the horsemen would laughingly ride after and shoot their arrows at first from afar and then closer in a contest of skill. Wolves and predators came out of the forest to follow the trail of deserted animals and people. Eyes from the woods, ravines, and high brush watched their passage. Sometimes a child, ill and deserted by careless guards, was snatched up to the bosom of some crying, hungry heart whose own child was lost. Such hearts would not be denied, and if the guards observed from afar, they shrugged. If the child lived; well and good. Next summer they would return. Finally, they arrived at a huge, new yurt encampment on the river Don. Keke had carried Volf several hours at the end of every day, but every day they both grew stronger, if scrawnier. A small but determined remnant arrived at the training camp.

Drill in language, use of the bow, riding and trailing started. The day was full of chores, lessons, testing and punishment for failure was severe. Praise was rare, but given when merited. Soon all strove for praise and the small rewards that accompanied it. Failures were taken away and never seen again. Some said they were sold; others said killed. Life was crude and hard. After three years some of the children, boys and girls, were sent to the soldier's barracks to work. Keke, at twelve, was among them. She tried prayer once again in desperation, for she knew what would happen to some, but there was no answer that she detected.

Volf stayed with the school to become a soldier and at ten, as tall as a Hun, started riding summer patrol with the horde. She never saw him again.

After a week some of the girls and boys at the barracks became sick. Vomits, jaundice, diarrhea and listlessness were part of the symptoms. Keke faked the same sickness, using other girls' stained garments. The group was taken away and sold as a bargain to a Byzantine merchant from Crimea. They were transported there by boat and wagon and dosed with medicine. Keke was one of the first to recover. Those who responded were graded for looks and ability. Accordingly, they were taught cooking, serving, sewing and weaving, or dancing, singing, elocution and manners. All were taught to talk Byzantine Greek. Life was strict, but pleasant for three years.

At fourteen she had to start to earn her keep, the merchant said. He arranged special parties with rich men as paying guests. At these events she sang and danced and was introduced to less pleasant activities of drink, drugs and sex from which she earned a small part

of the take. When she had met the young, high living Onder, she recognized her opportunity. He was idealistic, but undisciplined, and she could wrap him around her finger. They hatched a plot to take his uncle's goods and make their own fortune. He bought her with stolen money, and taking the great golden stallion, had made off to the lucrative Eastern markets, which proved to be so far and so difficult to reach.

Now she found herself at the end of the road. Onder gone, dead, as he deserved, for betraying her for the horse. She was at her wit's end, the wife of a tribal chief, held hostage to a threat of trial and execution. Who would dispute the denunciation of Erkan? If she ran, they would have her before a day was out. She needed security and respect. She tried to pray, but only one word came: 'Help.'

She moaned and felt the throb of her head. She had not been able to care for herself these last days as she had been taught in Crimea, and her body felt different, a strange nausea pulled at her stomach. She laid her head on her arms and wished for Volf or Mother.

The Khan dressed in long black robes and black fox fur pill-box hat, began to gyrate on the broad rock walk and wall-to-be of the tomb. Oboe and flute began the sad, stirring music and accompanied the khan. The stage of pounded earth, standing on the north side of the tomb was part of the wall. This wall was part of the supports on which the rafters, reeds and skins were to be laid before burial. Both inside and out, the tomb would be a replica of the yurt, which was a replica of the dome of the world. The whirling motion coincided with the motion of earth, counter-clockwise. The man in darkness grieves alone and night dominates. As he began his movement, he reached one hand, the right, with palm up to receive a blessing from the sky, the other dropped to a tipped-palm gesture behind him to spill the blessing to those on earth. His movements were slow and steady; there is no rush or haste.

Then slowly a pale whirling eminence joins the dance. Several figures in silver and black robes and tall pointed caps join the ritual. Figures of mountains circled the brim, above that the moon and star symbols, and near the crown, the sun. They whirl, counter-clockwise before him and pass him in a clockwise direction circling round the one living representative and the recent dead. The onlookers understand that the stars and moon join with man in solidarity. Finally a torch-bearing figure of the worshiped and welcomed sun in bronze and copper ornaments and colors joins the swirling parade. He holds the torch up above his head so it moves, yet seems not to move. He too, circles slowly as the midnight sun moves round the horizon in the arctic summer, the grieving man has ceased to gyrate and stands dejected, head and body bowed. Three whirling circles of the burial mound finish the heavenly display and the whirling figures disappear and the mournful music fades to silence. The heavenly procession is finished. Tanra understands and consoles his people.

The valued traditional dress would be returned to the now scorched trunks for the next occasion.

The Khan paused. Looking from his position standing near the wall, he could see the living and the dead. He looked on the figure of the woman he loved and the shaman he hated. He was confused by a rush of emotions and filled with guilt. There was both gladness and sadness, relief and regret. How strange the way of God, mingling these feelings.

He signaled and two horses, both injured in the fire and not likely to recover, were led forward. They were placed at the right and left corners below the warriors facing out and killed there. Thus, the tribe gave its best, though not in the best condition.

The horse sacrifice was a borrowed ceremony, inherited with the horse from the western peoples of the steppe. It was practiced from Britain to India as the best and highest offering. Sometimes, the sacrificed animal was called the representative of the gods. Special colors were selected for special occasions. They gave what they deemed to be the best.

People have usually offered that which their society has most valued to heaven: precious metals and gems; animals and goods; virility and marriage; children and life itself. In exchange, they pray their own will be done for things on earth.

Erkan nodded to Vashtie, who had become his wife's favorite in the months since her coming. She was to start and she, Yuzbasha and several others, including Keke, repeated the 'Lord's Prayer' in the hearing of all and ended with the words `deliver us from the evil one, Amen,' and then crossed themselves from right to left in the manner of the Eastern Churches. They had practiced in their meetings beyond the camp in privacy and were ready.

Then, a startling thing happened. The group started to sing: all of them, together at the same time. The astonished tribesmen listened with incredulity to the strange words and foreign sounds. Four men's voices of different timber and quality sang the verse in unison.

VASHTIE'S NIGHTMARE (PAGE 70)

The higher musical echoes were repeated, softly in chorus by women in the group. A sweet child's voice completed the last phrase of each verse. The burial hymn was translated in their ears into a wailing farewell to the dead with something of their scale and familiar rhythm, yet the verses' contents, meaning and the echo effects were foreign and strange. They listened, fascinated and attentive:

1. Have mercy on your servants, Lord;
   Your servants, Lord.
   Who humbly come before your throne;
   Before your throne.
   Grant us salvation for Christos dear sake;
   Christos sake.
   And be forgiving of our sins;
   Forgive our sins.
   Free us from all evil; And rule our hearts.
   Yesu, the Savior, shed his precious blood;
   Shed his blood.
   That we might see His glorious kingdom come;
   His kingdom come. Let it come.

A sigh passed through the band of listeners. Was this what they were committed to by the wetting in the river? Was this the heavenly being who would rule their action and decisions in the future? What could they expect from this new allegiance they had accepted? Some were disturbed by this reminder of responsibility taken on during the time of emergency. Others were resentful of the commitment. All listened carefully to the sacred song as the singers continued their presentation.

2. Remember and receive your servant, Lord;
   So faithful, Lord.
   At her life's end she comes before your throne;
   Your throne, Yesu.
   Grant her salvation by your sacrifice;
   By your grace.
   And be forgiving of her sins;
   Blot out her sin.
   She loved and served her last days;
   You ruled her heart.
   Yesu, the Savior calls for her to come;
   Let it be.
   And enter in His glorious Kingdom come;
   His will be done. Gladly go!

3. Yesu calls for all to be God's servants now;
   He seeks for you.
   We will all be called before His throne;

To stand alone.
When He cleans our hearts we have confidence;
We are saved.
We must repent and leave our sin;
His power within.
Yesu provides all we need;
He rules our hearts.
With His precious blood He paid the price of sin;
On the cross.
That He might bring His glorious Kingdom in;
He's at the door. Let Him in.

MISERERE

Vashtie, head veiled, entered the sacred walls of the tumulus and placed a rough, wood T-shaped cross on the breast of her friend. She made the gesture of greeting and farewell used by her people, palms together between her breasts, “Rest well dear one, in Yesu's garden.”
The prepared beams were slotted in the walls and the felt vault rounded above the dead. Earth from the ramps where the people sat or stood was carried forward by everyone and the tomb was completed in half-a-day. Rounded with over a foot of earth, it would last for decades.

> - - - - - - - >

Vashtie lay in feverish exhaustion on the makeshift bed of sand and skins. She had hardly rested since the day of the child's birth. Little Kaiyam lay beside her with her own girl child, Yownja. He seemed to have thrived on the neglect and was sleeping soundly, though he was still losing birth weight. She had little milk to give and was too tired to eat. Sometimes she was feverish.
She moaned in her sleep and tried to pull away, "Quick, before it's too late!" She heaved a deep sighing breath. "The knife, pull the knife!" She felt his body heave up against her. She could feel the handle of the knife, and the blood between her fingers on the knife. "Blood! Is he dead? Trouble now." Her body started to thrash on the bed. "What to do! Where to hide! They're coming... quickly. See in the dust at his side, shining? Don't leave the coins! They must not have them." She made a strangling sound as Yuzbasha leaned over and lifted her up.
"Vashtie, *jan-um*, my dearest," he cried, "you are safe with me. Wake gently, don't fight so." He blew on her face, for the tribe feared to wake someone suddenly. When awake, he soothed her face with his hand. "Don't cry so dearest. I won't let them hurt you." He kissed away her tears, and she slept, but he slept no more that night.
Yuzbasha stared toward the corner where the velvet cords once hung; where the woman he loved had placed a T cross and some sketches that showed bits of the life of Yesu. The first was as a child with his mother. One showed a man praying in a garden while guards drew near, led by a traitor. Another showed a man hung from a cross beam nailed on top of a squared pole. He is slowly bleeding to death under a darkened sky. Also, a woman stands before an empty tomb with angel messengers. The last shows a shining figure ascending into the clouds before awed followers. They are small parchments attached to a hanging *kilim*, a cloth matting. They were prominently displayed on the wall, pre-empting the place of the ancestors.
“ Why did I do it? Why argue and fight? I should have continued on the back trail. I would have had it all without guilt, had I trusted and kept quiet – let others solve my problem for me -- but I, a warrior, was afraid.”

> - - - - - - - >

Cool weather came and large hunts were staged to bring in sufficient meat. The warm, dry days and cold nights were ideal for drying meat. The lost and strayed animals were still being sought. Hunts were staged starting from the borders of their territory, ranging inward to keep the game from going out into other tribal areas. A large appearance on the border also warned off aggressive neighbors who might have misunderstood any rumors about weakness.

They collected debts from friends and trade associates and made promises for ready money. They hocked heirlooms or sold them to another distant family member with a lien to buy it back later, perhaps.

Praise God! Another fall caravan came. It paid well for safe passage and protection. Then, winter fell and hunger came to stay.

JUSTICE OR MERCY (PAGE 77)

PEOPLE, PLACES & PLOTS IN CHAPTER 7

Cha'vush: a vocal defender of the accused and a friend of the needy.
Dar: a counselor from Silk City, a suave oriental diplomat.
Day'day: a harsh traditionalist leader of the opposition.
Er'kan: hard pressed by circumstances, past and present.
Ghen-chair: a literate member of the tribe.
Ke'ke: she can't be found when the law is around.
Mer'yen: the doctor stands to lose a son no matter how the facts are interpreted.
On'der: though he is a dead master and rival, he comes back to haunt the living.
Peck: a city representative seeking compensation and justice for his client.
Vash'tie: a quiet observer of tribal justice.
Yuz'basha: the lieutenant has his past mistakes thrown in his face.

GLOSSARY HELP:

***deli kon'la*: literally it means 'with crazy blood'; youth; teen-age; a teenager.**
***git dish' are ah*: go outside; get out of here; leave.**
***goul'lay goul'lay*: go happily; keep smiling; good by; farewell.**
***hak'suz*: unjust; without justice.**
***kismet*: fortune; fate; one's lot in life.**
***ya'sa*: the law; based on tradition and updated by practice.**

EXILE OR DEATH

It was almost the third anniversary of the murder of Onder bey when Erkan called the council. They sat on the quilt-cushioned trunks that rested against the walls of the yurt. In the place of honor near the pillar of tasseled ropes sat two men; one fair, the other Eastern. There had been letters of inquiry from the small city state of E'peck Kent, located south of the Tanra Dah or Tien Shan mountains. A relative of one of its prominent merchants had been reported murdered in the district. His personal goods and justice were demanded. The *yasa*, law, was to be obeyed. Noncompliance would meet retaliation by loss of trading privileges for Erkan's people and goods. City guides would recommend other more reliable routes of travel to passing merchants. The two men had come as embassy with the threatening letter, an ultimatum. The tribe would be declared *haksuz*, without law. A lawless people become outlaws to all nations in short order.

Erkan had the letter read off by Ghen-chair, their youthful secretary, first to be so trained at the Hermitage. Every man listened with care. Such sanctions would make life harder. Injustice in a community not only damaged its reputation and treatment by other tribes, but affected the `*kismet*', fated future, of the tribe. Tanra was reputed to treat badly those individuals and tribes that were careless of fundamental justice. Not even the rich could neglect such basics, lest they cause their own destruction.

Day-day rushed ahead, as was his custom. "I have repeatedly

urged action on this matter. We are now both smaller and weaker by our delays in handling fundamental matters. Our Khan holds part of the merchant's goods. Restitution needs to be made."

Erkan cleared his throat, "Goods are restored after justice has been done. The signs were not clear at the time. Now the time has come to administer justice."

Erkan continued, "I have twenty gold coins for the price of the women, his property, for the deceased one's relatives. However, thieves robbed the bodies before they came to our possession. The jade knife and any monies are lost along with the animals and whatever the Hun carried. That is outside our responsibility. Two mounted men with a donkey seem to have escaped. Such a pair were seen by sentinels, going west, when our searchers were seeking Hunnish raiders to the east. We give the gold now, in value of the two women kept by ourselves."

Day-day made a gesture as if to speak, but the Khan moved on quickly. "We know of the quarrel between the two young men. It was over the woman Vashtie. We know he lacked the money necessary to pay a bride price. We all recognized the black hunnish arrow that has been the part of a ‘medicine bundle', a sacred symbol to keep their raiders from the heart of our territory. It is powerful magic and would have been greater protection had it not been used for harm and left without further damage to the young man. It was shot in self defense, after Onder had drawn his great jade knife to extort more money from the youth." Erkan smiled wisely, "Greed for gain is the cause of most violence, and jealousy makes up the other part." Day-day interrupted hastily, his querulous voice accusing.

"The man is proud by hasty promotion over others, making free with another's property even before he tried to buy her. She delivered before her full term. He hadn't the money, so he killed the owner to get the slave without cost. He fails to keep the way of the ancestors and brings foreign blood into the tribe. So, the Huns had success in their raid. The curse of the arrow falls on him."

"Our suspect may have had some plot in mind to make the death appear as by a Hun raider. He may have killed the Hun, a merchant, for there were two Chipchak arrows in him. The suspect denies killing either man though he admits to the quarrel and wounding of Onder bey," Erkan concluded.

"The other man killed by Chipchak arrows is not our interest in the case, an unknown, perhaps itinerant or vagabond," interjected ambassador Dar suavely.

"Let our friend Yuzbasha come forward and give us his version of what happened," interceded Chavush.

Yuzbasha stepped into the council circle and looked from eye to eye. Many averted their face or smiled down at the ground. "I would request the withdrawal of the women from the yurt," he said quietly, "What I say is for men's ears only."

The khan nodded. Chavush yelled, "*Git dish are ah*, get out." in his fiercest voice. The women scurried out, but lingered near the door and a few sat outside and rested their head against the felt tent.

"It is true that we quarreled about the girl and the price. It is also true that I had taken the medicine arrow with dark, evil thoughts of damaging the youth again. He had esteemed his life at two gold coins given to my mother in payment. I thought I would return his money and give him again his wound, but I forgot these things in angry words and would have left without acting against him, but he drew his knife. My hands were empty. I didn't have my knife, but he drew and I, evading him, drew bow and arrow on the instant. My purpose was not to kill. So I injured him and mounting, rode out in haste."

"Was it then his own knife that was used to pierce his chest?" questioned Erkan. "My Lord," the youth replied, after a pause, "I don't know. I had left, and since no weapon was found, I could not say whose weapon did it, nor when after my departure. When I returned, the man was dead. That was not my doing."

"Did you see the Hun alive? Did you kill him because he was a witness?" continued the Khan.

"I saw him for the first time, dead and robbed, when I entered the grove with Chavush. I swear it."

"This much is clear," said Erkan, "you went in with strung bow. This means you purposed damage. You admit acting provocatively and angrily. With words you caused the man to draw so you could attack him. You left him wounded, perhaps to die of the renewed wound, helpless against another's attempt. You killed or helped kill a guest of the tribe. Hospitality and protection are the bonds of honor. The Hun could have been attacked by the thieves, and he is not our concern. Have you a ransom?"

"No, My Lord, my family is poor as you know; service, not money, is ours."

"How well I know," Erkan replied, "if we had done justice before the fire, I could have ransomed you, but now I can scarcely pay the lesser ransom for two women. I can only guarantee to sponsor your child, assuming all cost, and your woman will stay with your mother. I appeal to our distinguished delegates," he continued, turning, "what punishment will satisfy you?"

"*Deli-con-la*, crazy youth, jealousy and rage, be merciful, My Lords," interrupted Chavush in his booming voice. "This is no bandit king robbing you of millions, nor professional killer awaiting your lone travelers."

"Yes, but his uncle, Jomer is prominent and will expect something just," Counselor Peck replied in a cultivated accent. "Otherwise, the townsfolk will say the tribes do whatever they please with travelers. It's bad for trade," he smiled knowingly, "Your trade and ours."

The Khan frowned, "Would yoking be adequate justice for the family?" he asked.

"You mean seated on the sharpened stake?" said Peck, with a look of avid interest.

Chavush raised his voice in anger, "No, he means cut loose to wander, a chance to live or die as the spirits guide ... as the Lord decrees," he corrected hastily.

The talkative Peck smiled, "I have little faith in spirits, but a man with a knife could change one's fate."

"You have never ventured unprotected into the forest," snarled Chavush, pushing his face close to the city man. Peck laughed unconcerned.

"I guess it's the best we can hope for, yoking and exile. I'll agree to that, but a curse on anyone who turns him loose," interceded Dar.

The Khan's voice was steel, "Anyone who looses him takes his place; it is the law."

And so it was arranged. The punishment was to yoke a man with a heavy pole across the neck and shoulders with arms and wrists tied to the pole, which stood out almost a foot beyond the hands on each side. The arms from shoulder to wrists were wrapped in raw hide and left to dry and tighten.

With the yoke placed, there were a number of possible alternatives: if he were seated on a sharpened pole he died in a few hours in a pool of blood, in agony. If he were hung with the yoke supported by a pole, a T shaped crucifixion, he died in a day in slow, relentless torture. If he were set free to wander with his yoke, he would probably die in his exertions, but he might just live. If he freed himself, well and good, but if someone else freed him, they suffered the same penalty.

The sentence was immediately carried out, and a small log the size of a woman's neck brought before the yurt. Fresh raw hide strips were wrapped tightly about the man's arms to the wrists. Notches were cut into the log to prevent the easy passage of the hide thongs up or down the log. The man was stripped to the waist and tied on. The only sign of grief was the weeping of the women.

Chavush taunted, "This will be a fine autumn birthday excursion for you, but you are now twice twelve years old.

"Happy memories are a light in the darkness," Yuzbasha replied.

"No comfort for the condemned now," Erkan spoke sharply, with a sidewise glance at the face of the ambassadors. The thin-faced younger man looked happily at the execution's proceedings.

"I've heard lots of stories, but never seen it done before," Peck stated with satisfaction.

"In E'peck Kent we follow the enlightened executions of the Son of Heaven and the people of Han, quick, and simple," Dar, the suave man made a motion with his hand on his neck, illustrating beheading.

"You are sure he can't work that soft leather loose now?" Peck said anxiously.

"We use thick thongs for the shoulders and wrists, my Lords,"

Chavush assured them, tugging at the parts in indication and rocking the condemned in the process.

"Only a knife would free him."

"Or a quick death in the river," stated the suave Dar, "The ways of the Han are better: everything is final."

"Men do not easily surrender life. It is about the struggle that our Epics are composed," stated Chavush flatly. "Now run, man, to exile or death." He pushed him.

The Khan was staring intently at the smug ambassadors and not at the departing man.

> - - - - - - - >

The man moved steadily forward: walk and run, walk and run. The pace was tireless and ate up the miles. He had three hours to cover the distance a horse would do in one. His sweat would keep the rawhide moist and lax. He had today to try for freedom. Salvation was today, not tomorrow. Each day would prolong the agony and make it less possible to gain freedom. If in three days he had not found a way to part the cords, weakness and pain would capture him; caught in a grove of trees, among the rushes and brush trying for water or rubbed raw and bleeding among the rocks. No one ever lasted a week.

The words of Chavush came back to him. Autumn, a birthday excursion, twelve years old and counted worthy for a trip out with the old man. Shade by rocks and trees, a gentle beach to cool fresh water, a place to delight the heart of a child counted grown. Fresh, firm trout roasted on sticks over the coals. He licked his salty lips and pressed on. The sun moved steadily forward.

It was falling night when he arrived at the place. Dry now and hot he went down to the water. On his knees, he put one end of the yoke on the bank, the other he lowered gradually into shallow water.

TWO GOLD COINS (Page 80)

He was now pressed, knees into chest and face nearing the water surface. The weight behind his shoulders and head over-balanced him, and he fell forward into the water. It was shallow and by arching his back and neck, he could clear his face for air. He managed to drink too, but the effort was tiring.

He lay forward on his face trying to immerse his yoke in the water. He was only partly successful. He leaned his weight onto the bank side of the yoke and got to his knees and then to his feet.

He moved to sit between the stones of the embankment. Finding one that was a bit sharp sat so he could scrape his leather thongs against it. Rubbing the leather against the rock, he rubbed his own skin raw under the ties, but he could not stop, except sometimes to doze.

It was just before dawn when he heard the sound of two horses coming. He was uncertain whether to call out. Then, he heard the voice of Chavush.

"Halt, you daughter of *Shaytan*, why such a hurry?" he growled. "I have a young fool of a friend here. Great Tanra, what some men won't do for a nice piece of silk baggage."

In the gray light, he saw the man dismount, draw a knife and move toward the rocks. Chavush crept stealthily forward.

"Hist," he whispered, "I may have been followed. This has to be fast... take the horse, yoke and thongs with you, get to the Irtish River, and drop them there to be taken away. Yesu keep you safe. *Goul lay, goul lay*, go happily; keep smiling."

As the thongs parted, Yuzbasha, gathered them and walked uncertainly to the extra horse to mount. He carried the pole in one hand, stiffly.

"I will never forget you," he promised.

"There is little enough good an old bandit like me can do in this world," Chavush hissed, "now get out, stay away for about twenty years. See the world. Then, you can come back. There will be a new Khan and few will remember your stupid crime or your payment of it."

"Care for the woman, Vashtie," the man pleaded, but the old man had mounted and was moving away.

It was mid-morning when Chavush returned to the yurts. He had been lucky in finding migrating quail and had managed to net a respectable number. He was met by the Khan and one of the city ambassadors at the chief's yurt. The smiling ambassador Peck was exercising a golden falcon on his glove.

"Good hunting, worthy Chavush," said the ambassador. "You've had a profitable morning, I trust?"

Chavush held up his brace of birds for inspection and dismounted. He walked to the medicine woman's yurt and dropped them by the door. As old Meryen came out, he nodded toward them, "These didn't get away."

"But the biggest and most important one did get away. Is that what you are communicating?" smirked the ambassador. "We followed your trail you know. We were doing some hunting too, but you led us. A little too late for the big bird we intended to capture, but enough to find proof." He held up a section of cut rawhide.

"Darkness is a bad time for clean up. You missed this." He threw it toward Erkan who grabbed it out of the air. "See the faithfulness and obedience of your sergeant?"

Erkan suppressed his anger. They were almost past the losses of the fire, with the good will of the trade center they would pass a comfortable winter. His face a violent red, he tried to think of an excuse, a face-saving exit from his dilemma, but there was none.

"Well," laughed the ambassador, "what is his reward?"

> - - - - - - - >

It was near noon when all was readied. Sobs came from the yurts. The ambassadors glowed with satisfaction. The men of the tribe stood about in small groups muttering and staring at the ground. The women peered out of the yurts into the central area. There Chavush was yoked and bared to his waist. His graying hair blew in the wind. His paunch was full and tubby.

"You knew the consequences of your action ... You have been foolish ... You leave us no choice but to obey the law. Tanra searches our hearts. We must do what the law declares right." Erkan's voice dropped, "May He show you mercy."

> - - - - - - - >

Walk and then run, walk and run, eat up the miles, sweat will keep the rawhide moist. There was a place Chavush had known as a boy.

He liked the cool shadows of the glen and the cave, a shelter from the wind that blows cold at night.

Chavush stopped for breath. He remembered the itinerant who came preaching. He knew the trade language, and he was full of sincerity, but his Chipchak was so full of mistakes. It made everyone laugh, of course, and they put up with him even when a few were angry and wanted to drive him out. The men hung on his words for mistakes to laugh over.

Once he had quoted his Master as saying, 'Take my yoke upon you and learn of me.' The men had laughed till they cried. Such a stupid, funny thing to say. It was no mistake, the man insisted.

The Chipchaks were not agriculturists as some of the western tribes were, who plowed the ground every year with oxen. There was only one use of the yoke among Chipchaks. That is what had struck them as funny: who would take another's yoke? Yet, here he was taking Yuzbasha's yoke. Perhaps the yoke was easier if taken for one loved. Is that what He meant? He thought he would like to learn of Him. He smiled and started to run again. Mustn't let the muscles cool and tighten now. Run and walk would get him there. Just another hour, only one now. The evening chill was sharp in the wind.

He slowed his pace. Riding everywhere cuts a man's wind.

His muscles strengthen towards gripping a horse, not running. His arms hurt. He had some discomfort under his arm lately, little chest pains. They were present now.

He could see the little glen in his mind's eye, the nice dark, warm cave out of the cold. There could be danger, even bears, but there were flint rocks on the floor, perhaps... He started to run again.

> - - - - - - - >

After crossing the Irtish, Yuzbasha had stopped to rest. He had thrown his yoke away into the river with the cords. He knew he was truly an exile now. He could join another tribe far away, or go to one of the cities on the silk road. If he went to a tribe they would expect him to take one of the local girls to wife. It was proof or guarantee of loyalty to the new tribe. He could not do that. The alien life of the city would be more difficult and no one would guarantee or provide food and work. Limited provisions were in the saddle bags, a breakfast wrapped in a woman's head scarf with white mares' cheese and dried meat, seeds and berry fruit. Tied in a corner in a small silk handkerchief were two golden coins, sent for his needs. He gasped as he recognized them, Byzantine! The ones Onder had given his mother for her healing care. The ones he had flung back in Onder's face.

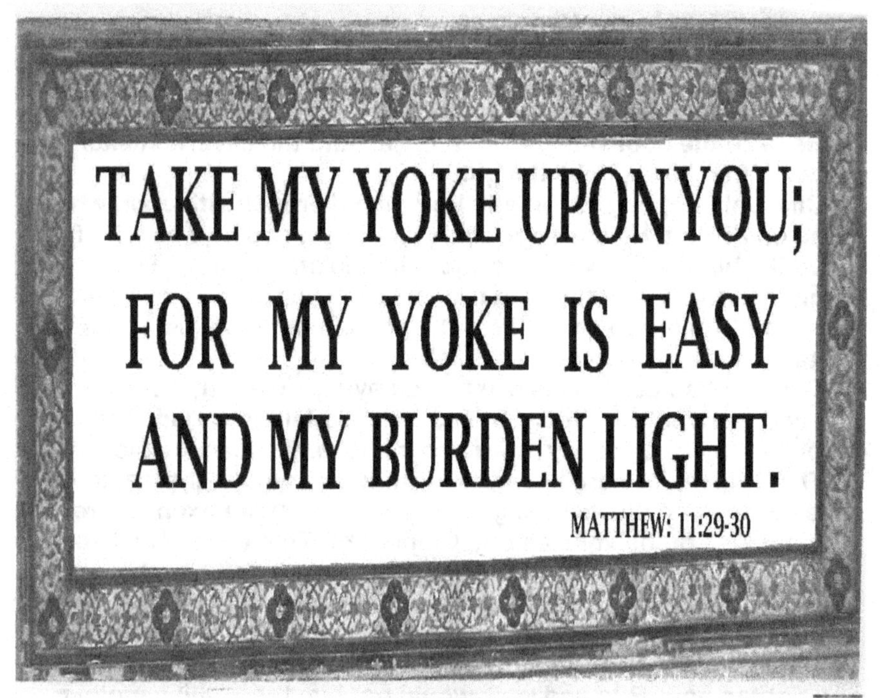

WALL TEXT (PAGE 79)

BEACH AND BEAR CAVE (Page 87)

PEOPLE, PLACES & PLOTS IN CHAPTER 8

Ay'ya: meaning bear, the new baby of the family.
Brun: the faster and cleverer of the twin bears.
Bronz: the stronger of the twins, a yearling friend.
Ghen-chair: a youthful helper on a work detail.
Hock'dale: a lieutenant in charge of a Tartar slave raid.
Kangal: a huge dog used for herding or hunting.
Ka'ya: forgetful of his baby name; the adopted son of the family.
Mer'yen: gathers herbs and useful medicines in the woods.
Mother: aging provider and matriarch of the three cubs and Kaya.
Tar'tars: a neighboring, linguistically related tribe of fierce power.
Vash'tie: a willing worker and loving mother to two children.

GLOSSARY HELP:

vah-she: A beast; wild thing; savage animal; abandoned child.
Ye'su gel: come, protect me; help me, Jesus.
Ye'su sin-in-lee ol'sun: God protect you; God be with you; may Jesus look after you.

WOOD GATHERERS

The ambush was laid with great care, and the Tartar band took their positions carefully hidden in the forest brush. They had watched the boat come down the great river Irtysh that flowed north to the Artic Ocean. The party of Chipchak wood gatherers, largely women and children, fastened their boat to shore, and they spread into the woods with hatchets and knives in hand to gather wood. For the Tartars to be detected would result in the scattering of their prey, and personal loss would be repaid by an angry Tartar Khan. However, the women and children would have to go against the current to return to the grasslands. That fact alone gave the Tartar raiders a great advantage.

The group leader was tall and fair; a contrast to the smaller darker men with him. He had been a captive when a child. Hock-dale knew the taunts and bullying of those whose position was secure. Indeed this was the reason of his command. He had no relatives, wealth or standing, other than his successes, to support him against the tribe. His obedience must be complete and successful gain his only objective. Injury or slavery would await any failures.

It was a venture of great risk just above the heart of enemy's country. Not one movement would be allowed. No fly or ant could be brushed. No cramp soothed; only this would assure absolute surprise of the victims whose movements were heard through the woods.

It was the end of winter, and the ice was starting to rot under the renewed vigor of the sun, each day a little longer, a bit stronger. The cold wind still shook the sides of the yurts and bent the trees, but its power was failing. Winter wood was a camp need, and women were the gatherers and haulers of the winter supply. This supply was now short, as winter continued to hang on.

The Chipchak women were happily talking and laughing as they moved down the hill trail, single file, toward the river, a huge bundle of wood and brush on each back. Children scurried ahead or lingered behind playing, some of the girls had little bundles on their backs in imitation. At the rear the tall, skinny youth, Ghen-chair, came with a few heavy branches in his hands and a little boy on his shoulders. Below, at the river, two old men sat sharing a leather bottle of kumiss to warm their bones, as they guarded boat and party. Little Kai-yam's mother called to the boy kneeling by the trail spinning a rotting leaf by its stem between his fingers, "Run ahead to the boat, careless one," she scolded, "Leave your dreaming and run; see if you can bring it in to shore."

The boat was tied, but had drifted out between the pans of breaking, rotting ice, flowing steadily north to pile up in large dams and flood the low country in spring. It was more work than a sturdy five-year old could do, but it developed strength and was a help for the tiring women. Perihan and Vashtie quickly completed the work started by the child, pulling the boat to the bank. Old Meryen got into the boat to help with the loading. Kaiyam and another child were placed in the stern. Ghen-chair, dropped his branches and bent to the ground to leave the child on his shoulders with Perihan.

At that moment, with an ululating screech, the Tartar raiding party struck. An arrow sped to the heart of each of the gray-haired men. The bending youth was caught by the flat of a sword on the head before he could straighten up. The women loading the boat, with arms full of wood, were caught, thrown down and tied by the laughing men. After which they caught the screaming, running children to tie them near their mothers.

The tall young man in charge caught up Vashtie's hair and laughed, "I should be tempted to keep this little partridge for myself." One of the older, small dark men said, "Don't damage the goods. The Khan will decide their disposition." The group of about ten men had their hands full and did not notice that old Meryen had pulled her knife and cut the shore rope. It was only as they finished taking their captives that they noticed Meryen. With her paddle, she was over 30 yards away and being taken by the current. The band leader with a howl of fury called the attention of everyone to the escapees. They shrieked! Kaiyam's foster mother was able to say "*Yesu-sin-in-lee olsun,*" before she was dealt a blow on the head. The shower of arrows from the short, recurved, horn bows reached the boat at about 50 yards. Old Meryen fell with several arrows in her body. One of the children screamed and the boat began to bob vigorously as Meryen toppled into the water. The current of midstream caught the large vessel and wheeled it round north down the river. There was no movement or sound on it. The Tartar party let it go without the loss of more arrows.

>-------->

The cold wet boy shivered as he sought the rock face hoping for a shelter from the wind. He was shaking and moaning as he came close and saw the icicles and ice sheets clinging to the cliff side. He moaned again "*Yesu gel,*" as he looked for a tree clump to burrow into. Suddenly, he saw a heavy juniper clump with some birch growing through it. He ran toward it hoping to find shelter and leaves. Then as he worked his way under the boughs he saw the cave entrance dark and dry. It ran into the cliff and turned. He did not hesitate but immediately followed it to the end of the passage on hands and knees. After the turn the cave seemed pitch black, but the air was a bit warmer and there was no breeze. The heavy scent of animal permeated the air. As Kaiyam crept forward, his hand touched fur. It was warm. It seemed to be resting over some soft earth. He burrowed and got slightly under it and sighed. His trembling ceased gradually as he created a warm spot, and his hand encountered some branches and leaves he pulled toward himself. Then, he fell asleep.

Kaiyam woke suddenly. His stomach growled and ached, and he sat up. He could hardly contain his hunger, and he looked about him. His eyes now accustomed to the dark could make out several lumpy shapes around him, and he detected a slow deep breathing. He then heard a high squeaking sound, a whine with urgency, and he watched a large paw move a tiny black ball of fur to a spot facing the boy. The bear whelp caught the teat and pushed vigorously against the mother's side and made contented sounds. The boy watched fascinated and moved closer. Many of the tribes revered the bear as almost human and respected their strength. He felt the urgency of his stomach and moved timidly forward. He found what he needed nearer his side and leaving a vacancy next to the vigorous cub, satisfied his hunger. Than he slept.

Kaiyam felt the movement beside him, as he woke. Something huge and strong filled the space of the cave. He was afraid and feigned sleep again. He felt the sniff of a nose above his head. He did not move and held his breath. The cub made a contented sound near his head. The nose transferred to the sound with a satisfied grunt. The form of the bear moved to the entrance of the burrow and squeezed its bulk through the hole and under the cedar spread.

She was nursing and now hungry. She would hunt for the supply of her family.

When the old mother returned later, she was wet and cold and smelled of fish. She bore a large 12 lb. trout in her mouth. She had fished through the ice and eaten her fill. She dropped the fish and called loudly. Two yearling twins awoke and shuffled forward sleepily and ate some of the fish. They avoided Kaiyam, but they did not act afraid or angry. He took the tail of the fish and peeled off the flesh on each side eating it slowly and carefully. The mother had assumed her place and the cub, too small for flesh still sought the comfort of his Mother's renewed supply. As Kaiyam approached, she raised her head and growled. He whined in piteous disappointment, and she lay her head back and let him approach. From that time on, he was one of the family.

The strengthening of spring brought more frequent excursions, and as they ate buds and bugs, the little bears became more active. Kaiyam was something of a misfit, naturally. He was nursing companion of little Ay-ya and active play companion to Brun and Bronz who exceeded him in weight and strength. Their wrestling matches were both fun and challenge. Any hurts were unintentional and could be broken off by one or another taking to flight or even climbing a tree. Kaiyam was the faster runner over a distance, but in the short dash anyone could win. The bears' claws aided climbing, so they were faster, but Kaiyam could go higher and ride the waving tree top where his brothers, for this is what they were now in his mind, would whine and back down.

The summer strengthened the body of the stocky boy and the yearlings reached toward, what was for them, adolescence. Now, thoroughly oriented toward the ways and habits of bears and integrated into the family, he prospered. Even the distrust of this furless bear was overcome, and he was cuffed by the mother, just as the cubs were, when they were noisy or out of place. One learned, by doing or from brothers and mother, the limits of life. He called each by name. He remembered to call himself Kaya.

By the end of summer as they fed on the late berries and fished salmon from the creeks and rivers, Kaya was muscled and strong. Ay-ya was weaned and was large and vigorous. Brun and Bronz took longer trips and excursions away from the family, sometimes accompanied by Kaya. They would return to the cave, yet another winter, but they were maturing. Mother would expect another little one or two. The cave would become crowded. They were building confidence for the break, coming in the next year.

The winter was full of differences. Mother was pregnant and irritable, even threatening with little Ay-ya, and the others remained even farther from her chosen back corner. Mother was getting old and white hairs were spreading among the brown. On two occasions she drove the twins out of the cave, and they were forced to sleep near the door. Kaya, unable to hibernate as his brothers, was forced to take trips out most days and while taking care of his natural functions, hunted and fished a bit. His recall of winter protection in the band, brought him to the saving of furs. The use of wrappings learned earlier, but forgotten in the naked days of summer, led him to attempt sewing. The art of making fire was remembered and experimented with until it was accomplished.

The tools found in the swamped and beached boat provided the flint and iron. His bear family did not appreciate the benefits of fire so he would make his fires some 100 yards from the cave in a shallow scoop out of the rock floor facing the weak sun of winter. There he resumed the neglected skill of cooking, doing as he remembered old Meryen and his mother doing as he fed the fire and watched the cooking flesh. It warmed one's insides and kept the meat longer.

Kaya reverted to his throwing games formerly practiced with other children and was delighted that the skill came with renewed strength and accuracy. He armed himself with rocks and a bone-bladed knife, which he scraped to a reasonable point with rock tools. He made sounds with each thing that he made. Somehow the sound and article were the same, but he couldn't remember why. He did not realize he was replicating a culture. He was simply doing what he had seen done, the way he had seen it. That he practiced women's skills did not occur to him as he sewed furs into a robe, or strung ornaments for his neck, but his long hair was unkempt, matted and inhabited. He remembered combs, but, boy-like, had never loved them, and his poor imitation was used only to scratch inside and to keep the damp mop away from his scalp. The comb stuck out above his right ear.

The twins did not sleep the whole winter through. Warm days would sometimes wake them, as did the constant coming and going of Kaya. They would come out and steal some of his food, if he were away hunting or would mooch some of Kaya's meal, hardly able to resist the tempting smells and wait till the food was done and cool.

Disagreements usually resulted in frequent wrestling matches. Their strength against his quickness and skill, but he rarely won and usually resorted to a quick run to the river or a tree. They were heavier now and less able to follow. In the water he had placed stones at appropriate distances to run across and the bears, disliking winter wetting, would not follow. Mostly they slept, and Kaya learned to live alone and fed the winter visitors to his camp. However, at times he went hungry, and he became increasingly careful about the preserving of food caught and its placement in tree tops and clefts where Brun and Bronz could not raid them.

It was the time of rotten ice again. Mother had a long and laborious birth of a single, slightly deformed cub. Its left paw was twisted outward either in development or at birth. Mother had moaned for days and driven the twins and Kaya out of the cave, even little Ay-ya, now a yearling, had to sleep at the entrance. The new cub moaned for weeks and found no rest. Mother's nose was full of white hair and she seemed less successful in fishing and hunting. Little Ay-ya moved to camp and slept between his brothers, full of self-pity and complaints. Mother drove off any attempts to accompany her on her outings and even Kaya's occasional offering of food left at the cave's mouth did not change her hostility or improve her strength.

Kaya had recalled the efficacy of traps during his long winter. He placed snares in the woods and nets in the river. Although his knots were clumsy, they frequently held their catch. He returned to camp after clearing his nets of a spring salmon. It was large, but thin from wintering in the pools. Suddenly, with a roar, Mother burst into camp; raised to full height, she towered over Kaya's head and moved menacingly toward him. Bronz and Brun ran off at a full gallop, and Ay-ya cowered against the rock wall whining piteously. Kaya dropped the salmon and ran for the back wall where he scooted up a large crack. At about two meters up, he pulled out some cached dried fish. He flung this down to her, but lost his balance and fell at her feet. She roared again, but went down on her forefeet to nose Kaya who lay limp and bleeding, out of breath and frightened. She picked up the salmon and departed. Ay-ya did not wait but ran off in the direction the twins had taken. Kaya, still trembling, gathered his winter accumulations and trudged away with a poorly constructed basket on his back. They never saw Mother again that summer or fall. They became rovers without fixed territory, sometimes threatened off by bear families or dominant males.

It was just after the first snow, falling on the colored leaves and leaving deer tracks in the deeper forest that Kaya and his brothers, now pleasantly fat and padded, sought out the trail. It would be a last kill before the real cold came. They had worked out a hunt strategy in the last months. Kaya, the faster, would go upwind of the deer, while Brun and Bronz waited beside the several trails downwind. The deer would catch the bear-man smell and move quietly down and away. If he ran towards them a few would panic and run away to the trap. Brun was quicker, but Bronz was stronger. If he managed to hit their head, he broke their neck. Brun might have to hit the stunned animal several times, but he rarely missed. Two or three tries a day assured at least one kill, a substantial benefit to the wanderers, for the deer too were fattened for winter.

As Kaya moved across the wind, the heads of the herd came up in unison, but they seemed to be looking not upwind where he crept, but rather up the side of the ridge near the glade. This would mean he might get close enough to kill on his short dash. He had no sooner launched his attack, when two arrows swished out of the hardwood ridge and took two bucks just behind the shoulder. Kaya found himself running in the midst of the herd when a third arrow took a young yearling he had selected, just a few paces before him: this from a conifer cover on the opposite side. He almost stumbled over the fallen animal. Another animal fell somewhere behind him at the same time. Kaya was single-minded. He changed his target and caught another yearling behind the head with a short wooden club, a substitute for a hard bear's paw, he had selected some months before. Without pause he caught the staggering animal and plunged into the brush at the meadow's edge just as three other arrows took the last stragglers of the herd. A fourth arrow plunged into the deer he had scooped up under his arm.

Kaya made no pause after entering shelter, but continued breathlessly up one of the deer trails. Behind him a tumult of shouting and noise had arisen. "Vah-she! Vah-she!" The sound penetrated his mind. A wild, savage animal? He shivered and almost paused to look about him, but he heard the savage roar of Bronz before him. One from the panicked herd had almost run into the great bear, and Bronz broke its back with a blow. Behind him the noise redoubled and began to move in their direction. Bronz was excited by his kill. He showed no disposition to leave his legitimate prey, and refused to follow Kaya down the trail. Kaya dropped his deer and seized Bronz by the ear, an affectionate way they had developed of guiding him to some special treat. However, Bronz was too emotionally wrought up to follow. He shook the boy off impatiently as a blast of a hunting horn sounded just behind them. Bronz rose to his hind legs and roared defiance, a three-year old just coming into strength impressively tall and angry.

A shout of surprise, followed by one of warning came just behind Kaya and he slipped under the bear's upraised paw to escape down the trail behind. As he did he heard the excited sound of hounds, three great kangals as tall as a man's waist burst into sight as Kaya cast a look behind him. The leader running too fast to stop, sprang for the bear's throat. Bronz smashed its head. Kaya turned and ran when the unforgettable sound of arrows touched his ear. Cold shivered down his spine, again the smell of blood, the excited chatter of hunters, the shrill exclamations. Blackness followed momentarily, and he found himself still running down the trail with all his remaining strength. Behind, the mortal roar of Bronz filled the forest, and was followed by the thud of a fallen body. A wave of guilt, shame and anguish flooded over Kaya. He had abandoned his brother.

STEPPE FLOWERS

MOTHER IS HUNGRY (PAGE 88)

HUNT IN DEER PARK (PAGE 89)

PEOPLE, PLACES & PLOTS IN CHAPTER 9

Bin'basha: title of a general, a taunt used by Kove.
Commander: the position of the man leading the hunting expedition.
Hermitage: a place of training for young boys, financed by a prince.
Hock-dale: the personal name of the commander of the Tartar force.
Jon'ny: boy squire and dog handler of the Tartars.
Kaya: lost again in a new wood, searches for security and refuge.
Kootsal': a title of a hermit, director or priest of saintly reputation.
Kove: second in command of the hunting party, teases his chief.
Kutch: a new, young, but brilliant scholar and attendant of the hermit.

GLOSSARY HELP:

a-fee-yet' ol'soon-lar: may they enjoy it; take advantage of it.
ah'ne: mother; mom; ma; a cry for help or of need.
chay: hot tea or some herbal equivalent.
do'er: stop; halt; stay where you are.
gel gore: come and see; here take a look; see here.
hoe'sh gel'den-is: welcome; we're happy to see you; happily you've come.
hoe'sh boll'duke: happily I found you; I'm happy to be here.
kangal: a huge dog used for herding or hunting.
kim ore'row-da?: who's there? who's out there?
kim'sin?: who are you? identify yourself.
tesh-ek-koor': thanks; much obliged;
vah'she: wild thing; savage; wild animal or person.

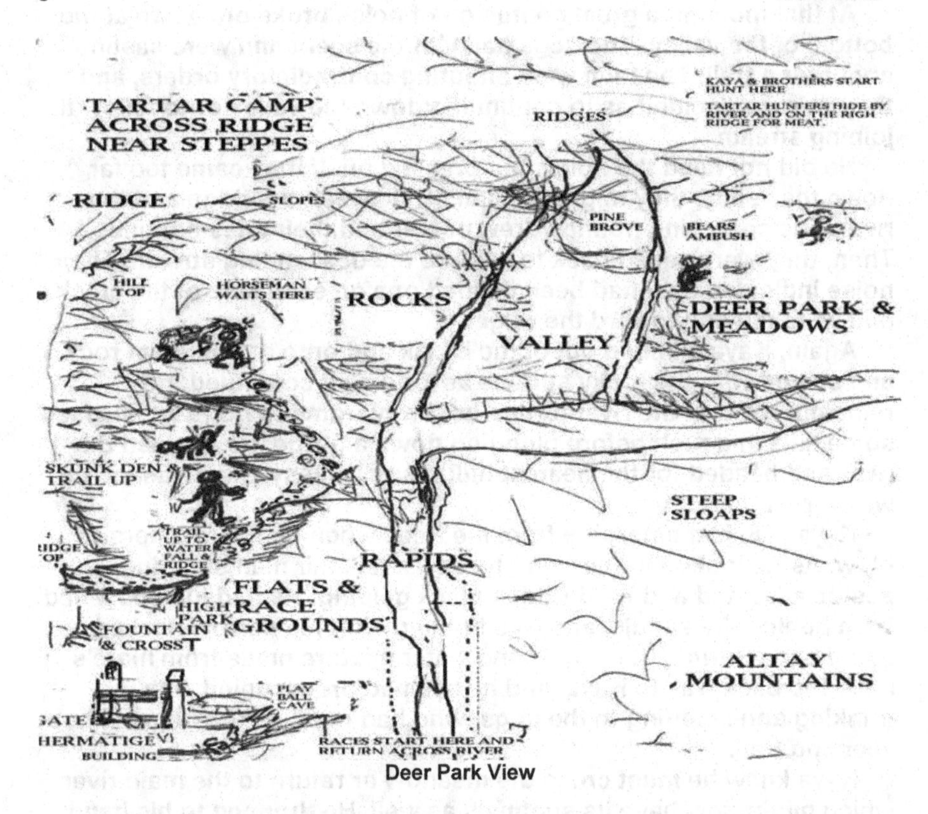

Deer Park View

Kaya was forced by exhaustion to stop and rest several times and tried to find ways of covering his tracks. It did not take much time for the hunting party to get on his trail.

Only a few men and the two great kangals traced him, but they were steady and purposeful. He shivered and, unbidden, the almost forgotten words of protection came to his lips, "*Yesu gel.*"

The excited roar of the dogs grew louder, and Kaya decided to go up toward the ridge. He found a shallow stream and worked his way under the overhang of tangled vegetation and up the firm bed of the rushing torrent.

He went almost to the edge of the hardwood when he saw a movement higher up on his right. Men were moving along the ridge, staying parallel to the sound of dogs at the bottom of the valley. The gaunt trunks of the open, deciduous forest offered scant protection and great visibility.

Turning to the bank of the stream, Kaya caught the overhanging branch of a great pine and worked his way up to the trunk, around it, out, and over to another pine and then another. He did this for about twenty yards and then dropped to the ground. Staying within the conifer cover, he ran, paralleling the ridge to another stream, which he entered and ran down for about twenty yards more.

At that moment a great confusion of noise broke out down at the bottom of the valley. The dogs had lost the scent and were casting about for a trail. The men were shouting contradictory orders, and they were undecided as to continuing down the valley or to follow the joining stream.

He did not heed the noise, but pressed on. If they came too far down the valley, they might cut him off between the ridge and the river. The searching hounds drew nearer and their cries continued. Then, they were called back to explore the descending stream. Their noise indicated they had been divided one on each side of the creek and were moving toward the ridge.

Again, Kaya climbed out of the brook and onto a prominent rock and stayed with the rocky surface as long as it continued. He remembered that the river turned left away from the ridge and passed some hills in a rush before plunging down a gorge. He avoided the river and headed for the nearest hill; it was grassy and pleasant, he would rest there.

Kaya was just emerging from the trees when he heard a horse blow. As he looked to the right, he saw a tall, fair man standing beside a frothed and hard-ridden black gelding. He had just loosened from behind the saddle, and was holding aloft his narrow-necked ayran bag to drink the yogurt and water mixture made from mare's milk. His back was to Kaya, and he seemed preoccupied with drinking and listening to the dogs, who had reached the ridge without scenting trail.

Kaya knew he must cross the meadow or return to the main river which might now have its sentinels as well. He dropped to his hands, running in a slump and crawling behind the tallest grass. He started to work his way across the meadow, clumps of willow and birch aided his progress.

The dogs were widening their circle as they cast farther and farther from the stream. Suddenly, one roared with the excitement of discovery as it caught scent beyond the pine grove. The hunting horn gave voice to the discovery, and the encouraging shouts of men echoed the sound. Now, they would have their prey. The drive was tightening the net; the quarry would meet its end in a shower of arrows.

The fair-haired warrior tied up his bag and strung his recurved, horn-reinforced bow and selected the white feathered arrow, made of the shinbone of a horse. The prey should break at any instant now. He turned to face the meadow.

Kaya paused in his progress. The man's preparations had caught his attention and he rested briefly while considering his chances. He remembered the size of the men on the river bank when they hit old Meryen in the boat. The distance was but little more. He seemed to remember the men of his clan at practice; he had to get out of range.

He was not sure where that would be.
The dogs again gave voice to frustration. The trail was again lost in water. Kaya thought they would again put a dog on each side of the stream, and he was not sure the rock trick would hold them long. It was 'chance it now or be caught here.'

As he rose, the man turned his head to listen to the dogs. Kaya moved quickly, running for the nearest shelter. The dogs, still frustrated, were working separately toward the bottom of the hill.

The whispering of the dry grass betrayed him. The man's head snapped back to view the meadow, and he had drawn the string full arrow length and loosed it before the desired haven was reached. Yelping with fear, Kaya lunged and fell as the arrow brushed his shoulder; he rolled and jumped again.

The tall Tartar leader already had a second arrow in the bow, but the gentle rise of the hill almost hid the lower part of the boy. His arrow slammed into the trunk of a small pine, inches above its intended victim.

The cry, "*vah-she, vah-she,*" sounded from the meadow, and then a horn called the huntsmen to the leader's side. The wild boy had been seen and the excitement mounted; everyone wanted to be in on the kill.

The leader cursed his carelessness. This was good training for the men, but it would not do to be found at fault. He would have fined one of his men for what had happened on the hill.

He swung into the saddle and, as the first men appeared, indicated the direction taken by the *vah-she*. He, however, rode toward the river to wait at the gorge, just as the sun touched the top of the western ridge.

Kaya was still running from his fright on the hill when he saw a sudden move in a small glade before him. He stopped abruptly and paused to adjust his eyes to the darkening trail ahead. Staring at the white spots before his eyes, he suddenly realized that he was three yards from an agitated black and white spotted skunk.

Every bear knew that to annoy this little neighbor was to court disaster and to annul any hope of escaping detection while hunting for a week. Kaya made an apologetic bear sound and backed away into the path through the woods.

The skunk after a pause to consider, continued up the trail toward the hill. Kaya slipped up wind and up a small rise off the trail. At about ten yards distance he threw a rock at the skunk just as the baying of the dogs started at the top of the hill. The skunk wheeled and raised his hindquarters in Kaya's direction and let a small stream of yellow liquid scent shoot vigorously at him. Kaya was already running away with renewed energy and the liquid did not touch him, but the scent did. He almost gagged, but could not find the liquid in his stomach. He was, again, empty, dry and failing fast.

Just at that moment the hounds, blaring down the trail, hit the scent and the skunk almost simultaneously. With a yipe of surprise they braked, but too late. The thoroughly annoyed skunk fired in their faces, effectively spraying them with the vile liquid. The great kangals whooped and whined like frightened puppies, as they turned back to the hill rubbing their eyes and sneezing.

The huntsmen, too, beat a hasty retreat, exclaiming their annoyance with the turn of events. The skunk, whose evening stroll had been so rudely terminated, returned to its burrow in the pine hollow.

Kaya's short burst of speed soon ended, and he limped forward continuing on the higher trail from the glade. He was driven by the escape-and-hide syndrome, but he didn't know where he could go to take refuge. The cold now penetrated his consciousness of the need to lay up, to hibernate.

He was so far from the den, so far from the yurt, so far from mother. "*Ah-ne*," he cried, but his voice was cracked and weak. He could see her now in memory, long, black hair and white shoulders that shone in the light, and long white teeth holding a salmon for him.

He whined piteously and stumbled forward as the trail led higher. He could see the base of a cliff ahead; home would be here. His brothers must be waiting. Perhaps there would be a kill and stomach-warming, strength-giving meat. He pressed forward salivating.

The cliff loomed over him as he heard the whiney of a horse below and to the left. He crawled to the edge of the trail; there just in arrow range, where the lower trail passed over the gorge, was the tall, fair warrior. He drew back with a moan of fear, "*Yesu gel*." The enemy had found him.

The waiting sentinel was alert and vigilant. Hock-dale had been made aware of the encounter with the skunk even before his arrival at this new post. The howling of the dogs and penetrating smell had reached him and given him pause to think on the uncertainties of the chase.

Even as he waited here now, he seemed to smell the odor, faint, but not far away. A slight moaning of the wind came to his ear. The forest seemed to move restlessly about him. Such a wary being would not come to the main trail he reasoned. It would be better to walk up the bottom of the cliff and meet the men on the ridge.

Then, as one of the river guards and a young page, Jonny, came into view, he called them over to take his post. Leaving his horse to crop at the verge of the river, he set off through the woods, up the bottom of the cliff.

Kaya was climbing up the incline at the base of the cliff. There was a kind of footpath that even had steps cut into the rock in several spots. This he followed until he suddenly heard the sound of splashing water. Then, a small rivulet sprayed his face with bone chilling refreshment. He opened his mouth and drank.

Kaya started to shake again so he stopped, and stared up the cliff.

Dimly, he saw what appeared to be narrow footholds just above the waterfall. Crossing the small stream, he came to an embankment, behind which, a few carefully cut footholds led upward. The sound of a breaking limb and a curse behind him sent him scurrying up the cliff.

> - - - - - - >

"Doer, *Kim sin*! Halt, who goes there," came a challenge from the ridge top.

"It's me," the Commander cried. "It's hard to see in this half-light."

"You're fortunate, *Binbasha*. We might have shot first," came the derisive reply.

"And you would lose your lucrative gains as friend of the Khan's favorite," the commander warned. He ignored the sarcastic reference promoting him to a General, *Binbasha*!

But between the stream and the embankment Kaya clung to his handholds and felt his way forward and up, all sounds covered by the waterfall. He eventually came up to a path between the rocks, overlooking the ridge and forest. At the end of the path, a flat place where gravel could be felt. There Kaya slumped down in the blackening night.

He felt the rock beneath him and then a fur -- bear fur! He whined like a cub, but there was no reply. He nosed into it, but it did not move or yield to him. He felt over it and could discover no legs. It was not alive! But it had shape and some material stuffed inside. There was a deer-hide rug under it, like the robes he made himself for winter. He shivered and still hugging the thing, he fell asleep on the robe wedged between it and a square tree that pressed against his back.

The commander strode up to the vantage point of Kove, his second, in charge of the ridge group. He paused to catch his breath and looked over the darkened forest.

"You can send the men back to camp for dinner. I'll pay my respects to the hermit and later eat at the camp," Hock-dale commanded. Kove looked at his tall companion obliquely, through narrowed eyes.

"What happened on the hill, Binbasha?" Kove said, "We had a sure catch there."

Hock-dale bey stared at him coldly, "Never mind what happened. Those dogs you trained were fooled several times. They lost the scent and the prey. You deserve to have them sleep in your tent tonight." With these words he turned away and walked to the top of the ridge where a path wound round the cliffs to the sheltered Hermitage on the southeast side of the descending slope.

The commander's mind was dark and angry. Kove had his position by family importance and influence. He was greedy, incompetent and insubordinate. He would deal with him as he deserved, some day, when he himself was secure.

>------->

Hock-dale bey came to the south gate of the Hermitage. There were no windows or openings other than the gate for the first three stories, for the building had been built into the cliff and the lower rooms were only for storage. The windows were alternately constructed of parallel horizontal slits one over the other, and then the next window had vertical slits that also paralleled each other. Each board in the window turned on an axis and could be closed in winter or opened in summer. These Venetian blinds could catch or exclude the light and heat.

The commander reached for a small rope beside the gate and a silvery, tinkling bell voiced a warning which had a penetrating, insistent quality.

After a short wait a high, childish voice came from a small, enclosed balcony built out over the gate. It was on a level with the third story, below where the windows begin. "*Kim ore'row-da*?" the voice challenged.

The commander summoned a pleasant, warm voice to answer, "Hock-dale bey, servant of Bata Shah, the Tartar Khan, wishes to talk with Kootsal bey, your master briefly."

The balcony over the gate was silent and the commander resigned himself to more delay. Then the bell tinkled an invitation, and the door set in the right panel of the gate opened. Light from a torch flooded down the stairs and a small six year old boy peered down from the second story landing.

"*Hoe'sh Gel'den*, Welcome Sir, I'm Kutch," his thin voice piped.

"*Hoe'sh boll' duke*, gladly here," came the pleasant reply. The commander from inside realized the door was controlled by pulleys from the balcony and there was a shaft above the gate for the hauling and lifting of material to the rooms up higher in the cliff.

As he followed the child up the stairs, his admiration increased as he realized that the stairs were also controlled by a pulley device for raising and lowering it from below the floor of the third story.

It was on the fourth level that he left the stairs and was conducted by his guide to a small room on the northeast side of the building where the hermit waited, sitting on a cushion on the floor beside a low table covered with parchments and scrolls. On one end of the table were wild goose quill pens and brush, bottles of China and India inks.

The hermit rose as the commander entered and made the sign of greetings and obeisance. He held in his hand a rosary of white stones; a sign of peace. A man with his hands full of prayer could not easily fill it with weapons of death.

The hermit's face held vigor and alertness, but the man was evidently older than he looked. He was agile in his movements, but seemed to think out each action and then to rapidly perform it. This gave an impression of hesitation, and then commitment in all his motions. He seemed to jerk.

"Why are we honored by your presence, commander?" He said, "You reach far in your raids."

At this the commander smiled coolly. "Kootsal bey, We are only a small hunting party today," he explained. "Getting supplies for the trek home. We had a splendid catch today," he continued. "I will send you some venison for your large community."

"*Tesh-ek-koor*, Thank you," the older man replied, "you are generous." When the commander gave a self-satisfied smirk and nod, the hermit added, "I heard your dogs and smelled their encounter. I trust all have survived the incident."

The commander's face went red. "It was of no importance," he said, "We chased a *vah-she*, a wild boy; vermin to be exterminated."

The hermit paused long before saying, "Perhaps we should give thought as to why these unfortunates are roaming our woods."

The commander changed the subject by observing, "How do you come to have knowledge of what happened today?"

"It is possible to have knowledge of much in the world by diligence and observation," the hermit evaded. Then, suddenly he conceded, "I have a place of meditation and prayer that is also a lookout. Would you like to survey the field of your day's activities?" He motioned toward a narrow door behind the table. "*Gel, gore.* Come, see," he said.

The hermit loved this favorite spot. It overlooked the high valley with its dark forest, hardwood ridges and mountains beyond. It also looked across the gorge and the lower forested hills toward the grass-filled plains to the south and west.

The spot was too exposed to be used as living quarters, but the flat, plateau-like, expanse of about twenty yards contained rocks, trees and bushes that had been made into a kind of park with walks, benches and a kind of bolster, made of hide, on a large flat-topped stone at the foot of a T-shaped cross of squared wood.

It was a starlit, night sky that greeted the pair as they moved into the garden walk, moving with care past the darker shapes of benches and rocks. Away, the faint horizontal lines almost outlined mountains and very little more. The faint scent of skunk still lingered in the cold air.

With his arm the hermit described the vast panorama as if embracing it, "This is a small, but beautiful part of our world."

"There's my camp," declared the commander, pointing to a number of fires burning near the ridge beyond the hill. "The preparations for dinner are being made."

"*Afee-yet olsun-lar*, leave them to enjoy it," said the Hermit. "We have soup tonight. If you will, join our humble house, and you will eat well."

The commander made a small grimace into the night and said, "I would not trouble you, Kootsal; you have mouths to feed." He did not add that the prayers, company and conversation would bore him beyond endurance.

But the Hermit insisted, "You have hunted all day and are weary, We have chay, tea and good soup; come and drink then, and be refreshed. I'll have them bring it up here."

"Don't bother," declared the guest, "It's chill, and there is still the after taste of the evening hunt in the air."

"Did you know that the Greeks, our learned brothers in the far West, equate air and wind with the word spirit, to signify qualities that are felt but rarely seen? Wind blows, but we don't know where it will go or where it started. This is the way of the spirit world: a land of changing winds. Winter now and Spring comes surely later. The wind of God blows upon torn and frozen hearts. Can you feel their breath?"

"Save your homilies for the classroom, Prince," said the guest dryly, "I follow the ways of the ancestors; what they had is good enough for me. Their riches are mine."

"If their gold and treasures; lands and conquests; women and households are enough, why do you come unbidden to the land of the Eastern Mountains? Surely you seek and find where your heart leads, but let the wind lead your heart."

"I have heard the story of your loss, oh Prince," said the Commander, drawing back toward the door, "but I have no time for sentimentality and semantics. I have my religion and my gods; all rivers lead to the sea."

"Gods of violence and death," warned the hermit sadly. "What sea do you refer to Commander? The Caspian Sea is salty as is the Sea of Aral, the Black Sea less so, and the Sea of Balkhash is alkaline, the Baykal Sea alone is fresh and drinkable. To what sea do your actions and devotions take you? You already feel their effect. Do you enjoy your choices?"

"I am hungry now," stated the guest sourly. " I will go to my camp. I cannot accept your hospitality. Come, dispatch me."

"A thousand pardons Hock-dale bey," said the Hermit contritely. "I never come to this sacred place without a prayer at the cross. If you will not join me, may I crave your indulgence, for just a brief moment?"

The commander's haughty face wore a mask of scorn. "Quickly," he ordered. taking command by nature. He was out of patience with the old hermit and found no joy in the verbal fencing, which usually gave him pleasure.

His heart filled with contempt for the man who had once enjoyed great power and wealth, but had used it to build such a place and live this kind of a life. He would not draw near the cross as the old man did.

The hermit's head was bent in meditation. He suddenly knelt, leaned his hands on the bolster, which was becoming visible by the rising in the east of a big harvest moon.

The hermit remained hunched over in prayer. "Our Father in Heaven," he mumbled. He untied his cloak, which fell to the ground beside him.

The Commander stirred as the breeze brought again the faint odor of his defeat. He turned to face the rising moon away from the man who arose and went back to the guest.

"If you but knew the power of the risen Lord," he said with a touch of awe in his voice as he led the way for his visitor, from the small exit to the stairway, and out into the night.

The Commander noticed with contempt that the old fool had forgotten his cloak in the garden.

GARDEN LOOKOUT (PAGE 100)

PEOPLE, PLACES & PLOTS IN CHAPTER 10

Binbasha: head of a 1,000; general; used in flattery or derision.
E-ven'ke tracker: Siberians that combine reindeer herding & hunting.
Hock'dale: a captain of Tartars hunting in the Altai Mountains.
Kaya: meaning rock, is firmly embedded in the hermit's affections.
***Koot'sal*: the hermit's name as head of a school of useful arts.**
Kove: a cynical and derisive lieutenant serving in the Tartar force.
***Mookades*: meaning holy, a title of respect for the hermit.**

GLOSSARY

***hi'yer:* no; not at all; definitely not.**
***oh'tour:* sit; sit down; be seated.**
***vah'she*: beast; wild creature; lost child.**
***yam' yam*: cannibal; those who eat human flesh.**
***Ye'su gel*: come Jesus; God help me.**

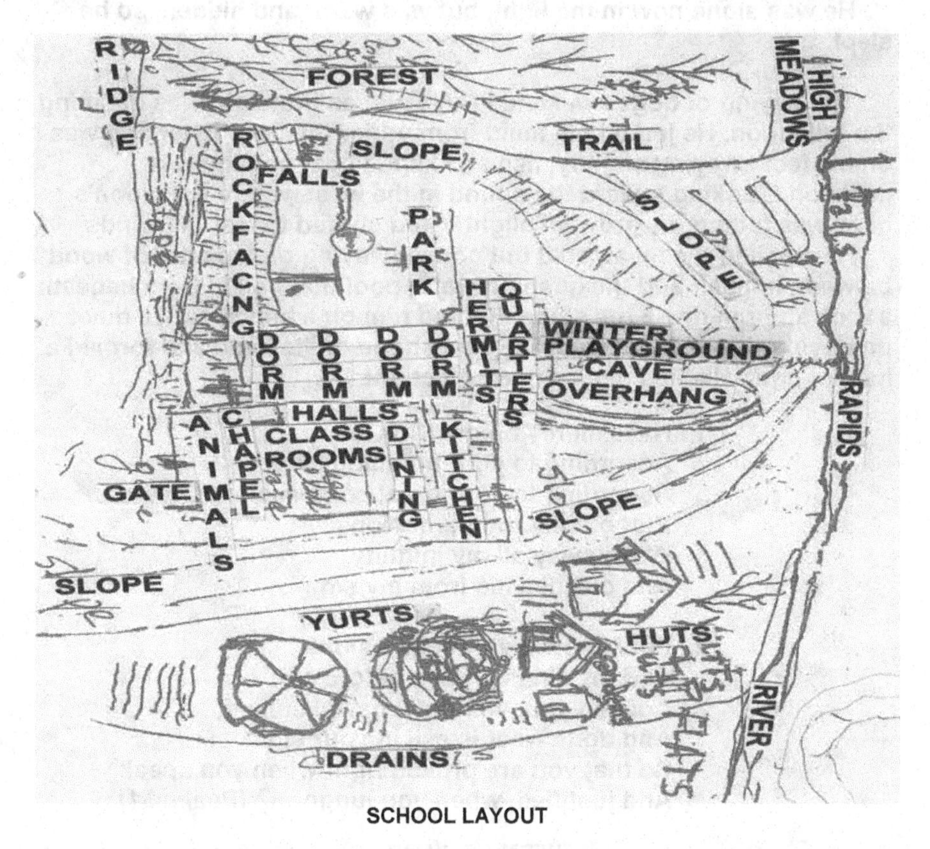

SCHOOL LAYOUT

Kaya found himself in a dark cave. Outside somewhere he could hear sounds of men. He tried to straighten up, but found that something lay on his arm. It was another bear! He tried to growl and push it off his arm. The sound froze in his throat; the smell of the skunk penetrated the cave and with it the voice of the enemy.

He heard a whisper, `*Vah-she*, wild, savage,' it insisted. He jerked his head back and up, `no, *hi'yer*, no, never.' He hid in his mother's arms, `Be good, little one,' she warned, `If you are bad the *yam yam*, , will eat you up,' and she pinched his cheeks between her fingers as if testing his fatness. He squirmed as he always did and sought her breast, but she was gone and the voice of the enemy came again.

Fear trickled down his spine. He wanted to run, escape, but his mother held him down by the arm. She was always angry now and would cuff him roughly if he disturbed her. `*Yesu gel*!' He lay frozen and afraid.

Something approached and it grew lighter in the cave. There was a soft sighing sound, a murmur; like a wish unfulfilled, but still sought, and then, soft weight, warm hidden feelings as the light dimmed yet began to increase.

He was alone now in the light, but was warm and hidden, so he slept.

>------->

The baying of dogs awakened Kaya just as first light was dimming the full moon. He jerked his hand from under the fur bolster and was on his feet swaying slightly, like an excited bear coming to a decision. Looking toward the sound in the west, where the moon's glow was fading, he growled slightly and sniffed to test the winds.

He smelled the meat, cold but cooked, laying on a platter of wood between himself and the gushing water pool that boiled from beneath a rock and ran down the slope. Behind him on a bench sat an quiet unmoving figure. Light from the east shone on its head and formed a halo of light. His lips moved in a soft chant.

1. Have mercy on me, Oh God
   According to your unfailing love.
   According to your great compassion,
   Blot out my transgressions.
   Wash away all my iniquity,
   And cleanse me from my sin.

2. For I know my transgressions,
   And my sin is always before me.
   Against you, you only, have I sinned,
   And done what is evil in your sight.
   So that you are proved right when you speak,
   And justified, when you judge. (Psalm 51)

HERMIT'S CHANT

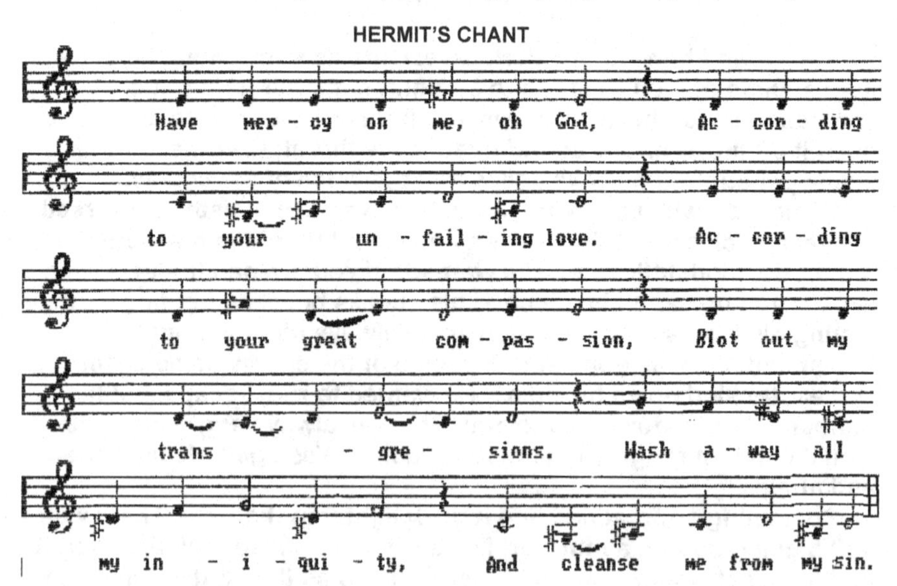

Kaya had all the assurance of his adopted kind. The danger was not immediate, so hunger took first place. He nosed the meat and took a few bites, then as he frequently did with his brothers, grabbed his part with his hands and ran from the figure.

He stopped near the pool, and seeing the figure did not move, grew bold again. He turned his back and drank. Looking over his shoulder, the figure still had not moved. Something fluttered in the hand of the man; the wind moved it. Kaya stared fascinated at the thing. It looked like a great leaf.

He stared at the man again in the increasing light and saw gray hair and remembered old Meryen and Mother's muzzle. There was no danger in this man, but he might be irritable, so he waited while finishing his meat. He walked behind a bush to answer a call of nature. This was not a custom of bears, but seemed to be something previous in him that he did not try to resist.

The figure had not moved, but was making some kind of noise, and looking at the thing in its hand. The noise was pleasant and soothing. It seemed to please his ear and give confidence to his heart. It chanted words only half understood:

He drew toward the figure. When he was but an arm's distance, the man smiled in his reading. Kaya stopped immediately, for the showing of teeth means to take care. ‘He is an old one and wants respect,' thought Kaya.

>- - - - - - - >

At the camp there was a flurry of sound among the hounds, the high shrill sound of whippets, fast hunters of small game. Excitement was contagious as the hunt began. The shouts of men and the bark of dogs spilled from the ridge. Moving in a circle, two dogs to the river side and two to the ridge, they started backtracking to the meadow where the deer were killed and took up the trail again.

More bear tracks were discovered, leaving the valley up river. The way they had evidently entered. A large set and a smaller set, two bears. No human tracks were found.

Kove's sardonic face greeted his commander on the ridge. "Your *vah-she* must have thrown himself over the gorge. Hock-dale bey." He said, "Or perhaps you smuggled him out under your cloak after you had a friendly chat on the grassy hill." He baited him knowing his own position was too secure to invoke strong reprisals.

"He is holed up in the area under the cliffs," affirmed the commander, "Search through it again." Kove scanned him obliquely before speaking.

"If he is holed up with the skunk; you may well lose more dogs, Binbasha," he said, exaggerating the man's military title to General, "even the Evenki trackers, don't want to go through yesterday's spray area." He held his nose, comically.

"A gold coin will get one to do it," the commander affirmed, ignoring the jests.

"So much expense for a wild boy? Is this a blood feud or a love affair?" Kove asked, intrigued now.

"Do it, now," ordered the commander, "and I want him alive."

As Hock-dale bey walked away, he knew that he was being unreasonable and that the story would spread now. Everyone would talk, and it might even get back to the Khan. His men were not so loyal as to resist a bit of bribing by the agents of the Khan, but he could not change what had occurred.

He sighed as he recalled the details. He had seen the frightened face of the boy as he loosed his second arrow; he was sure it was him, the object of his quest!

>- - - - - - - >

The dogs and trackers were sent down the ravine toward the hills and plain, but no trace or scent was found. The hours passed, tediously, as when one awaits bad news. Activity slowed to nothing.

An almond-eyed, powerful, Evenki tracker appeared before the captain, he bowed and awaited recognition. His face and hair were washed, and he wore unsoiled clothes, but he still smelled of skunk.

"Well" the commander said, searching his face, "tell me all you found."

The man nodded, but remained silent.

The Tartar lord reached into his pouch to remove a small gold coin. "This is for information," he said, holding it up between two fingers.

The Evenki stared unblinking. "They say gold coin for enter skunk den, I kill skunk, enter den, trace boy."

Hock-dale bey was exasperated now. People would be watching. He had no intention of letting himself be taken for information as well. However, he smiled and nodded in agreement, placing the coin in the man's hand.

"For your bravery in entering such an unpleasant area and your report as a good soldier," he said.

The Evenki relaxed, but did not warm too much. "Boy smart, pass skunk on high trail. Throw big rock." He produced the double fist-size rock. "Skunk shoot at boy, dogs come, spray dogs plenty. Boy go high trail, look see ravine."

The commander looked startled, "But I was at the ravine; nothing passed. Jonny came with the dog, we saw or heard nothing."

The tracker smiled for the first time, looked down at his hands and shrugged. "Boy above you, good boy, not kill you. Not bad boy!" He motioned with his hand, "Boy go up to waterfall. Commander go up to waterfall." He put his hands before him, one crossed over the other by way of illustration. "Commander footprint over boy footprint at bottom of falls, where boy drink water."

"Just a minute, how do you know he drank?" He objected. He had a feeling the man was making a fool of him.

The guide continued to illustrate with his hands, "See

Commander, boy print face falls, your print go up. I push spear into falls: no cave, no place to hide, must drink."

"But where did he go after that, before I got there."

"Tracks say you come one big hurry on boy, He go up or down water, like deep wood spirit no more tracks!"

"You mean he vanished, fooled you, and you can't say where he went. I wasted my money on you," the commander fumed.

"Men say money for find and enter skunk den, not for find boy. I kill skunk, find den, enter, trace boy you step on." The Evenki rose to his full height and width and declared, "I no work for you more, I go home country, give silver coins work promise, now."

"Don't get smart and uppity with me, you scum, or I'll have my gold coin and your head too," the commander snarled.

The man's complexion became dark and his face impersonal, a mask. His hands were clenched at his side.

At that moment Kove walked up and looked inquiringly at the two men stiffly facing each other.

"Am I imagining things or have we come to an impasse. Perhaps the lack of evidence has curdled our stomachs. Ah well, an infusion of sweet herbs will cure that, given time." Kove stood savoring the moment. He chuckled maliciously. "I took the liberty of ordering the men to break camp, Binbasha. Unless you wish to order a day of prayer and repentance at the Hermitage for us all."

> - - - - - - - >

At the Hermitage, Kaya lay near the fur bolster at the foot of the cross and watched the activity below as the camp was folded away and the attendants, men and women, packed their parcels and goods into several two wheeled carts and a number of pack horses. He was completely taken up by the sight of three large Bactrian camels being loaded. In his excitement he spoke in Chipchak baby talk.

"See, two-mountain-back horse, carry big load," he said, chuckling.

"Its name is Camel; it has two humps," said the hermit carefully. "You must learn many new words and how to do things. We will start in the morning, when the sun is there," He pointed to a spot just over the horizon, "and you will work at hand tools till there." He pointed to another spot near the western horizon. "All winter we will work and learn."

"Eat every day, not hunt?" asked Kaya incredulously.

The hermit smiled, "Yes, food every day, but not often meat."

> - - - - - - - >

Hock-dale bey, dressed in his travel clothes, sought out his busy lieutenant who made a hasty salute, the right palm forward at shoulder height, which demonstrates the hand without a weapon. "Yes my Captain?"

"You started the packing, so you can see it through. I have some instructions for the hermit. Start without me; I'll catch up on the trail to our western base," he stated, cold-faced and sour.

"Say a prayer for your humble lieutenant, left with all the work," mocked Kove, with a smirk.

>------->

The wait at the gate was longer this time, and there were dozens of eyes peering down through the slats at the impressively dressed captain. Orphans, servers, and students lived inside the building. Refugees, working for their own support and protection, had built a number of yurts and shack-like structures near the protecting presence of the Hermitage. An incipient town, or city of refuge was growing round the sanctuary. The blessing of love and considerate sharing for the broken and hopeless, brought them. No one starved, and no one was unduly prospered, but there was a warm comfort of stability and hope based on firm promises of a future heavenly bliss.

The captain was finally led to the office of the hermit, who stood beads in hand to bow a greeting to the visitor. The captain extended his hand to grasp the hermit's hand and after kissing it and touching his forehead to the back, stood erect awaiting the opportunity to speak.

"To what do we owe this unexpected honor, Captain," the hermit asked in a kindly way. "I saw your hunters and goods departing just now. You have meat for the winter season. I've thanked your hunters this morning for their generosity in sharing your bounty."

"I've need of your garden overlook," stated the officer, "I want to review the activities of yesterday for the possible hiding places of the boy."

The hermit advanced to place his hands on the arms of the captain, and looking deeply into his eyes said, "Why all this preoccupation with a wild boy? One whose parents were doubtless killed by marauding bands."

"It may have been one of my raids that produced such an orphan. If it is so, one parent is alive." muttered the official with a blush of shame.

"Here lies a troubled conscience and the need for talk," replied the hermit, eyes wide with astonishment and pleasure. "*Oh-tour*, sit, my friend. Sit and tell me what troubles your heart."

The story was a familiar one: "I was a war prisoner and orphaned by the Huns in the early skirmishes near the Caucasus Mountains. I passed my early training at the Volga school and was posted to guard the northeast border tribes, the Finnish speaking peoples of the Ural mountains. I learned bits of their language, and it grieved me to see them forced north by Hunnish exploitation and Tartar advances from the east.

"In a border skirmish, I was unhorsed and captured by the Tartars. Had I been a Hun they would have killed me, but being a trained captive they knew my loyalty was not absolute. I would be loyal to those who fed and clothed me, always on a mercenary basis.

"The Tartar Khans have no trust in the prominent families. They are potential replacements and rivals. But my promotion, by merit alone, would make me a more loyal servant, and the jealousy of the rivals would keep me true. So, I have continued to serve and strive to better my condition and to please my master."

There was a long silence as the man sat staring at a point above the hermit's head. "I have sickened of being the Khan's executioner. I'm hated by the high families and am an outsider to the tribe. There is no homeland left for a return, but I'm rich enough to have many envy my wealth. When the present Khan goes, they will make sure I and my wife do, too. I suspect the family of my lieutenant is about to strike the blow. What am I to do?"

"One thing is needful," stated the hermit firmly, "God alone is sufficient for your dilemma, are you willing to trust Him for a solution?"

"Perhaps He is the cause of my dilemma," sighed the captain. "I did not chose to place myself in any of these conditions. What I am, is simply a reaction to what has happened to me -- the demands of my situation. I could do or be nothing else."

"You fail to answer the question, sir," the older man continued, "I have asked if you are willing to accept a solution from Him, or do you prefer to seek your own resolution?"

"Do you mean I'm to accept the guilt of that which I did not create, and blame myself for all that has been brought upon me?" The captain replied indignantly. "Am I to absolve Him, simply because He is more powerful?" The captain sat bolt upright, "What I do, I do because I must, what choice is mine?"

"Your choice, my friend, is whether you will trust God or try to judge Him. Will you condemn Him for flaws that you suppose are of His making, and excuse your known flaws, that are definitely of your own making?"

"I don't wish to condemn God, but how could a good God permit such a hellish world? I do not preen myself at the expense of God, if that is what you are implying, but I find myself at one with an imperfect world," emotion flushed the cold handsome face.

SCHOOL TOOLS

"Will you then cling to this known, evil world or trust in One who remakes it into His own image? Do you love this world to the exclusion of another or would you wait and work for one in which righteousness reigns?" The hermit's face held an intensity that almost glowed.

"I came to look from the terrace, not to answer philosophical questions that have no bearing on the day-to-day world." The captain stood upright. "With your permission, Holy One."

"You seek a boy to share your dangerous world, to be taken prisoner as you were and teased into submission and slaughtered when you are? This is the kindness you would do a wild, but rational child? Do to others as you have been done by and perpetuate the system that has damaged you? This is your choice: blindness to your own warped condition, and the imposition of the same on another?" The hermit's face glowed with anger.

"It is not for myself," frustration showed clearly on the captain's features. "I was alerted; I must comply."

"You obey every interest but God's. Your men have searched every niche and cranny of the valley. It is enough. You may go. We will speak no more."

"Farewell, Kootsal, may your awaited world come."

"Goodbye, and may God have mercy on you and your present world."

>------->

For a week Kaya hovered between leaving and staying. The climb behind the rocks beside the falls became so used that Hock-dale bey himself could have found it at night. Awaking every morning the boy would find the bowl with porridge waiting, warm and fragrant with a small portion of honey mixed into it. The old one would appear and bow before the great tree and make sounds. They jumped and soared and were sometimes loud and sometimes soft. He would close his eyes in sorrow and mourning and then open them again bright with tears, excitement and exaltation. The boy sat quietly watching, curious to know the source of this strange power. Then after a time the old one would turn and show his teeth. Kaya then knew that such things were to be respected and not intruded upon. He would have to wait and learn.

After this the man would open the door to his room, and the boy would thrill to the strangeness of this cave. It had flat walls of wood and stone, and high openings for light where one could look out over the lower landscape. There were long reaches in the cave that led to the sound and smell of other humans, but he could not go there, to a place of mystery yet, the hermit said.

When Kaya tired of mysteries he went down to the falls and the high valley until evening brought him back to a great bowl of hot soup and bread laid on the stone table. The old one would come again and teach new words for things almost forgotten. He slept at the foot of the square cut tree, by the large bear that once was. The old one's woven wool cloak covered him. The wild called to Kaya, but the hermit held on to him with prayer and love.

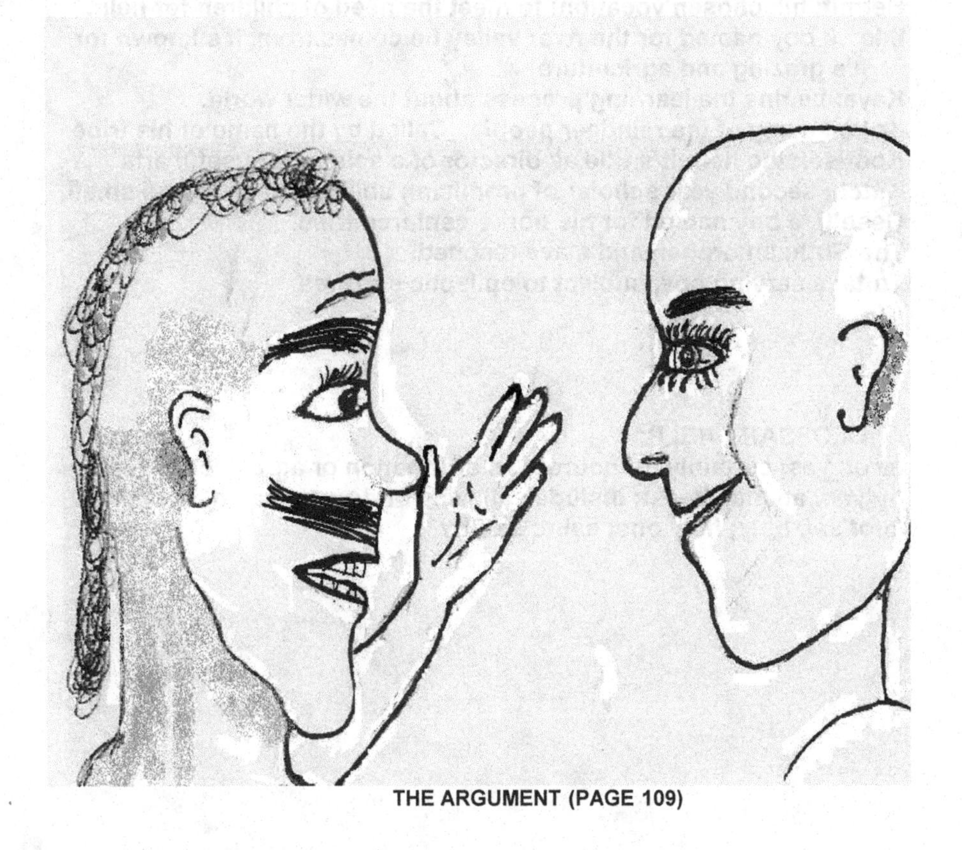

THE ARGUMENT (PAGE 109)

PEOPLE, PLACES & PLOTS IN CHAPTER 11

Cook: a big smiling man of good food and uncertain temper.
Cook's wife: a worrier and talker who requires no audience.
Hermit: his chosen vocation: to meet the need of children for help.
Il'le: a boy named for the river valley he comes from. It's known for it's grazing and agriculture.
Kaya: begins the learning process about the wider world.
Ko'mi: a boy of the reindeer people. Called by the name of his tribe.
Koot'sal: the hermit's title as director of a school for useful arts.
Kutch: second year scholar of promising ability, but timid and small.
Osse'ti: a boy named for his horse-centered tribe.
The Goth: an orphan and slave rescued.
Tu'ta: a serving boy, subject to epileptic seizures.

GLOSSARY HELP:

***ev'et*: yes; certainly; of course; an affirmation or agreement.**
***hy'van:* animal; beast; includes all, wild or domesticated.**
***koot'sal:* holy; holy one; saint; saintly.**

SCHOOL PLAYGROUND

At the end of the week, a great storm of snow and cold arrived to ice the descent by the falls and block the path below with ice and snow. Kaya passed the day in the office and private rooms of the hermit. He was shown the wonders of an indoor privy, hung over the cliff's edge. He was persuaded into the baggy pants and blousy shirt used regionally.

As evening fell there came a timid knock at the office door. As the hermit opened the door, he directed, "Come in, Kutch. Put the tray on the table; don't be afraid. This is the new boy, Kaya, from the deep woods. He speaks Chipchak, so you can talk to him. I would like you two to be friends."

Little, squint-eyed, pale-faced with straight black hair, Kutch shivered and stared fixedly at his slippers. News and speculation had been the main pastime this last week among the orphans and students of the Hermitage, just as the arrival and hunt of the Tartars had occupied them the one before. The presence of a *vahshe* was suspected from the time the hermit had started bringing two soups to his quarters.

"*Evet, Kootsal,* Yes, holy one," he murmured. The hermit continued, "This is Kutch, a small boy with great ability. He can tell you anything you wish to know, Kaya." Sweat stood on the small boy's face, and he became even paler as he continued to look at his own feet. Kaya examined the boy closely, sniffing his smell of spices

and food. Kaya suddenly uttered a small chuckle and said, "He smells like good food." The boy, Kutch, swayed as if to faint. "But he does not smell of forest. He does not hunt; he prepares others' prey," Kaya continued, without realizing what was afoot.

The hermit understood it all and with a smile, which silenced Kaya in respect and reassured the little servant at the same time, moved forward and took the child by the arm and directed him to a couch-like projection from the wall. "Sit here! Don't be afraid! Now look at him; he is a boy like you. The boys in the quarter will ask you, so you must be able to tell them." At the master's word and touch, the child took courage and looked.

Kaya's strength lay hidden by his clothes and only his wide round face and thickness of neck and frame showed. His feet, face and hands when exposed showed a crisscrossing of brown, with white and pink scars. His face was generally expressionless, but his mouth was slightly open and his breath audible because he was excited. For like most animals, he used his mouth to breath and his nose only for smelling. This he did in an obvious pointing way, sniffing delicately, as he did now, detecting fear. "Why you big scare? Old one good fellow," his voice was loud and coarse, but a trace of a smile played around the lips.

The boy, Kutch, snorted in disgust, "Baby talk! You're just a big, fat baby." He was relieved that Kaya was too stupid to know who he was afraid of. Suddenly, he thought of a way to establish his superiority. He pulled a hank of string from his pocket and made a simple cat's cradle with the string between the two hands. "I bet you can't do that."

He grew delighted when Kaya looked very carefully at the hands, string and pattern created and watched him make the string move. Then Kaya reached out with thumb and forefinger felt the texture of the string and smelled it. "Not wool or hair! What this and how make?" Kaya demanded. Kutch looked disconcerted and murmured, "Cotton from Persian or Hindi lands." Kaya immediately asked, "Where lands?" By the time the questions were answered, they had illustrated the twisting of fiber for string, the nature of the plant and its fruit plus extensive geography, half understood, using a sand table to show mountains and rivers of the south. The hermit contentedly sat on the cushions behind his low desk and slowly ate his cool soup while the two inquiring minds met and learned respect.

When Kutch returned to the dormitory hours later, he was strangely quiet about the new boy. He remarked that Kaya was big and smart, and they would study together at the holy one's direction till after the new year.

Every day after the dawn meal, Kutch answered questions, and the hermit's quarters were explored, articles handled and named, origins and use explained and illustrated. Excursions were allowed into the corridors and the play yard when they were not in use by the other staff or dormitory occupants.

The play yard was an increasing necessity, as the hermit's park became more windswept and cold. The falls were frozen into white columns of clear and colored ice and ooze as new water and attracted moisture appeared to force its way out of the hill or attach itself to the existing serpentine of sculpture. The beauty was breathtaking, but there was no room now for activity and play.

The play yard was cut from rock on the south face of the cliff, shaped like a lazy V or Y. The top was open end faced the sun. So a low angle winter sun would enter and warm the cave-like structure and a high summer sun would be excluded except at rising or setting. There was a low two-foot wall toward the outside edge and a drop of about a foot to a small terrace about four feet wide and then a bright red ochre painted six-foot wall with desert spines and wicker fence holding netting, fixed beyond the top.

The small wall was the favorite place to play or sit and watch the others on the higher ground that slanted up toward the back of the excavation. Balls would roll unerringly back down to the small wall. At the end of the rise of floor at the back, the rock that rose toward the roof was cut in alternate flat, curved and angled planes so the balls would bounce in different yet determined directions off the backboard. A ball would rebound to partners and away from the butt in a game of keep away. This provided hours of entertainment and the development of good eye, arm and leg coordination.

If the ball jumped the small wall, the larger one stopped it. If it passed the outer wall and net, it was lost till the next day, and a punishment accompanied its loss. In fact a red smudge on clothes or body usually invoked a severe ear pull or a bastinado, a switching on the bottom of the bared foot. The second wall then was the children's great challenge. How close can you get to show off and dare others, without its mark showing and punishment deservedly falling on the guilty.

It was popular with a few to get others into trouble and get them smudged without themselves bearing the sign of transgression. Tears and crying would get some of the younger off, but the older ones would bear their punishment and plan how to pay back the enemy. So fights and rivalry were often accompaniments of the boys' process of education and growth.

A door was cut through the rock at the end of the platform and a wide tunnel led back to the main building. A stout gate open only at playtime guarded the tunnel entrance. It was opened for Kaya and Kutch every day while the other children were in class or work. Here came Kaya and Kutch to toss the skin-wrapped bladder ball and throw it to see how it would bounce or roll. Kaya's skills quickly returned. They also practiced wrestling on the thick mat woven of bulrushes. Kutch was small, but agile and wiry in his strength. Kaya looked big and fat until he made body contact, and then he was found to be all muscle. Kaya found himself in the role of his bear brothers, too large and strong to fell, but outwitted and molested by smaller, faster Kutch. Trip, dodge and swing out and away and then attack again, sometimes laughing and yelling they roughhoused and played. The sound of pain or anger usually advised him of his small companion's limits and he immediately relented, while lots of pretense and show went into the effort to give a good account. Kutch loved it when Kaya would let him hold him down and pretend to groan and writhe with frustration to overcome his small friend. "Wait till we show the others this one," Kutch would say panting and out of breath, practicing a new hold.

Kaya came first to know the cook and some of the kitchen staff. The cook was an old man, and he was assisted by his talkative wife whose seamed and leathery face was round, grim and determined. The old woman talked without ceasing, to herself or whoever was near enough to be addressed. She did not often wait for a reply, response or even a look of acknowledgement. The cook's wide, round face was fixed in a beatific smile, and he rarely ever talked, but occasionally shouted a loud command, and every one would immediately respond with a clatter of activity while the wife made comments on everything. The helpers were some of the orphaned or abandoned boys, some with physical or mental defects. The tall chief assistant had a harelip and speech defect. Another had a goiter-thickened throat. A scrub and washer was noticeably idiot, and in the corner by the wood supply sat another, Tu'ta, whose one job was to carry and stack wood, animal chips and starter for the fire under a line of great kettles used for cooking.

The head of the Hermitage, Kootsal himself, took time when the weather permitted to accompany Kaya after morning prayers or more especially after vespers in a kind of nature walk to think and exercise. It was a time loved by both participants and increased the mutual respect and dependence.

As they walked Kaya hummed a tune he had liked from the worship. It was to him stately and jumped about curiously. All music was like walking up a hill of sound and suddenly swooping down from on high and bumping around in a valley of low notes to begin a smooth climb up again. Kaya had fallen in love with music and so was never without it. His voice was coarse and not always on pitch. Although not loud, it seemed to come from within and fill him. He sang about his new knowledge:

1. God is so good, He sends the rain.
   The sun comes up and goes down again.
   Though days may be numbered,
   They're full of delight;
   For God made all to be joyful and right.

2. God is so strict. He tests us all.
Winter will come soon after the Fall.
Though seasons are fickle,
we enjoy the change;
For God made all to be within our range.

3. God is so great. He made us all.
Each living thing, both great ones and small.
Though life holds hard moments,
It's filled up with thrills;
For God made all to be just how He wills.

His face would bear a bemused, contented expression as his singing or humming occupied him. His volume dropping if the hermit spoke as he often did of the sights observed on the short walks.

Kaya's listening, when alerted tended to be directional and with a suspension of breathing until his mind was put at ease. His movements were relaxed and deliberate. He was at home outside, but winter was not his season, and he came to prefer to drowse indoors rather than spending time outside. His interest flagged as most of the mysteries were explained inside the wooden cave in the course of the winter.

The hermit introduced Kaya to the other students gradually and to the class room. There were three classes divided by age and ability. At first Kaya went with Kutch to his age group. They were the middle course, but Kaya found them talking of things he did not understand. Then he was sent to the class of younger and smaller children. There he was bored. Kaya seemed a thick, dull child, a typical butt for jokes and pranks by more established young scholars. Only his constantly moving eyes betrayed the restlessness of the spirit and the occasional flashes of humor and recognition in them: the intelligence that lived behind the mask.

He was a problem from the start. Unused to long hours of listening, he would move to where his eyes, nose and ears told him of activity and especially of food. When not hungry, he would listen and watch any activity and would participate in it. But when attracted by something else, would leave immediately to investigate. Tidbits, dried fruit or meats, sweets tied in handkerchief corners or tucked in waist cloths, all were soon detected and investigated by Kaya and usually eaten before the owner could protest. The teacher's threats were answered with growls and the showing of teeth. If backed into a corner, he would stand with arms outstretched like a rampant bear ready to charge out at a tormenter. He fascinated the small children, who alternately mauled him lovingly and fled from him with screams of *hi-van, hi-van*; beast.

He could sleep anywhere, and frequently did, if the material discussed was above him, or if the memorization was too long. The hermit got him to learn psalms, and he liked arithmetic, but he undermined the activities and discipline of the classroom and he was soon relegated to the position of helper of the smallest children, butt and playmate in the yard.

While in the play yard, he would carry some of the younger children and help them throw a ball. Some of the stronger would try to get him smudged with the red powder of the forbidden wall so as to involve him in punishment. Here again the boy would accept no punishment: a pull of his ear resulted in a powerful blow on the wrist of the puller. If the punisher persisted, Kaya went into the wide-armed rampant bear stance. A bear hug and tussle ensued while the other children screamed encouragements to one party or the other.

At meal time for food servings, the boys formed a line before the kitchen to receive their gruel of wheat, barley or oats as the season and supply dictated. The boys supplemented this with private food from each little larder, with special bits that excited the appetite, curiosity or revulsion of the others. Kaya too formed up with the others to get his portion of porridge and bread. They sang heartily their grace with these words:

1. Lord, we thank you for your goodness;
   For food that we eat.
   Lord, we thank you for our people:
   Tribe, clan and family.
   Lord, we thank you for our teachers,
   And world where we live.
   We thank you Yesu for grace

2. Lord we thank You for creation;
The care that You take.
Lord we thank You for the clothing
And shelter that we make.
Lord we thank You for the challenge
To live out our best.
Thank You for faith, hope and love.

THE HERMITAGE GRACE

Suddenly, the little woodcutter, Tu'ta, who was serving a gourd ladle of milk into the bowls of the children, lost his bright vacant smile and dropped to the floor. He was moaning and convulsing, his eyes staring and unfocused.

The line of children leaned over the serving table to observe all that occurred to the little servant. They did not interfere or help in any way. Each drew conclusions different from the others.

"The fool had his wits stolen by the mountain spirit," said Komi of the reindeer people.

"He lived an evil life and insulted the Buddha in a previous life," said the farmer boy from Illi.

"His mother ate the wild honey of Azalea Mountain," said the Osseti from the hills.

"No, he had a fever sent by Ahura Ahriman, the Evil One, when they let the sacred fire go out," shouted the boy from the great southern valley, pushing the plump farmer and the hill boy.

By this time several were pushing and pulling in succession, and the line began to lump and wind with several struggling figures.

"Unhand me you horse-eating fool!" screamed the farmer's boy who ate no meat, at the Osseti, for whom the horse was milk, meat and liquor.

"Get your fat ass off me, you big yak," a boy retorted from the bottom of the pile.

An East Goth refugee, rescued from slavery, from beyond the Ural mountains for whom the horse was sacred, turned in righteous anger, screamed, "Who eats horse? Horses are a sacrifice for the gods; eat and be damned." He slammed one of the southern boys on the chest causing him to fall over the group already on the floor.

Quickly, the monitors moved among the boys pushing them apart and cuffing some who did not respond rapidly to the commands for order. One in particular, Koosta of the East Huns, seemed to enjoy the work of subduing the smaller children and usually left many bruises and tearful faces. At the same time the kitchen help had picked up the body of the little woodcutter and taken him through the kitchen to his little cubby hole near the outer door where the hermit brought medicines and attended to his needs.

The order to sit and eat was given and holy words were read to give point and order to the meal, after which a general grace was sung. After that offenders were to apologize or go up for punishment. All was done in an orderly way.

> - - - - - - - >

Then it came to the spring of the year and the annual time of games and departure for the summer at the home yurts. There they participated in the tribes' traditional summer activities. This meant: following the grass for the nomadic tribes, tundra moss for the reindeer followers, tending the ground for the agricultural tribes and movement to hunting grounds for the forest and arctic bands. Before moving, they would come in bunches and families to the grounds of the Hermitage, neutral ground where peace was the rule, to meet. They would gather their children and return to their way of life.

Few indeed of the tribes were Christian. Most followed the ways of the ancestors and were directed by a shaman. A few were influenced by Buddhism or Zoroastrianism. These beliefs were concentrated in the trading towns and agricultural villages of the south along the Amu Darya, Syr Darya and the Tarim Rivers, but the offer of literacy and geographic knowledge persuaded many a khan and principal man to send sons to learn with this holy man: for what he had been, if not for what he had become.

Here at the beginning of summer when the work of calving and planting were over and the ravages of winter repaired, the tribes could come together in peace. The children would return after helping in the fall harvest and preparation of winter food. When the ground froze, there came the time of study and discipline again.

Kutch was elated by the news that he could return home with his new friend. The hermit would have preferred to keep Kaya, but the summer was producing increased restlessness and day-long escapes from the school; he wanted to find his brothers, Brun and Ay-ya. The Chipchaks would come for Kutch after the June dismissal. It was better, Kootsal decided, to get Kaya back with the tribe. He asked Kutch to let Kaya go with him.

TUTA'S SEIZURE (PAGE 119)

PEOPLE, PLACES & PLOTS IN CHAPTER 12

Jo'mer: a rich merchant with a heavy burden of guilt and troubles.
Kaya: seeks a good thing, but finds a bad one to strive against.
Koos'ta: an older student of the Huns and attendant of the hermit.
Koot'sal: a name or title of sanctity given to the hermit.
Onder: although dead, he is still a source of sorrow and confusion.
The Prince: the hermit tells the story of a man of wealth and worldly wisdom.
The Princess: receives a desired gift, for which she thanks everyone but the giver.

GLOSSARY HELP:

hy'van; animal; a wild creature; beast; dangerous.
jo'mert: generous; lavish; bountiful; the root of Jomer's name.
koot'sal: holy; holy one; saint; set apart.
Tanra dünyaya sever: God loves the world; on wall hanging.
tau: The Greek letter for T; used as a cross by some, in the first Christian centuries.
Tufan: a depression in the Tarim Basin where water accumulated for agriculture.

TREASURE SEEKERS

The Tokhari trader appeared a few days before the gathering, and it was evident that he had separated himself from his caravan to seek out the hermit and to visit the Hermitage before the great gathering. He requested the time for the visit and was of course invited to tea in the office. After the usual courteous preliminaries, the rich trader, Jomer bey, made known his business.

"I have been seeking information concerning my nephew, Onder, who was murdered south of here in the Chipchak area," he said. "The tribes do not accept the presence of inquisitive relatives, so I have come to the only source of information available."

"You do well, for I remember the incident, but you come late. It has been at least eight years." He gestured with his hand, "justice was executed three years after and compensation made. The tribe would resent the opening of the case again."

Jomer paused, shook his head ruefully, and replied, "Yes, I was shorthanded at the time, hurt and angry. Until I got my present caravan manager five years ago, I was in constant journeying. Then I heard rumor that there may have been a child."

"Tell me about yourselves," pressed the hermit.

"We are from the region of Tufan, a land of grapes, which produces skins of wine and fruit that we dry for export north and east to the tribes. We trade the furs, gold, dried meat and hides to the south or to the Chinese children of Han. We commerce west to the Mother of Rivers, which flows south to the great inland Caspian Sea where we trade silks, jewelry and fine lacquers of the East for gold coins and the great horses of the Caucasian steppes, which we export to the Han of the East. My nephew was assigned to the western end of the route to search for stallions and mares of unusual qualities, for such lordly creatures bring their weight in gold from the great Chinese Emperors." Here he paused and considered the formidable if slight form of the hermit. He dealt with Buddhist monks and now Christians on his home ground and the leaders of the great temples to the east. Some ruled small religious states; others were robber barons on the silk road. The hermits and brothers were more varied, and some had strange ideas of what was proper in trade. So he delicately phrased his words, "We buy young women for sale as wives and concubines in the East and West as well as other trade goods."

The hermit permitted a slight lift of the eyebrows and said, "You get your weight in gold from young virgins I understand." The merchant, Jomer nodded his head and licked his dry lips, "disease free and guaranteed; the others go at much lower prices and serve as concubines."

The hermit sniffed," Not as cheaply as you pretend, and they go to the houses of pleasure and theater for a brief season. You frustrate the purposes of God for married happiness and procreation for them."

"Not I, *Kootsal*, holy one," objected the merchant. "I sell to honorable men who promise good husbands and worthy enterprises; some of the girls become famous and are showered with jewels and gifts; they purchase their freedom and buy estates. They can chose their own husband and marry a rich man."

The hermit frowned sadly, "One in a thousand; the rest of them contract disease, suffer abuse or disappointment and grief. What will you do with your great wealth?" He asked thoughtfully, "Is it for this you seek a child -- for your heir? Money gained without God's purpose or blessing will bring tragedy to all it touches."

The Tokhari considered his porcelain tea bowl carefully as if for the first time. It was elaborately designed with gold scrollwork around the lip of the bowl, Han, no doubt. "I have thought much on this. Perhaps I will give riches for one of the holy houses of our faith," he said slowly.

The hermit raised his index finger, "You will want us to pray for the repose of your soul when you have filled it with blood and gold, so your fat greedy little self will enjoy the best of both worlds. This is your idea?"

The man twisted in his seat. "We are taught," he said, "that there is forgiveness of sins in the name and power of the Christ." The smile on the holy man's face was beautiful.

"Yes, it is true, but when sin is recognized, action must, at that moment, be taken." He leaned forward intently, "Repentance and forgiveness must be now, not when your coffers are full or time convenient." A thin line of sweat appeared on the man's forehead, and he sounded out of breath.

"You mean change everything now?"

The hermit smiled beatifically again. "From the moment recognition and repentance start, the changes will flow from God through your heart. You will know what to stop, what to continue, and how to rectify mistakes and sins. Trust Him. He will make it clear."

The merchant weighed two bags in his hand. "Which will you have?" he sighed, "Gold or jewels?" The hermit seemed to become taller and severer as he sat before the merchant who seemed to diminish.

"Salvation is not purchased," he said grimly. "It is a gift of God. This is the message of the church 'Today is the day of salvation'."

It was the Tokhari's time to smile, "But the cure for a greedy soul must be the giving away of that which one loves too much; and to find a worthy object as the recipient must be the aim. One who will not be corrupted by its possession. *Jomert*, generosity," he said, making a play on the meaning of his name, "always demands responsibility."

The hermit bowed his head, "You do us honor. The gold is more useful here." He placed the bag near the brushes and paper.

He sat lost in thought, head down, for a long moment. Then as he lifted his head, he looked at the merchant with troubled eyes.

"You said, `The loss of that which one loves too much.' You have truly hit the mark, for it takes me in the heart, and I find myself defenseless," Kootsal said pensively.

The merchant looked at the older man carefully, "I have heard conflicting reports about your past."

The hermit sighed, and shaking his head began to tell the story of a studious, bright son of the ruling family of a large city on a river whose supply of water never ceased, and in that land of fruit and agriculture learned the ways of those countries, south and east, whose civilizations were admired. Born to a ruling family who doted on their own, no pain or expense was shirked to give the young heir the best: education and travel, languages and arts, war and diplomacy.

A great dynastic marriage was arranged with a family as rich and privileged, after long personal contact and interviews by trusted friends and advisers. The match was to be the talk of all Central Asia for the next year. It was auspicious in every respect, and astrologers and forecasters of every variety predicted greatness and blessing for the match. Even better - the young couple fell deeply in love, and both found their expectations met fully.

For the first several years, they found themselves well occupied, but as time passed, the lack of an heir began to produce moodiness on the part of the wife. She began to consult 'experts' of every kind and to collect theories of procreation from them. This took her into the realm of religion as well, and she became a connoisseur of creeds and religious practice. Everyone was full of advice and helpfulness; they spent great wealth in the process. The distressed wife took less pleasure in parties and high society and went on retreats to Buddhist nunneries and temples. She learned the sevenfold path and found she could not put the desires of her heart from her. She tried the Taoist temples and bowed to numerous goddesses and gods with appropriate gifts and offerings.

All this activity proved of little value and perhaps some hurt. A famous shaman was called in. His familiar spirit recommended a special hot springs and drink. About this time she acquired a woman who had the reputation of curing many ill and sterile women through prayer. This woman became not only an advisor, but a friend who would take nothing until a cure was effected. The next spring there was a boy child. The spiritualist claimed the credit and so did the Christian. They paid them both and offerings were sent to all the temples and congratulations poured in from all.

The lady healer was the only person to worry. She told her mistress plainly that Yesu shared His glory with no one and that those who received favors were expected to offer themselves to his direction and power in obedience. However, the prince and princess were taking no chances with their treasured acquisition and refused to heed her advice and honored all deities with their thanks.

It was August, when the child was in his seventh month when, while bathing the child, the mother and attendant noted a sudden change of color and shortness of breath in the child. He was dead when the prince received him into his arms. He was prepared for burial by the time the Christian friend arrived. Enraged, the prince had her chained.

He had shouted and threatened, and the woman, crying, said, "I warned the princess that Yesu is at war with the spirits of earth. He will rule alone and with none other. Your worship became unacceptable to Him. His glory He will give to no other. The child will wait for you in Yesu's garden where He is, and another may be sent if you take this lesson to heart."

At this the Prince started to rage again. The arrogance of the statement startled him. Just who did this deity claim to be? The wisdom of the Buddha had been taught for hundreds of years. Taoism was even older and all of these religions competed on friendly terms. Visits between temples was considered normal behavior.

He put his face before the prisoner's and snarled, "Who is Yesu, that He should claim so much?"

"Yesu is Lord of lords; he will end the present age and its lords. He controls life and the future."

The prince's face twisted with a grimace-like smile. "How did he become all these things?" He smirked sarcastically, "Wasn't He killed by Roman justice?"

"He was rejected by the religious leaders for his claims to be the expected Messiah of God. Condemned by the unjust political considerations of governors. Killed brutally by foreign soldiers. God intervened to give Him life through His resurrection to a new more powerful life and to preach forgiveness of sins and new life for all who believe." She spoke this in such a calm, steady voice that the prince was shocked, and somewhat awed.

"If this were true, it would be the turning point of all history. Then why are your numbers few and believers insignificant?" he responded, now curious.

"The evil prince of this world blinds the eyes of those who do not seek God with a humble heart," the woman answered. "I did not realize that He would require the return of the child when you did not obey Him." She was weeping now and acting as women should under condemnation. The prince felt his pride and anger return.

"You will pay for what your God has done to me. No one gives and takes back from me," he stated arrogantly.

> - - - - - - - >

The hermit sighed deeply as he remembered and turned again to speak to his visitor, now become confessor.

"I will not tell you of the sadistic satisfaction I experienced: the thrill I felt during her torture and death. I will not sleep this week if I open the door to that sealed room of the past. But I won no victory." The hermit continued, "My wife went into a continuing decline, calling for her Christian friend to come answer her questions. Kissing the Tau cross, calling continually for the child and asking Yesu's pardon and permission to enter the garden and play with the child." The hermit was crying now, as was his guest. "I died with her. My ghost wandered purposeless through the northern waste lands until, on this spot, I found a new life and purpose. Here, where I found spiritual riches, I poured my earthly riches, that others might also become rich."

He sighed and rose to his feet. He was now acting as fellow petitioner and not as a preacher condemning the guilty. "God will accomplish his work in you and through you. We will have a moment of prayer together in our garden on the ridge and after we will speak of the loss of your nephew."

The older boys of the school took turns serving the hermit, for training in manners and court etiquette, Han Chinese and Sassanian Persian models were still the mode.

As the hermit and guest were delayed outside, Koosta, the largest and oldest boy in the school, came into the room of the hermit and started to gather the porcelain and carry the lacquered tray with remnants of rice cakes and wheat muffins, expensive imports. He was finishing off the bits of cake when his eye fell on the leather pouch. First hefting and then greedily opening the purse, he removed several coins and open-mouthed stroked the gold coins. Then, startled, he looked up to see Kaya at the door. Kaya too, had learned that crumbs remained from the reception of guests and had been guided by his hopes and nose to investigate.

Koosta had closed his hand over the coins and slowly moved his hands down to his sash, while moving around the writing table and leaving the tray and cups where they lay, walked over to the boy in the doorway. Koosta, confident in his newly acquired height and strength sneered at the boy, "What are you staring at, you little dumbbell. You had better get away from here and keep your mouth shut." He swaggered with arrogant self-display. He felt assured of his strength and ability to handle anyone at the school, adults included. He started to move away from the place with his new gains.

He was startled by the blow of one of Kaya's arms across his back and the other wrist on his adam's apple. He was caught in a bear hug, and the child was climbing right up him and his legs caused Koosta to trip and fall. The growls of a bear came from his back where Kaya hung and pulled him down. Koosta fell on his back and tried to roll and get an arm behind himself to get some kind of purchase on his little opponent. In this he was not too successful at first; the boy was heavy for his age and strong. When he thought he had a hand hold, he found his arm being twisted. Indeed, the holds Kutch had taught Kaya were very useful. Eventually, the greater leverage and weight of the youth, enabled him to break free.

The door to the outer park opened just as Koosta had taken hold of the child's neck and was slamming his head against the wood floor. He paused and still on his knees gestured to the two men there. "See, Holy One, this *hi'van*, beast, has taken your gold," he exclaimed, palming from his sash and demonstrating with a flourish two of the coins.

The awkward hermit moved with sudden energy and skill. He separated the two with one motion and had them side by side, each held by one arm in a squirm-proof grip shaking the coins on to the table.

"Explain yourselves," he demanded. Looking first at the older boy.

"When I came in to remove the tea things, this beast-child was stealing the gold from the purse. He tried to run and I caught him here at the door."

The hermit looked doubtful, "Beasts run away," he said, "Any beast would have chosen the outside door."

"But you were there outside, Holy One; he would not dare intrude," the youth insisted.

"He has never shown fear of me," the hermit smiled, "or anyone else. Nor does he value gold. What did you see, Kaya," he asked.

Kaya was still breathing hard and sounded sullen and angry though his voice was low. "Koosta eat cake bits, look in little sack, eyes open big. He take bright shine things in sash. See me, come to door and growl at me."

The merchant had been counting the purse while this happened.

He broke in with the words, "Two coins are missing still. Search the big one first."

The hermit released Kaya, who stayed in place, and ran his hand along the sash of the big youth, who was starting to move away from the searching hand. "Those are mine," he protested, "from my father."

"Then they will be Chinese coins won't they? Your father gets pay from the Northern Kingdom as an ally."

The youth began to cry in humiliation as the coins were taken from his sash. "I could have gone to the Buddhist monastery near the wall among the Huns of the left hand and been near the land of China. Why did my father send me here?" He grieved.

The merchant was examining the gold pieces. "Greek like the rest of them," he stared accusingly at the boy.

"Your father knows that you would have been a hostage," said the hermit. "You would be part of the schemes of diplomacy used to divide the Huns against each other again--those near the wall from those in the north--just as the Han Chinese divided the right hand from the left, and drove the right hand from Kansu province starting them toward the far West."

"The money is restored, Kootsal bey," said Jomer, "Now what?"

"The lad has finished the year and must return to his family. He is not apt nor promising, but perhaps God can make him into a good warrior, if he has the sense to repent."

The hermit looked at each of the boys, "Go first," he told Kaya, "when you are inside, bar the door of your room. I will send food and tell you when you are safe." He turned to the merchant, "Let us talk of your lost nephew tomorrow in the morning, before the races." He turned to the sullen Hun, "we will talk a bit now, before you depart with your family tomorrow.

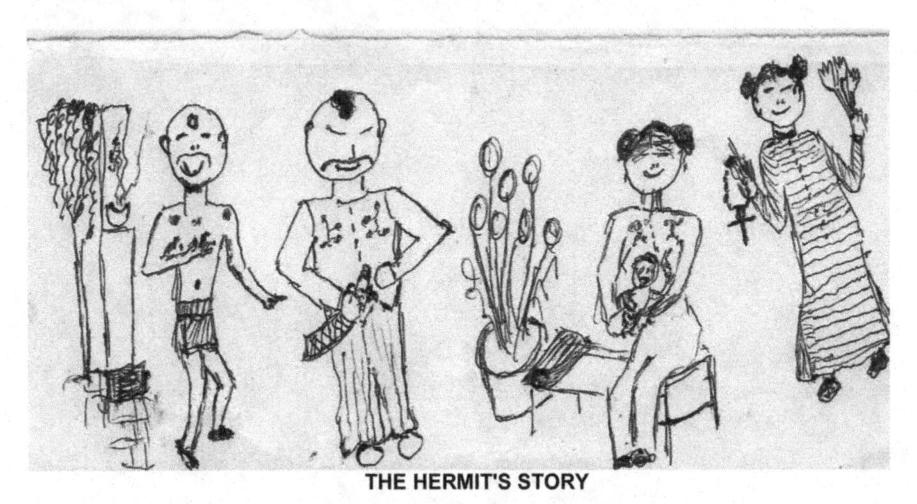

THE HERMIT'S STORY

PEOPLE, PLACES & PLOTS IN CHAPTER 13

Jo'mer: the uncle of Onder of E'pec Kent.
Kaya: has time off with his friend Kutch to sing and celebrate the gathering.
Koos'ta: leaves the Hermitage with a damaged reputation.
Koot'sal: a name or title of holiness given to the hermit.
Kutch: is excited by the races and the coming of his tribe and family.
On'der: wayward nephew of Jomer, impatient for success, met death.
The Hun: a messenger of forgiveness sent to contact Onder bey is now dead.

GLOSSARY HELP:

op'tal: fool; clown; stupid; a funny person.
vah'she: wild; dangerous; untamed.

GRASSHOPPER GAMES

The days were turning warmer and longer with only a touch of chill at the noon hours. Easter had come and gone at the Hermitage. It was a beehive of activities as the preparations for the gathering of the families and wide dispersal of the students drew near. Some of the chiefs would come; others would send trusted servants who would observe and report everything that happened. Some would represent groups that preserved great equality of condition within their tribe, and others would be aristocratic in nature or achievement oriented. Most contained elements of all these systems of human relations.

The strictly hunting tribes saw little use in writing, so those represented were largely herders and a few who combined their activities with agriculture or commerce. So, every one rode: yak, reindeer, or horse. Many tribes refused to hunt on foot even in the deep wooded taiga. Naturally to these kinds of people, the race was the most attractive activity and the climax of the spring dispersal.

Since each riding animal was adapted to a very different kind of terrain, each ran against its own kind and in as appropriate a setting as the mountains and flats of the Altai Mountains could provide.

Kaya was filled with excitement as he and his school friends went to see the horses exercising for the afternoon races. As they walked, Kaya hummed a tune he had liked from the morning prayers, It was to him stately, but he made it change and jump about curiously. His voice was low and steady, but wandered on pitch and broke with his voice at unexpected places. He was completely uninhibited. He saw a grasshopper in the grass, and he started a song about his favorite season, matching it with the new music of the altered tune:

GRASSHOPPER SONG

1. **God is sending summer,**
   Grasshoppers will come --
   J-U-M-P, J-u-m-p, soon now.

2. **God is sending warm days,**
   New life is springing all around --
   J-U-M-P, J-u-m-p, how nice.

3. God is sending long hours.
   Watch big grasshoppers, see them grow --
   J-U-M-P, J-u-m-p, watch them.

4. God is sending light rain.
   Green grass is so high now, see them hide --
   J-U-M-P, J-u-m-p, catch them.

5. God is sending sunshine.
   They go so high, some jump, off they fly --
   J-U-M-P, I eat them.

6. God is sending summer, Thank God.

He did just as he said, he jumped, caught and ate a small green one, grinning at the laughing Kutch. He dodged Kutch's swing at his face. Kutch wrinkled his brow and wrapped his arms round his own face to pull his own ear and nose and make an ugly face. "*Optal,* fool." he added, and both were laughing again.

They passed by the line of horses selected to race on the meadows. Most children rode well by the time they were six-years old. Kaya had been an avid learner while with his human foster mother. Indeed all the tribe had gone out of their way to train and care for him. Now in touch with a faint memory of the nature of horses and his earlier experiences, Kaya confidently touched one's muzzle and fed it a handful of dry honeycomb. It was a beautiful three-year old mare of a reddish yellow color which the horses of the Chipchak had acquired these last six or seven years. This was the one that he liked particularly.

"Why don't you race this one?" said Kutch to his friend, "I'll take the black, and we'll have fun. It will give the East Huns a good race. The big bullies have everything their own way too much."

Kaya stared at the beautiful animal before him and wondered if he could hold on until the finish line. Kutch seemed to understand for he said condescendingly, "We will put footholds on for you." The leather loops were tied under the saddle for the benefit of little ones to keep them on the animal.

"I don't want to be tied on. I'll rest my feet on them," said Kaya modestly, stroking the horse.

"She likes you," observed Kutch, "you will have a good race this afternoon."

"But will the grooms allow us to use the horses?" inquired Kaya.

"Of course you can," assured Kutch, "all I have to do is give the order. Mother says I'm the Prince of the tribe, and everyone will have to obey me someday." His looks belied his words as he stared at the ground. "They aren't often very prompt or nice about it, though. Mother says they are stupid animals, but I don't think some of them like us."

As they started back toward the food and goods market set up temporarily near the Hermitage entrance, the large, red-haired merchant in rich clothes of Oasis style -- tight pants, boots and embroidered vest-- pushed past them. Suddenly he stopped and looked at the boys again.

"You're the boy, Kaya, who fought the big boy in the Hermit's chamber," he stated, "well fought and thanks." The big man put a hand to the boy's face and pinched his cheek between two fingers. "What is your family and tribe?"

"I am Kaya the bear, and apart from being Chipchak, I know neither family nor clan. I'm *vahshe*," he spoke as if proud of his condition.

"Bravo," smiled the merchant, "a man's condition depends on the man's quality, not the circumstances. We will meet again," he promised, taking leave and then without noticing Kutch, he strode purposefully toward the entrance to the Hermitage. There, of course, he would have to ring for entrance, for the door never stayed open even at festival times. The people were too turbulent and the needs too desperate for presumptuous confidence. In short, treachery was a present reality. It was necessary to live cautiously.

The hermit himself answered the summons to the door for all his charges had departed for the fair. Koosta, also, had departed with his goods.

When they were comfortably seated in the hermit's room, the trader, Jomer, began again. The story was an old one of confidence misplaced and goods and money stolen. The nephew, entering his twenties, impatient for life, wealth and experience and seeing little value in apprenticeship and learning, had run away with fifty gold pieces and in connivance with a pretty prostitute had taken a prize horse of mixed Arab and Alani stock with the intention of selling it in the East.

"They crossed the great Volga River that year, evidently buying another girl from the Sassanians and were following the great northern horse road to the Altai. In July they should have been arriving from the north to the Black Irtish. They would pass the Dzungarian Plains to winter in Tufan by October. From there he could have gone by the Kansu road to the East to the southern Kingdom at Nanking; or to the Northern one at Loyang or to one of the war lords that have arisen. So much chaos in this barbaric age! Two hundred years ago the great Han Dynasty brought peace and a greater China to the whole zone." He paused, sighed and continued.

"I had received notice first of the theft and then, the movement of the thief. In June, word came of the destruction of the caravan he joined. In July, I heard that Onder was still alive after the attack. So I sent an emissary with a letter of pardon, peace, reconciliation and an offer of travel money to the home base in the Tarim Basin, if my remaining goods were returned to me. The youth would be put back to work for the family. An affirmative reply was received. Advance notice was sent in an early letter with a notice of pardon from myself, his maternal uncle, by a traveling friend. The rendezvous place and day were stated in the letter. The agent who was due to receive the submission and horse was dispatched in August with 40 days to travel north. The agent was instructed to kill Onder if he resisted. It was uncertain if the lad would wait for him, but the net was spread. We were close on the trail. The key to restoration was the return of the horse and submission of the youth."

The hermit was completely fascinated. He asked breathlessly, "What happened?"

"The agent was an East Hun and an astute confidant. He had always been able to complete any assignment to the letter, but three months passed without any word or indication of what happened."

"But rumors and gossip precede all the caravans even to the numbers and cargos. There is nothing hidden from prying eyes. How could you not know?" asked Kootsal.

"There is a way," Jomer continued, "though rare; it must be a tribal matter, something they wish kept so secret, that the man who told it would die."

"Yes, of course!" exclaimed the hermit, "something affecting their wealth or honor."

"The tribal yurts do not receive strangers kindly for everyone is considered a spy," the entrepreneur stated, "but God had mercy on my anguish and sent me news in winter, through the arrival of two gypsies and a bear. They gave me this." He produced a beautifully jeweled bronze dagger. It had an incised metal deer on the handle leaping toward the point, front legs folded and rear legs extended, the big turquoise eyes wide and a jade stone on the end of the handle as foundation for the hooves.

The hermit let his breath out slowly and extended his hands. "May I?" he asked. He regarded the weapon, which had been laid across his upturned palms. He shook his head as if at a loss for words. Finally he said in wonder, "They gave this up?"

The big man chuckled, "The worth is in the art and poor gypsies might be suspected of theft or murder if they sold it at the Bazaar. No, they had my name, and it was easy to track me down. They expected and got generous rewards." His expression was sad now.

"The news was not good then?" inquired the holy man sympathetically.

"The worst," confirmed Jomer shaking his red head slowly. "The young thief dead, killed by a knife, but not this one, another, they said. My agent dead, two arrows in his back. Chipchak arrows... but a black hunnish medicine arrow in Onder's right front shoulder. The two men swear they saw someone departing through the heavy brush. The knife was on the ground as if it had been dropped. They grabbed it and the letter and ran just as a troop of horsemen arrived outside the wood."

"You're sure of the facts?" his listener queried. "They may be telling lies for money."

"The knife confirms the person. I gave it to Onder on his becoming a man. The letter confirms the agent. They met and talked in the wood beside the northern road near the tribal border."

"How do you interpret the fall of events?" persisted Kootsal.

"It is possible they met and when Onder refused, my man struck the fatal blow. I have killed one I loved." He bowed his head and started to cry, "I was so angry I could have killed him myself! The stupid fool! What did he know of the problems, the long journeys, the hunger and cold to earn a bit of comfort and honor for later years."

"Could not Onder have killed your man? Perhaps he had lost money and horse. Arrows would be available from the tribe," countered the little man.

"But my nephew is dead. My agent is dead. My business with the horse and the Emperor of the north is dead. My heart has died with them. I repent and pray your forgiveness," he grasped the hand of the awkward little hermit and pressed his tearful face to it.

"My dear man," he sighed, "I have done worse. It is God's forgiveness you need, and you have it through The Christos who died for us sinful men." He placed a hand on the bent head and said, "Be comforted. When we seek Him, He is seeking us." The big man nodded his head to show that he heard, but did not respond. He seemed to be praying. After a time he raised his head.

"It is possible that another outsider killed my Hun and took the knife from Onder. Or did a tribesman kill Onder and my agent? Others may have had reason to dislike my nephew. He bragged a lot and was haughty, but he was in the Chipchak camp only three months. He wouldn't have made blood enemies so fast nor were his riches so great to provoke robbery. The jealous quarrel over the slave woman may have caused my man to have used the Hun arrow first and then stabbed him. But a bow is for distance. If Onder ran, the arrow would pierce the back. Was he shot previously, then found and finished by another, as ambassadors Dar and Peck thought? Stabbed by my agent? Did some guardian friend then kill the Hun? The two musicians were not able to add to my knowledge here. They heard running feet in the woods and the corpses positioned as I have said. It is all so confusing."

"Did the gypsies mention other signs or give you anything besides the letter and the knife?" inquired the hermit.

"I have questioned them closely. They swear that there was only time to look, take the knife and letter, and run before the horseman entered the wood. They said they were terrified that the tribesmen would recognize them from their visits to the camp. They went to gain coins from the entertainment of merchants recovering there."

"But," insisted the little man, "they were acquainted with the tribe and camp. They would know of any bad blood between them. They know more than they are telling."

"Yes, they know more than they tell, but I refused all reward until they cleared up my questions. They told all they knew of the camp. The Chipchaks did not permit them to stay in the camp. They were allowed in camp for several hours in the mornings and afternoons for fortune telling, musical entertainment with a dancing bear and juggling feats. The merchants were kept apart on the edge of the tribal encampment where they were fed but not free to wander. Those well or recovered were sent to the next tribe in groups as soon as possible. The very ill were kept in the yurt of the medicine woman as were several young women. The gypsies had never seen Onder or the Hun before when they found the bodies. The letter was the key that led to me when they found a reader, and the knife was the verification of the owner. They may have robbed other things from the corpses, but if so, they are not telling. There is no way of knowing short of torture. Their dress and care show little of money."

"Is there a possibility that they killed either or both?" persisted the hermit.

"Why come to me with murder on their conscience? Why give up the knife? Why, if they got the great horse, not go on to the East and sell it? These men are clever scavengers, not bold warriors," said Jomer. "But I did learn something else of interest. When the two left the Chipchak camp and were returning west, they discovered and visited the camp of the Persian marauders outside of the tribal territory. The brigands had sick and wounded to evacuate as well as a portion of goods, booty to be carted south to the cities for sale.

LOOTERS' FIND (PAGE 135)

Many of their horses had been taken in the fight with the Chipchaks. They promised a large sum if they could obtain animals to transport their goods back to their lands. Our entertainers knew their summer was over and they wanted to leave the area. So, leaving the bear, they returned to see what they could get from the Chipchaks in the way of animals. They admitted trailing my Hun there, and they watched him enter the woods. My man travels light, so he would have had a beast for carrying food perhaps another for riding, one or two animals. I suspect they stole whatever animals there were and ran back to the marauder camp. Rewarded for the animals, they would accompany the group south. From my reward for the knife, letter and the information, I deducted the price of two animals. Naturally, they complained, but I could see they were satisfied."

"So that's an end to it." The hermit shook his head regretfully. "It seems unfair not to know the truth in this life. We fail to see God's justice on evil men."

"It's not all, however," continued Jomer, "the leader of the bandits was called Gooch, a giant Persian. The men said he harbored a particular hatred of Onder for organizing and fighting a defensive action and delaying the seizure of the goods. He is especially angered by the fact that Onder released the golden stallion and sent him flying ahead into Chipchak country, warning the tribesmen. He blamed all their troubles on one man and swore to avenge himself on him. After he had interrogated the gypsies about the tribe's camp, he may have reconnoitered and penetrated the margins of the Chipchak land. His men wanted nothing to do with more fighting and were content to keep the old hilltop fort they had occupied.

There was a long silence. "Why then, do you accept the guilt for something that is still in mystery?" inquired Kootsal earnestly. "Most men avoid any suggestion of complicity in evil."

Jomer looked down at his hands and replied slowly, "I have become conscious of my willingness to murder or adversely affect the lives of others, if it is to my gain." A gentle smile greeted Jomer's eyes and the old head nodded, "Welcome to wisdom. You have arrived at the point of repentance and salvation. Now, Yesu can help you." They went together, again, to the pinnacle garden.

STEPPE FLOWERS

THE BOYS RETURN (Page 151)

PEOPLE, PLACES & PLOTS IN CHAPTER 14

Er'kan: watches the race and plans special rewards.
The hermit: is the awarder of prizes and accolades.
Jomer: finds hope and gives his knife to get an heir.
Kaya: his first race is full of unexpected moments.
Ke'ke: finds her fears revived by a familiar sight.
Koos'tah: cheats anyway he can, to win the race.
Koot'sal: the name given to the Hermit by his admirers.
Kutch: proves his bravery and persistence to everyone.
On'der: haunts the living by the memory of his death.
Ters'in: young East Hun groom and helper of Koos'tah.

GLOSSARY HELP:

deli-kon'la: literally, the one with crazy blood; youth.
hy'van: beast; animal.
jan'oh-var: monster; hideous thing; ugly creature.
tau: The Greek letter T; An early form of the cross.
vah'she: wild; savage; abandoned.

KAYA PASSES

The race was to be on the meadow near the river at the bottom of the gorge where the stream slowed through a widening valley. Some willows grew on the banks, which were subject to spring flooding. There were trees newly leafed out on the edge of the rise at the foot of the steep hills covered with conifers.

The people sat on the rise at the side of the hill to get the best view of the proceedings. Erkan of the Chipchaks was present with Onbasha, Dayday and several key men. He was wearing his badge of office, the great white swan ivory medallion around his neck. They sat near the starting line opposite the East Huns across the river at the finish line.

It was only fun and entertainment, of course. No one put much money on a race between children. That was reserved for races between tribal champions, where intense rivalries and great prestige were at stake. Ethnic, linguistic groups sat with their own in scattered gatherings to cheer in a tolerant easy-going way the children of their community.

The students themselves felt entirely differently about things, as personal rivalries and prejudices were to be given opportunity to demonstrate superiority. Also, it gave a chance to avenge wrongs. Feeling in the school was intense. The opportunity to demonstrate traditional accomplishments before the home folks and shame a rival, brought heightened tension to all.

The noise level was overwhelming as they surged into the gathering area. Horses shied and grooms tried to keep charges and horses in line, and bring some kind of order in the start-up. There was no actual line up of course, simply a mass of horses to run down one side of the stream, cross a shallow ford of pebbles, and return, clock-wise, left to right, to the finish line. The winner would receive a coveted award, given by the hand of Kootsal, the hermit.

After several false starts and much shouting, a bronze bell was struck and a flag waved, signaling the start of the race. The pack surged forward in a mass, and it was only after about three hundred yards had been run that the lead was successfully established. Koosta of the East Huns held the lead with Kutch of the Chipchaks close beside him. Kaya was in the mass behind.

Another three hundred yards brought them to the ford and Kutch was definitely pulling ahead; the light weight of the frail child proved an advantage that the larger Koosta did not have. Kaya had broken from the pack, more because of the superb qualities of the golden horse than from dimly remembered skills. As they entered the water, Koosta swung his plaited leather whip, backhand, hard across Kutch's face. The small jockey flinched and threw up his hands defensively, and his horse shied and faltered a moment.

The boy swung wide, away from his opponent, but gamely, after swerving, resumed his position at the side of the bigger boy. Kaya, meanwhile, had taken the right flank lead position, and Koosta found himself bracketed. When there remained but a hundred yards to the finish, he furiously kicked out at Kutch while bringing his whip across and swinging down at the head of Kaya. The edge of the whip caught Kaya on the temple and cheek. He responded with the startled roar of an infuriated bear cub.

Three things happened simultaneously: The roar stimulated Kaya's horse to greater effort to escape, plunging ahead. Koosta's horse shied left to flee the sound. The aggressive rider, off balance, foot in the air, his body and arms leaning right, fell off, and was passed, splashed and begrimed in the mud. Kaya won by a head. The other two horses, still bearing left, crossed into the stunned crowd of astonished viewers, scattering them. Kutch reined in immediately, but the riderless horse continued its unhindered run through the mob of Huns.

Meanwhile, Koosta had to scramble toward the river to get clear of the horde of horses bearing down on him. Even with all his efforts, one of the horses bumped him into the river. Wet, bruised and angry, he washed up at the edge of the ford. As he trudged toward his horse, now cropping on the meadow attended by Tersin, a tribesman, he planned his revenge.

Kaya had found his friend Kutch and reunited they walked, arms round each other, laughing and praising one another. They relived the race moment by moment.

"You were in the lead from the beginning," asserted Kaya, "everyone could see you were bound to win. If he had not hit you, you would have finished a full length ahead."

"No, my horse was tiring. At the half you were up even and ready to pass us both. You certainly chose the better horse and were the better rider."

"I am not a good rider yet, but I will be," promised Kaya. "I did not see your black tiring, only the unfair advantage taken by that *deli-kon-la*, when he hit you."

"You fixed him," chortled Kutch. "I thought a bear had joined the race." He laughed once again, "I guess one did." He pummeled his friend's back amiably, "after all you are *vahshe*."

Kaya nodded his head in agreement. It didn't sound so bad being 'wild' when people were not hunting you. His friend could have called him anything, and he wouldn't mind at this moment of joy.

"I chose the black to honor Fewsoon, the bright-haired one," continued Kutch. "She is the only girl in the home-camp that is even human. The rest are animals."

Kaya could not remember any girls in his life and there were none at the school, so he reserved judgment waiting for his friend to say more.

"She lives with Maya, the medicine woman, her mother died and left her the black as an inheritance. The horse is over ten years old. So you see she was tiring."

"When did the mother die?" asked Kaya, for the subject of mothers was a tender one to him.

"Three years ago, during a Tartar raid," Kutch explained, "The old medicine woman, Meryen and some others were killed too. Not all the bodies were found, so some may have gone as slaves."

"Did you see this thing?" Kaya's voice was low and tense.

"I was only a baby playing round the yurts, but I remember my father's great anger as he rallied the troop together and set out in search of the raiders. It occurred on a river to the north."

"Was your mother there too?" Kaya inquired breathlessly.

"The wife of the Khan does not need to go on wood gathering chores in the forest." Kutch stated smugly. "Erkan of the Chipchaks is my father."

> - - - - - - - >

Jomer bey sat beside the Hermit as they watched the race. After the finish during the excitement, he turned to the little man with flashing eye. "I would like the winner of the race to have this as prize and trophy. If the boy was a *vahshe*, he has become a horseman." The red-haired man held out the bronze knife with the jade, turquoise and silver handle. "I want this no more, and I would like to know more about this boy. You say he speaks with the dialect of the Chipchak? What about his people?"

The hermit paused, waited for the musical presentation to end before he began. He recognized the symptoms, a man clutching at straws, searching for an heir. He sighed and listened to the wander-lust expressed by the school chorus.

1. I love to go a wandering
In woods and grassland green,
Far from my yurt and my homeland.
Let me live in open space,
Under the everlasting blue sky.
Bright blue sky! There to be
In Tanra's great creation,
And pass my life there.

2. I love to go exploring now
In mountain pastures green,
Far from my yurt and my homeland.
I can live in tundra wild
Under the never-ending blue sky--
Clear blue sky. Let me be
In Tanra's demonstration
And spend my life there.

3. I love to go a-hunting out
In forest dark and dense,
Far from my yurt and my homeland.
I may live in open swamp,
Under the great eternal blue sky--
Dark blue sky. Let me be
In Tanra's presentation
And live my life there.

4. I love to go a traveling
In endless grass and hills,
Far from my yurt and my homeland.
I will live in open steppe
Under the transparent open sky--
Light blue sky. Let me see
Tanra's manifestation
And end my life there.

"The Chipchaks are a widely dispersed people, and the child could have come from any unfortunate family killed by disease or war," the old one began. "The people's origins seem to be to the north. The old songs and stories about the gray wolf and reindeer mention Tura, Turuk and the great north mountain where they hunted the great wild yak for their trophies and standards. The Kotuy, Anabar, Olenek and Tungus Rivers, the flat mountains and peninsulas of the central Siberian uplands, tundra and woods country, figure in all their stories. They resemble the far north people: round faces, short and stocky, large chests and heads, small hands and feet, pale complexioned with black eyes and hair. Stolid, determined, steady if sometimes irritable when crossed, they are hard workers and hunters. They are persistent. They are different from the Han people of China. They live north of their cousins, the Huns at the Great Wall. The Mongols live east of the Gobi and the Evenki live north and east of them with the Old Siberians in the most eastern parts and the little hairy Ainu people living on the coasts and islands. So the Chipchak

are the northern-most of the horse people. They now live west of Lake Baikal, occupy the steppes of Angara, Abakan, Minusisk, and Barabin to the Irtysh River. They seem to be drifting west over the Chipchak Steppes. Their history is different from yours," the Hermit concluded seriously.

"Your people, the Tokharians, on the other hand, are from the west and are agriculturalists and stock farmers. Your people create industrial products and arts for building communities. The Tarim cities are the products of your society. Can such differences be accommodated if you include such a boy in your inheritance?" The old man leaned back to watch the effect of his words.

"I liked his honesty and fearlessness in resisting the older boy," started Jomer, "I liked his courage to ride against more experienced youth." He stroked his chin, "If it is true, as our great faith teaches, that God looks on and values the inward part. Then that part should matter most." He raised his face to look the old man in the eye, "I feel an affinity inwardly with this lad and his outward look does not offend me. I want him for my heir."

"Well said," chortled Kootsal, "I would not have consented otherwise. One must be very sure in these matters." He laughed again, "Yes, I don't think you could find a finer heir."

"When can the boy come on a visit to the oasis?" Jomer asked eager to have the boy live with him and take advantage of city life.

"We must first consider the condition of the boy," stated the hermit. "He has lacked parental care, and a mother will likely be his greatest need for a short time. He will also need to be oriented to his own people and take up the skills and language he only partially learned." The man thought again and went on, "Your different world and language would confuse him at this point. Let us give him the summer with the tribe of his friend Kutch, then a winter more here. Despite all his alertness, he will never be a scholar, but he will learn reading and writing, and he loves music and arithmetic. After that, I can do no more for him, and he will be ready for another summer with the tribe. Then, he will go with you and learn something of the merchant's trade and oasis life."

"That is not very satisfactory to me," complained the merchant, "I had hoped for something more prompt."

"Long range investments take time to mature," countered the old one, "Trust me, you will get full value.

>------->

The presentation was simply done. The school children were drawn up before the Hermitage and the relatives and vendors stood facing them. After more songs by the students, the awards for personal recognitions were given.

The hermit simply called each child's name, repeated his accomplishments and gave a small bit of cloth with the acknowledgement in a dark waxy ink. It was tied to a small stick like a banner. As a status symbol flown beside the door of the yurt, it proclaimed the merits of the father of the house, and the diligent son's merits for official duties. Great was the status of the man with many flags, however faded by time, that waved by the entrance for all to see.

Kaya's turn involved few stated accomplishments, although, arithmetic and music were mentioned. Wrestling and the winning of the race were the emphasized factors in his recognition and the prize of the knife drew gasps of surprised admiration from everyone. The `dummy' became everyone's friend, and all wanted to see his trophy.

Kutch, however, got first in many subjects. His small pale face shone with pride; and his flag was large with the listing of his accomplishments. As well as being the best student in school, he got mention in wrestling. For second in the race, he got the Tau cross of polished wood the hermit had selected originally for the winner. None crowded him to see such an ordinary prize; so he joined the others looking at the dagger.

"The hermit has never given a prize like this before," stated one of the older boys (about twelve) who would soon start work as a scribe. "If I had a weapon like this, I'd learn to throw it." He exclaimed, and made the hand motion. "You'd lose it too, first thing," jeered another. Kaya stood watching his new treasure being handed back and forth. He looked up as his friend Kutch arrived. Seeing the wood cross he took it from the boy's hands, wrapped the thin red silk cord around his wrist twice and said, "We take turns with the prize; remember, you get knife today, I take this holy thing." He strolled off leaving his friend with those admiring the knife.

BULLY'S REVENGE (PAGE 148)

"Look" Kutch held the knife up with both hands to his parents, "This is our prize for the race!" His mother, dressed in her finest riding trousers and coat, turned with pride, to see her son's newest trophy. "What," Keke gasped, and turned a yellow-green color as she stared, hypnotized, at the bronze and silver dagger. "Get it away from me." she screamed. She hit his hand causing the knife to fall. She swung around and took refuge behind her husband, moaning and clinging to Erkan, as he stared open-mouthed at the scene he had witnessed. His wife, stunningly beautiful at twenty-four, was behaving like a terrified little girl. Kutch equally stunned slowly retrieved his dagger. "Let me see it, Son." said Erkan solemnly. Keke began crying on his back, "It's his, Onder's knife," she sobbed, "I would know it anywhere." Tight-lipped Erkan returned the trophy, "Give it back, son. You can't take it home to the yurt. I will get you a useful Chipchak knife. Get rid of that gaudy, foreign thing."

> - - - - - - - >

As Kaya walked by the willow bank, a figure launched itself from the brush and with an arm around Kaya's throat tried to pull the boy off his feet. Kaya reaching over his shoulder pushed his fingers and palm under the chin of his opponent forcing his head up, throwing him off balance. They both fell and Kaya rolled and was up on his feet. Koosta got up more slowly and was busy letting off hatred in his curses. "You animal. *Hyvan! Vahshe!* You are no rider. I can beat you any time. You made me fall, rammed my horse."

Kaya did not answer, but he was, now, thoroughly angry at Koosta and tired of his insults. The two assumed classical wrestling positions and faced each other head to head. Each trying for a head or arm hold on the other, faking a dive for a leg and circling, they spent a moment sizing each other up and looking for advantage. Then Koosta caught Kaya's hair and pulled him off balance and caught him around his neck and chest. They thrashed over the ground.

The struggle was to the older boy's advantage now and as they rolled and panted the longer legs and arms of the youth forced Kaya back on the new grass. Holding Kaya's body in a scissors hold with his legs and using his arms as weights on the upper arms of the boy. He had spread Kaya's arms so Kaya's hands could not reach his head, but his hands were over Kaya's face. He gave a snarl of satisfaction, "You see too much, you snoop. I'll stop you from ever seeing anything," and proceeded to dig his thumbs into the outer edge of Kaya's two eyes.

As quick as a dog that snaps at a fly, Kaya turned his face up toward the left hand and had seized the thumb in his mouth between his teeth. He was biting with all the power that his healthy young jaws, accustomed to eating gristle and bone in the wilderness, could muster.

Koosta's screams brought everything at the gathering to a hasty halt and search was made for the source of the sound. The East Hun gathering of relatives and attendants came rushing up to rescue one of their own.

They found them with both arms outstretched and straining against each other's, bodies still entwined, anguish and hatred on Koosta's thin face, grim determination on Kaya's. A crucifix of passion. Blood poured from the youth's stump, the severed thumb lay on the grass beside them. The grass and their bodies were smeared with the bright red of out-flowing life.

The rescuers descended with a shout, and a dozen hands grabbed the two boys separating them. Both questions and blows were aimed at the two, but only Koosta responded. "I'll kill you," he bellowed, "I'll kill you. You animal. You wild beast. *Jan-oh-var*. I'll never leave you in peace. I'll chop you in bits." His voice grew hysterical, and he fainted. He was borne away by relatives, while Tersin and some of the attendants slapped Kaya and beat at him. The boy jumped into the river and was carried down stream.

A wet, exhausted Kaya met a dejected, sad Kutch near the horse lines. The friends exchanged their trophies with explanations and apologies. They rode out on their horses, resolving to ride ahead of the relatives to the Chipchak yurts. Kutch reestablished his pride by leading. Kaya followed observing with care. A finely-dressed merchant, an elderly holy man, Chipchak tribesmen, and East Hun relatives also observed with care the departure of the two.

AT THE BEARS' CAVE (Page 167)

PEOPLE, PLACES & PLOTS IN CHAPTER 15

Ah jit': meaning hungry; a widely traveled caravan master for Jomer bey in Silk City.
Al'tom: 'my gold', a colt becomes Kaya's special care, which he shares with others.
Erkan: must show love in distant ways, gifts to each boy, a colt and a knife.
Few-soon': Kaya's sibling or foster-sister, and admirer.
Jo'mer: has the opportunity of training his prospective heir in the trade of E'peck Kent.
Kaya: enjoys new places, new faces and a new year.
Kutch: shares all, but wishes he had more.
Op'tal and Pesh: appear in the city with flute, bears, special deals.
Oz'mir: politician, and recipient of the favors of those seeking influence in town.
Ted'bir: a rich politician and owner of special entertainment facilities in the city.
Yown'ja: meaning clover flower; the baby name of Fewsoon.

GLOSSARY HELP:

***ashk*: passion; sensual pleasure, written on a wall plaque.**
***bayan*: lady; Miss/ Mrs; a title of respect, used before the name.**
***bosh' ooze-two nay*: I obey immediately; right away.; at your orders.**
***füsün*: delight; enchanting; charm, written on the wall.**
***hoe'sh gel'den-is*: happily you have come; I'm glad you came.**
***hoe'sh boll'duke*: happily I have found you; I'm glad to be here.**
***kar'desh:* brother/ sister; sibling; blood relative; companion.**
***lezzet*: savor, flavorful, delicious. a wall motto.**
***mesut*: happiness, written on the wall.**
***zevk*: enjoyment; sensuality. a wall motto.**

THE GOLDEN COLT

Word that a '*vahshe*,' savage, had come from the hermitage to the tribe, had gone before them to the encampment of the Chipchaks. It was easy arithmetic to arrive at the probable identity of the child. The whole village turned out to see the arrival of the two boys. Kaya, who could not remember clearly the arrangement of a camp, felt the hair on his neck rise as he rode past the silent, staring people.

Only when they stopped and dismounted before the yurt of the Khan did the yuzbasha, lieutenant step forward and give the official welcome. "*Hoe'sh gel'den-is*, welcome," to which Kutch answered, "*Hoe'sh boll'duke*, happily we have found you." Kaya too, mumbled over the required formula. Then the boys were invited inside to be served by the wife of the lieutenant. Porcelain cups held honey sweetened tea, as a special treat for the boys. Cakes of sweetened clabber thickened with rice starch were served.

All listened as the lieutenant asked leading questions, first about the school and life at the hermitage and then about the race and the prizes; finally they asked Kaya frankly about his early memories. Inside, this proceeded with calm, but outside, where women sat with their ears pressed against the felt wall, there was great excitement. They periodically conveyed the gist of all that was said inside. Tension mounted and the word went round. This was the 'child of promise'.

Suddenly, a red-haired girl of eight thrust through the crowd and opened the flap door of the yurt. "Brother," she cried, and fell clinging to Kaya's neck, knocking him flat in the process.

"Fewsoon," exclaimed Kutch, scandalized by her action and trying to help her to her feet.

"*Kar'desh*, Brother," she repeated again and again. She cried copiously and kissed his face, resisting Kutch's efforts to restore decorum to the disorder. Kaya lay with a bemused expression on his face, unresisting. He seemed pleased with his homecoming.

> - - - - - - - >

Kutch had talked at the Hermitage of Kaya sharing his yurt, but the arrival of his parents soon destroyed that dream. The matter was settled soon enough; Kaya was moved into the yurt of the medicine woman, Maya, where he would be with his sister. He would care for a small amount of livestock that had fallen to the family through the exile and death of their parents. Maya, now married, let them share the yurt, but expected work and contributions for their presence and food.

The Khan could have claimed his son, but his wife would not have accepted it with grace, and the possession of the knife of Onder seemed to make an impossible situation for the ruling family. Kutch was forbidden to visit the medicine woman, and the boys had to arrange meetings outside the camp at the mare's corral, where they went each day.

"You have been lost to the tribe, now you are restored and have brought honor by winning the school race," the Khan announced before the presence of the council and other onlookers. "I will reward and welcome you back with a gift. The sister of the gelding you rode to win the race, is expecting a colt, her first. It will be yours to keep and train." Kutch was given a beautiful Chipchak knife and scabbard at the same time.

Fewsoon would not permit Kaya out of her sight, so she tagged along happily on all excursions. She had her mother's gift with horses and all other animals as well. She certainly had Kaya at her beck and call, and he would meekly accept any task at her hand and cooperate with chores that boys of the tribe would have scorned.

However, no one challenged Kaya or teased. In fact, he soon became the pampered object of concern by all the tribe. He could do no wrong and anything he wanted he got, and some he didn't want. He was fed continuously and was free to investigate everyone's yurt. He stuck his nose into everything. Old treasures and oddities were sought out and revealed for his entertainment and Kutch, despite all prohibitions, managed to see things that no tribesman had shared before and to hear the old stories of how these things came into a family's possession. People pressed gifts upon Kaya. Kutch, Fewsoon, and all the other children could have been resentful, except for the fact that he shared with everyone. Did bayan Chavush cook thin pastry with cheese and wild green vegetables inside? Kaya must sample it, and so do all his friends and attendants. Has the woman with the freshened mare, lots of milk made into yogurt? Kaya must try it, or would he prefer it mixed with water and drink it as ayran? He prospered, and so did his friends. When the mare dropped her foal, she was a golden beauty. He named her ‘my gold,’ Altom, but she seemed to belong to everyone; they all fed and petted her. Everyone brushed her pelt.

By the end of summer, he was fully integrated into the tribal life, but he retained that difference that had come from his experiences outside. He still breathed through his mouth, and left the nose for important business. He still hummed his exotic melodies, between breaths, when thinking. He never lost his amiable disposition and curiosity, but he also brought to the tribe the hours, prayers, songs and Bible stories of the Hermitage. Kutch helped him continue practicing the writing and reading which he had started to learn during the winter. They wrote on the yurts, in the sand, on the tools and possessions; they labeled everything with names of owners and uses. Fewsoon rapidly learned as much as Kaya and Kutch could teach her.

When the days of frost had increased to permanently harden the ground, and the grass had cured on the stem, the time came for their return to school.
Sad farewells were said to Altom and Fewsoon, now in charge of the colt. She cried copiously again, and both Kutch and Kaya left their hearts in her care.

> - - - - - - - >

Again at the Hermitage, Kutch, the brilliant scholar, excelled in everything, but was still small for his age and plain of face. Kaya big, plump and strong was moderately good only at arithmetic and music, though he learned his prayers, doctrine and apologetics well enough, including chosen psalms and gospel portions. He seemed to like to understand another's ideas and to test them with close reasoning and pointed similes. He had grown to be a respected center of authority, as boys sought to gain his approval. No more boys came from the East Huns; their youth went to the Buddhist school near the Great Wall.

Kutch took first in the races of spring. Kaya was third on his family's black mare. The first prize was a brush, ink and a small red silk banner. Which they took back to the tribe that summer.

> - - - - - - - >

Fewsoon divided her time and honors between the two. Keke avoided Kaya. The Khan watched with pride the participation of the two sons in all the events, but for peace, avoided making much of one or the other. Kutch had his Chipchak knife and a new colt of his own. Kaya's mare was a playful yearling with a new saddle.

In the summer things seemed to be the same as the year before, but when both Erkan and the yuzbasha were away from the yurts, the people started to bring their problems and quarrels to Kaya to settle. The dapple mare had fallen and sustained a break in her knee joint;

`Is she to be killed or healed?' He heard both sides of the question and decided, always with the advice of Fewsoon and Kutch. Keke noticed with displeasure the displacement of her son to the role of advisor, but her complaints to Erkan fell on deaf ears. Her time was spent with her sickly little girl.

On returning to school Kaya found, with surprise, that he was not to stay the year. The good hermit put the matter in this way: "You are only a passable scholar, and I have apprenticed you to a merchant of impeccable reputation and character. He will give you a trade and allow you to see something of the world. So you will serve three years for food, clothes and a small allowance. Believe me, it is better than many tribesmen ever see." Kaya bowed and taking his teacher's hand touched it with his forehead, saying, "*Bosh ooze two nay*, as you command, sir." He was sent south to a town on the southern face of the Tanra Dah Mountains, E'peck kent.

The man who was his guide south was a tall handsome man of tribal origin. He knew the language of the Tarim, an East Iranian or Persian related speech akin to that used in north India and the Sassanid Empire. He spoke Chipchak and Hunnish flawlessly and even northern Han Chinese. He had traveled from the Caucasus Mountains to the Great Wall. His round, brown face and great mustache gave him a warrior's look, but his manners were gentle, his speech kindly.

"My name is Ahjit," he said, and seeing the surprise on Kaya's face, explained, "my master found me hungry and in pain, when he took pity on me and gave me work." He eyed the boy carefully, "I understand you write. It will be for that that the master wishes your service."

Kaya, riding beside him, responded, "It is the goodness of the hermit to obtain a worthy employ for his worthless student. I write and read slowly."

The caravan leader chuckled and affirmed, "My master is not fooled. You have some redeeming qualities, else you would not be called for." Then as the searching look continued, it fastened upon the dagger in his belt. The man's face changed and became pasty yellow with shock.

"Are you ill?" inquired Kaya, for the man now leaned forward and seemed to be resting his head on the neck of his great horse. But his hand moved out to touch the nose of the black mare Kaya rode. Suddenly, his hand caught the reins at the bit and the man was on the ground staring up at Kaya with the black stopped obediently before him. His hard eyes pierced the boy. "Where did you get the mare?" he demanded.

"Ahjit bey," he stuttered, "she is part of the family inheritance. She and her seven colts are the property of Maya, the medicine woman, daughter of Meryen the wise."

"You are a boy," the man said in an accusing tone, "what have you to do with the inheritance of women? Unless you..." It was the man's moment to stutter. "You are Kaiyam? That Kaiyam?" The breath seemed to go out of him. He took a deep shuddering breath. "But where did you get the knife?"

"It was my prize two years ago, for winning the race, not with this horse, but another. The prize was the knife, the first ever given by the hermit," the boy stopped breathlessly.

"Truly, that holy one is full of surprises," Ahjit bey exclaimed, "I wonder how much of this he knows?" He shook his head. "But now, little Kaiyam, tell me about Yownja she will be just your age, what is she like?" He remounted his horse.

"Fewsoon is my age and there is no other there younger or the same age." Kaya puzzled, "Kutch or one of the others would know her perhaps."

"Kutch? Is that Keke's boy child? He would be younger than the girl, she had fire for hair," he reminisced fondly.

"But that is my sister, Fewsoon," insisted Kaya. "She is alive and well."

Ahjit's face went hard, "Then her mother is dead," he stated definitely. "They change the flower names for another, when the mother dies." He reached across and stroked the mane of the black as if caressing his dear one. "Tell me what happened," he commanded, "leave nothing out."

>------->

The next summer, between journeys, Kaya entertained Kutch, who was allowed a month to visit the city. It was his first time, and Kutch was eager to see everything. They went to the markets on the special bazaar days and to the caravansary where travelers came through. They gawked and stared at displays of merchandise and questioned the guides and guards about far places. Since Kaya was also a traveler and had a bit of spending money for tea, the men were nicer than they might have been to tribal boys. Kutch already knew a lot of the East Iranian speech and improved rapidly. He was introduced to a Christian church building, the first he had seen. Indeed, there was a Buddhist temple, Manichean building, Temple of light for Zoroastrians, and a Han temple as well as a church for Arian heretics who had split with the Western churches. The town's political situation was always in turmoil, as ethnic and religious divisions competed for influence and authority in law making and enforcement, holidays and privileges.

One day in the market, they heard the sound of tambourine and flute; the melody was strange and lilting. People sang of a far-away land of luxury and mystery:

If you seek for wealth and pleasure,
Come, come to Hindustan.
If you long for love and leisure,
Come, come to Hindustan.

There you'll find great treasure.
All there in Hindustan.
There's wisdom without measure,
All there in Hindustan.

Jewels, spices, fabrics ooh,
You will find your heart's dream:
Cities, beaches, mountains, too!
There you'll be content.

COME TO HINDUSTAN

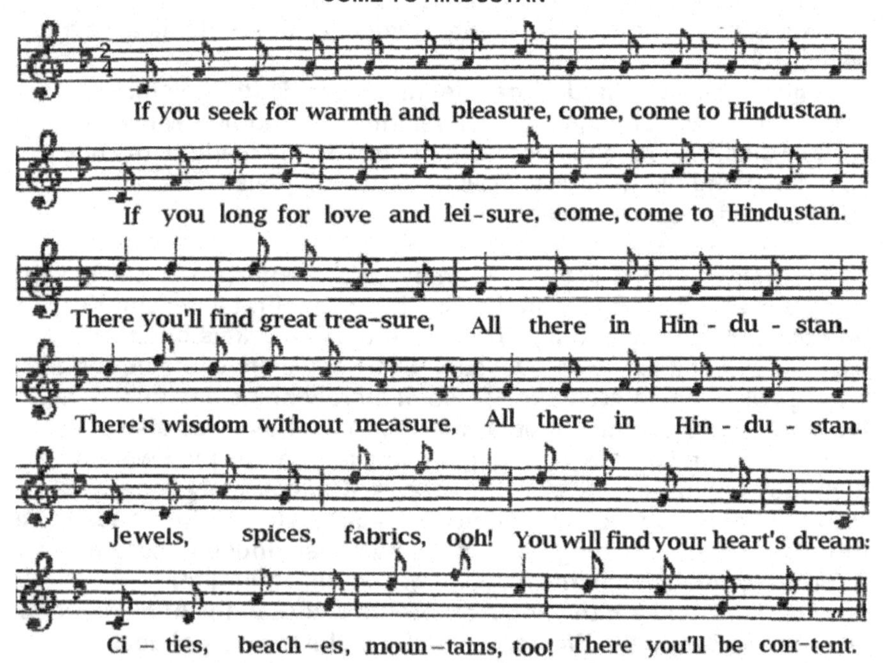

Standing in a large crowd in a wide place near the fountain were two swarthy men with a dancing bear. The bear master had graying hair which contrasted with his very dark complexion, but his mustache was black. The other man was juggling six wooden cylinders. The children were clapping time to the music and dancing. Some adults threw money at their feet. Then, the performer missed a cylinder, and the crowd laughed and hissed. Nevertheless, he gathered in the remainder and bowed. The bear master prodded his charge to stand upright again and give an encore; the song was about the pleasures of India. The bear, rather flabby with a gray muzzle, whined irritatingly and complied reluctantly.

Kaya stood hypnotized. He had never seen a captive bear before. The bear, a male, reminded him of Mother when she was in her last year. The state of its coat and teeth showed bad health. Behind, tied near the fountain, was an undersized yearling cub, the new apprentice. The male after one chorus went down on all fours and showed it's teeth defiantly when the bear master threatened to club it. Shrugging, the men finished the tune and retrieved their reward, meager as it was.

The juggler said, "I may have to go on with five. My eye and hand are not what they used to be."

His companion answered, "Four or five but the important thing is not to blunder. Come, we need some food. We have enough for soup and bread." He motioned toward an inn on the square.

The crowd had dissipated, but Kaya stood rooted and paid no attention to the restless Kutch. The juggler's eye was quick enough to see a prosperous boy entranced by the bear. Quickly, he came over with a smile, bowing and motioning toward the bear. "Would you like to feed our fine bear?" he said. "He delights in berries and fruit, bread and meat, soups and stews. Whatever you get him, he will eat out of your hand."

Kaya remained frozen, and Kutch seeing his friend's dilemma, produced a small coin. "Send the innkeeper's boy servant for fresh fruit," he ordered, "We will go in with you, if they admit the animal."

Kaya recovered as he fed the bear the fruit and bits of bread sopped in stew. The two men ordered a large meal while Kaya fed the yearling as well. The men insisted in ordering for Kaya and Kutch, too. The juggler did a few tricks with the spoon and knife. While they ate, the bear master plied them with questions. "So you are the Khan's son," he exclaimed to Kutch. "I picked you for a Chipchak. We were up in that country a long time ago, on the north horse-road." Well he remembered the stern old Khan. "You would be a child of his old age." But he stopped abruptly, and stared at the knife Kaya had drawn to cut the apples, pears and melon into smaller manageable pieces.

The juggler missed the spoon, and the men exchanged glances. The old one, whose hand developed a perceptible shaking, asked, "You are surely related to the merchant, Jomer? Yes, perhaps his heir?"

They did not believe the negative answer. "You wear the knife of Onder, the dead heir, surely you must be Onder's child," the juggler insisted. "The last thing he said, was to get it to the child. He knew he had one."

Viciously, the bear master slapped the juggler's face, sending him reeling back, "You heard nothing, fool, nothing, no repentance or last words. He was dead when we entered the woods." He glared at the man, red faced and shaking with agitation. He hissed softly, "We are sworn and our lives depend on it. He was dead!"

The adept juggler, nodded amiably, resumed his place and murmured, "Of course, I was just being dramatic. I have a weakness for overstatement." He buried his face in his plate and ate vigorously.

The bear-master turned to the young host and said suavely, "No matter, let me assure you of our interest and friendship; we are all lovers of bears and their music and rhythm. Tonight, we perform near the city baths where, incidentally, there are many other attractions for young nobles. Things to taste, smell and feel that open new worlds for young men. We can be the doorway to many delights. They call me Optal and he is Pesh. Just ask for us at the baths."

"We will consult my master," said Kaya, who was allowing the bears to finish his platter and lick it clean. "He will give us leave if it is to our advantage." Ever the correct apprentice, he bowed to the foreigners.

"But young gentlemen, there are pleasures that the old indulge and then distrust. Surely you should test for yourselves these waters of delight."

"A master as wise as mine gives only the best and protects from wrong. I trust him. So, good day." With that Kaya and Kutch left after paying the full bill.

> - - - - - - - >

Three full years had passed and the summer was drawing to a close. Kaya thought longingly of the pastures and his horse, Altom, now three years old, but his apprenticeship dragged on. Kaya had worked in the office taking care of accounts, and he was bored and sweaty with the work of drying fruit, packing it for export, counting, recording everything for the next caravan out. Hot and tired, long after sun set, he was directing his way to the baths. He usually went with the other workmen before this hour, but had tarried over some task.

Tonight there was entertainment in the outer court of the building. A giggling group of slave girls were preparing to dance. Their eyes were lined and faces painted vividly, and they primped and fluttered while an older man and woman supervised. Some idle young oasis dandies were sitting and ogling the girls. They motioned for Kaya to join them, but he waved them off and continued to the bath.

He noticed for the first time that one of the side rooms had been partitioned off, and some mats and divans were scattered about. Large braziers, charcoal burners, provided a nest of coals for cooking skewered meats, but the scent was not of food, cedar or incense, but of hemp and poppies. He stopped to look over a table with various powders and rosins rolled into pills in boxes. Wrinkling his nose with the strangeness, he passed on to the bath area where he entered a cubicle to change out of work clothes and emerged with a large towel wrapped around his middle and wooden clogs on his feet.

Inside the small steamy room, he seated himself on a marble slab and dipped water with a large bowl from a small central basin. He poured heated water over his head and shoulders again and again, relaxing in its comfort. He eyed the wall hanging slogan: a listing of the desires of men. *Mesut*, happiness (is) *zevk*, sensuality, *lezzet*, enjoyment. A writing near the door proclaimed: *Füsün* delight (is) *ashk*, sensual love. He hadn't noticed them before.

Suddenly, two large men in bath towels filled the doorway. They stared at him closely through the mist.

"Ozmir, is this the new boy?" the larger one asked in a Persian accent.

The small dark man with the beard wavered. tried to focus his eyes. "Don't know," he responded groggily, "can't see him good, Tedbir." The large man reached over and took Kaya by the wrists and pulled him toward himself. In the struggle the man's towel dropped, and the man bent over Kaya's face to see better. He grunted, nodding his approval,

HAMOM -THE BATHS

"You'll do, not pretty, but new." He grinned wickedly and began forcing the boy down, holding a wrist in each fist and pushing down. Kaya's twelve-year old strength was no match for the man's. His face at waist level, Kaya was suddenly filled with the understanding of what the man intended. He resisted and cried, "*Yesu gel.*"

The man blinked stupidly and shook his head, "You scared? You'll like it, get good money too. You need a smoke first?" He reversed directions and started to bring the boy up toward his own face. His breath was both sickly sweet, and acrid, as he puckered his lips and leaned over. Kaya placed his two fists together thumbs up and pushed up with all his strength hitting the man at the soft juncture of throat and chin causing the man to lose balance and choke with the force of the blow. Kaya brought his two hands down suddenly outside the man's fists breaking the hold. He backed against the wall as the man struggled to recover, but the smaller, fat, bearded man, Ozmir, stood blocking the door. Suddenly, Kaya pushed off from the wall in a dive that took him head first into the fat man's middle. As the two fell in the corridor, the nimble boy evaded the man's fumbling grasp. Kaya shoved the man, who cracked his head against the marble floor and lay groaning.

Kaya fled, naked, down the hall. He paused only long enough, at the end of the corridor, to grab his clothes in his hands and run, without his towel. Curses in Persian followed him. He ran into the torch lit courtyard where the dancers were formed into a chorus line, bumping and grinding for the benefit of the ogling boys and leering old men. Kaya exited through the middle of the line, causing a flurry of screams, blushes, coarse laughs, hysteria, knowing nods and angry curses.

One called out, "Thief," another, "He hasn't paid."

Kaya was halfway home, before he stopped and clothed himself in the dark of the church garden.

> - - - - - - - >

Jomer held the horse's bridle as Kaya finished with his preparations and tied on his belongings.

"I'm sorry it has to be done in this way, boy. The two men are prominent politically and Tedbir, the Persian, is fabulously rich. They were hurt enough to make revenge probable. They moved the council against us. I will send Ahjit with news on the next westbound caravan. He will take care of any needs you may suffer with the tribe. Take this for now." Kaya received the bag of coins meekly.

Kaya wondered that anyone would consider tribal life hard, but he nodded and mounted the black mare. Excitement tingled, raising the hair on the nape of his neck. In two weeks he would see Fewsoon and Altom; perhaps Kutch would still be home before his return to the hermitage. A happy sense of joy lightened his way. Soon he would be home with friends.

BEARS ENCOUNTERED (Page 168)

PEOPLE, PLACES & PLOTS IN CHAPTER 16

Ay'ya: Kaya's bear cub 'brother' now grown to full vigor.
Bayan' Chavush: the widow of the yoked and exiled sergeant.
Cha vush': the exiled sergeant of Erkan's band.
Dah': is a native Dol'gan hunter who speaks for others.
Dol'gan: a mountain tribe of hunters. living in the forest.
Kaya: searching the mountains for his father or friends.
Koot'sal: literally, Holy One; is a tortured prisoner of the tribe, a rival of the shaman.
Sha'man: is a leader, the spirit conduit, healer and advisor in the ways of the ancestors.

GLOSSARY HELP:
***a'jee-lay yet'*: hurry up; be quick.**
***ark'ah-dash*: friend: meaning one who covers your back; back up.**
***ay'ran:* watered yogurt, sometimes sour, a favorite drink.**
***ay'ya:* bear, used as a designation or name.**
***ba-bomb':* my father; daddy.**
***gel:* come.**
***soos:* hush; quiet; silence.**

STRETCHED OUT

A large stout boy about 12 years-old, dressed in oasis tight pants and vest, wandered among the smoking remains of the village of yurt-framed buildings. His round brown face wet with tears and his lower lip trembled as he searched the ruins running from frame to frame. Again and again he called her name, "Fewsoon! Fewsoon!" alternating with the demanding, but less urgent sound of "*Ba bomb*!" "Father!" "Altom!" and "Kutch!"

There was no answer! Just the crackle of fire on wood and smoldering felt. Here and there in the distance a few old crones rushed about trying to salvage the essential tools and treasures of the different homes. They were pulling what they could from the fire and screeching and cursing when it was difficult or the fire too hot.

The settlement was in turmoil as the old bewailed the dead who had resisted the Tartar raid or had not fled rapidly enough to preserve their lives. They cried for the women and children carried away into slavery.

The sudden surprise attack was typical of the raids on the mountain and meadowlands as the great Hun Empires grew in every direction. The tribes jostled each other as alliances changed; as warriors, for gold or glory, sold their services where they could and when opportunity arose. Chiefs were obliged to send tribute, usually in excess of what they could afford, to the all-powerful rulers of the steppes. Those slow to affirm their allegiance or slow in their tribute were immediately at risk from the dominant tribes. Vigilante groups, seeking to augment their own resources, attacked the weak or careless. It was a scramble for goods, to pass on to the Hunnish terror centers in the west or south.

>------->

Kaya found Bayan Chavush who sat on a rescued chest, beside her charred yurt, with a stricken expression. “Where are the men?” he asked, “I see few dead warriors. How could the enemy have made such a clean sweep?”

The woman made a vague sweeping motion with her hand. “They rode north to collect taxes from the Dolgan people in the mountains, to possess some of their goods: yak tails for the standards, hides for the seats, tribute for those we owe.” she shrugged her shoulders.

“And the medicine woman? My sister Fewsoon? My horse Altom?” he inquired insistently. She shrugged indifferently.

“Gone with them for special herbs, mountain herbs, good medicine.” She looked around with dull red eyes. “Where was God when this happened?” she started to cry, “I thought we would be protected from disasters.”

“Men and devils make our troubles,” said Kaya, “God only heals the wounds and makes new occasions for love and help.”

“We thought our beliefs, our faith and obedience would save us from this. We were wrong. They didn’t. Why didn’t God care? He is supposed to have the power. What did we do wrong?” She broke into crying again.

“Your heart will know the wrongs done, but He forgives and helps. We are His to shape and change, even through suffering.” Kaya repeated the hermit’s words. “Why shouldn't He care?” he assured her.

“We were prosperous and happy. Then this happened. Doesn’t it matter to Him?” she argued on bitterly.

“The hermit said, ‘We are all His creation, each individually shaped for special good things.’” Kaya leaned forward and touched her shoulder, “Trust Him now in the dark moment, light always comes with the new day. His mercies are new every morning.”

“They took our people, even the Khan’s wife, and her sickly little girl; where is His love or mercy in that?” Her defiance flowed over into tears and wailing.

Kaya spent the week helping with the salvage and burying the dead. When all was in order in the camp and some of the out-riders and special work crews had returned, he set out north to the far mountains to find his people. At the end of the steppes, he entered the mountains, leaving his black mare in the narrows of a long fertile valley where a few yurts spoke of Chipchak presence. Still hoping for news, he entered the snow-filled mountains and climbed to the higher lands there.

>------->

With great caution Kaya entered the clearing where the fire smoldered. He had waited for a long time, observing the comings and goings of the shaman and the tribal members during the day. A prisoner was being tortured. That, in itself, would not be a reason to interfere with tribal justice and taboo, but the man had called out in Chipchak. He had called on Yesu, certainly a reason to investigate, but no one walks into a hunting tribe's encampment without every precaution. The dense fir and pine cover, between the rocks of the hill top provided a good hiding place and the group seemed to be preoccupied with the prisoner.

They would talk long with him, then suddenly slap, pinch and cut at him with their knives. They would spit in his face and shout insults at him, trying to make him afraid. They had him strung up with hands tied above his head, dangling from two saplings, with his feet hardly touching the ground. He had to stand on the balls of his feet to take the pressure off his arm sockets. Finally, they had heated a knife and then burned some symbol on his forehead with two strokes of the knife.

Kaya heard the cry "*Yesu gel*" as the man, already bleeding from chin to groin, fainted. His full weight on his arms bent the trees. The shaman laughed, and the men picking up their weapons went single file, down the hill to the river where they had an encampment with food cooking.

The old man shook his gray head and tried feebly to get back on his feet. It was then Kaya showed himself and walked to the man. He had been branded with a T-cross on his forehead. Kaya stared and blurted out, "Who are you?"

"*Soos*, hush," the man replied, "They will hear. Quickly, cut me loose. They will come back to kill me afterwards." He looked at his bonds, "I'm Chipchak from Erkan's band," he continued, but seeing

AVALANCHE (PAGE 168)

the boy's bewilderment added, "In exile these ten years. *Ajee-lay yet,* hurry." The boy took his knife and cut both cords in two short motions. He thought the man would fall but he staggered and recovered. "Must go higher up in the mountains," the man said, as he went forward swaying unsteadily, "It's our only chance."

After half a mile they were forced to rest, and the man could scarcely gain his feet. After another half hour climbing in the snow, the man fell heavily, and they were forced to seek shelter. They found it near an overhang in the cliff and in the windbreak, they clung together and Kaya applied a handful of snow to the areas that still bled. The man took some snow to put in his mouth, but was soon shivering uncontrollably. Recognizing the need of nourishment, Kaya took out a small skin bag of ayran slung under his cloak to give the man. After drinking, he licked his lips appreciatively.

"A taste of home: the blessings of the yurt and civilization." The man crossed his hands over his chest and seemed to pause meditatively for a long instant. Swaying, with his eyes closed, he took three long breaths. When he opened them, he seemed much restored and stood up.

"Yes," he said, as if in answer, "You are right, we must pass the notch to be safe."

"I said nothing." Kaya responded, puzzled, looking around.

"You do not see Him," the strange man turned a piercing eye on Kaya, "Not all my friends are seen. *Gel*, come, we must move out." He paused again, and a wry smile lit his face, "They know I have escaped. They are searching. They see your tracks with mine. We must keep moving."

"My name is Chavush," the man stated, "an exile for the sake of Christ and love to my fellow man." They were moving up between two large snow-covered mountains. The snow cover, which had been but a sprinkle by the river, had become solid and continuous as they mounted higher. "Come now. We are *ark-ah-dash*, friends. We defend each other. Tell me your name and family," the man Chavush continued, "I know the tribe like the palm of my hand."

"I am called *Kaya-ay-a*, Kaya the bear," the boy stated definitely, "I live with the medicine woman, Maya, daughter of Meryen the wise, with my sister Fewsoon."

"The lines of the tribal families grow tangled," stated the old man, "Maya was but a maiden, her mother alive when I departed. She had no younger children."

"We were breast mates of Vashtie the good," laughed Kaya, unconcerned of pursuit, "Mother was taken in a Tartar raid six years ago, Meryen killed and I alone escaped. Fewsoon had been left with Maya in the camp."

Chavush looked with respect at the youth, "You must have been quite a boy to escape Tartars."

"I simply went where the boat carried me. No skill or wisdom of mine saved me." The youth continued, "My second mother was a bear and my brothers, her cubs."

"So you're the child of promise! Baby of Sevim," exclaimed the old one. "Well I remember the day of your birth."

"Listen," exclaimed Kaya, "your enemies are searching below and have just found our trail!" The call echoed again. Kaya stood sniffing the wind coming down the slope of the pass. "There is a bear cave ahead," he predicted. "They will be asleep, but it is warmer than here. You are in no condition to pass the snow peaks. The night is falling, and you need rest and food."

The old man nodded his head. "I have two Saviors now, one large and one small. Lead on little friend."

"Who is this big one?" questioned Kaya, as he turned to help the man stand and started to lead away up a dim trail.

"The one who took my yoke from off my back," Chavush answered from behind.

> - - - - - - - >

The cave was large enough to stand in the entrance and was sheltered from the wind. They had started a fire in a tiny corner that blew away from the smaller tunnel that went deep into the mountain side. The snow blowing and wind would not show their position, and the tracks were soon covered.

They had surrounded the fire with three tiers of rocks, placed one on top of the other. Beside it stood a leather bag full of snow. By dropping rocks, hot from the fire, into the bag, the snow was being melted. Steam rose and the rocks hissed as they were picked up with sticks and dropped into the bag where they boiled.

A stained rag of cloth tied up with tea and herbs floated in one corner. A bit of dried meat was draped over one side to get the benefit of the steam and splashes to soften. Kaya hunted for wood.

The old man lay in a stupor, licking his dry lips occasionally. He was in shock. The boy had covered him with dried leaves and had placed hot rocks near his feet and head to warm him. He filled the almost empty ayran bag for soured milk with the warmed liquid using a short handled spoon carved of wood. This warm bag of liquid was then fed carefully to the patient every time a new batch was ready. The meat when tender was cut into tiny bits and mixed with the liquid. Stones were heated and placed, removed and reheated and again added to the bag or to the extremities of the weak torture victim. Chavush alternately burned with fever and shook with cold. The boy had laid his short cloak over the leaves and sat huddled over the fire. The broth was now pure snow water and the fire wood finished as the dawn broke.

Chavush woke with the light. New sounds were issuing from the small cave. The boy looked alert despite the toil of the night. Complaining whines and growls were heard and a rasping 'huh huh' sound got louder. Kaya was ready to leave and had everything ready.

He made a gesture of silence, hand before his face and then motioned away, and they silently left to continue toward the notch.

Chavush took the lead now and started up a thin rocky trail under overhanging cliffs and almost vertical precipices. Now, the anchorite made the sign for silence. Kaya looked at the vast mountain above them and nodded his understanding. Behind them a sudden scream of triumph sounded. One Dolgan search party had found their trail and camping site. Answering cries indicated the others would soon come together into a pursuit of vengeance.

The pursued pressed on silently. Then, suddenly, there were additional sounds behind them: the roar of an enraged bear; the scream of an injured man; the roar of a second bear and the cries of surprise and confusion. Looking back, they saw a small party of four close on their trail. Behind the four a much larger group was dividing. Some ran away from the cave, others took defensive positions before the cave and some continued after the leading party containing the shaman.

Then the bears came into view out of the cave. It was a giant bear. The largest Kaya had ever seen, but the brown red color of his coat seemed familiar. A large pregnant female came out beside him. They still had their accumulation of fat and were twice as big as any hunter. The pair roared in harmony. The hunters yelled defiance, although they were falling back to decide what to do. Kaya screamed the name of Ay-ya, his brother and breast mate. The shaman gave a victorious war whoop as he rushed ahead of his trailing party and at that moment the heights above gave a low ominous growl like thunder coming closer. All other sound stopped or was drowned out. All motion blurred while the world turned white. Chavush had thrown his weight on Kaya and borne him down as a mass of snow pushed them ahead and buried them.

When Kaya came to himself, he was covered in snow. He started to push up and to dig lose snow from his sides and transfer it downward. He worked slowly and breathed slowly. He found the body of Chavush beside him, but he was unconscious or dead. He was stiff and cold. Kaya tried to burrow upwards, just beyond his head and transfer the snow down below him. It was lightly pressed together and held its form. After what seemed a long time, he could stand as he formed steps with the ice packed below him. The tunnel moved slanting up and the light increased, but he suffered dizziness and sleepiness. At last his arm thrust out through a hardening crust. Cool air touched his face with its blessing. He stopped and breathed deeply a long time. They were on the slide's edge and the snow was not packed.

When he felt better, he enlarged the opening and returned to try to bring out his friend. The man was too large and stiff, he had a blue color with white spots on his face. The boy started another set of stair steps at the top that would broaden the entrance, and it too, went over a yard, before surfacing.

Suddenly, a face appeared in the opening. A hunter looked in on him with an anxious expression. Seeing the boy, the man drew back and handed down a cake-like piece of food consisting of fat, dry berries, dried dark meat and other dried things mixed. The hunter patted his chest vigorously.

"I, Dah,' give food to Holy man; we do what he say. Shaman die today, just like I hear good man say," the man's face bobbed as if to give emphasis to his words.

Kaya was confused. He took the food automatically and nibbled on a bit to sample. Then, he gulped some more when his body approved and relished the nourishment. The anxious face of Dah continued to watch him nervously. Another joined him, and another cake of food came down.

"What did the Holy one say?" he asked the men and began widening the hole. They started helping eagerly. Dah continued talking.

"Brave man, he say, 'You wrong shaman. You follow evil road. If you don't turn back, you be dead tomorrow.'" The man tittered nervously, "Now shaman dead. We find broken body below." He motioned down the mountain side.

"If you want to help the brave man, you must carry him out," Kaya stated. "He seems to be in the presence of God, but he may come back, if we help and pray." The men descended to the burial chamber in the snow with great reluctance. The air made passage through the larger opening, but the air was still stale. They seized the body and in haste tried to exit up the passage, without widening the hole, and they managed to bang the body against the side and steps repeatedly, but they finally emerged. Kaya noticed that Chavush's color was better.

More hunters joined them, and they assumed responsibility for the body and carried it with care, straight down the mountain beside the slide area. More joined them where the body of the shaman lay. Kaya sat behind the body of Chavush his arms round the man's chest. He squeezed him regularly to aid his breathing and stopped only to pound his back and body to restore circulation. The two rescuers talked excitedly to the new group about their experience in an incomprehensible language. The others made affirmative sounds and, as they were able, each gave Kaya some provisions. They took up the still unconscious Chavush and started toward the camp. Kaya with his arms full of food packets, walked with the group. Suddenly, he stopped.

"Did you kill the bears?" he asked angrily. When they stared at him stupidly, he repeated, "What happened to the bears?" One shrugged, "Them go sleep like always. Guard sacred mountain. Why bears like you?" Another asked, "Let you cook on door step like friends."

"The cinnamon bear is my brother, Ay-ya." stated Kaya, matter-of-factly. There was a moment of shocked silence. Then the statement was translated into their language. Everyone stopped and stared reverently. Kaya now found himself in charge.

"We go down to river below shaman shrine where you found him?" They inquired solicitously, "We take good care, plenty food."

"How many were killed in the slide?" Kaya asked suddenly. The man who did most of the translating consulted the others then answered, "Three men die: shaman and helper, one warrior who kill many. One man have claw marks on shoulder, one other hurt arm." He smiled, "Holy one, can teach tribe now. Everyone listen plenty." He was right. They became guests and teachers while there.

It took three days of constant attention before Chavush regained consciousness. It was a week before he could move. He lost some skin on his feet and face by frostbite. Kaya fielded their questions and began to get some of their language, which in some ways resembled his own. As Chavush returned to health, he was able to help. Time seemed to race by.

"Why would you wish to stay and teach these people?" asked Kaya, "If you came home to the tribe, the Khan would pardon you."

"Laws can't be suited to individual needs or favorites," Chavush responded. "They have to have general application to be enforced and respected. God makes a place for me here. I'm content."

"But they tortured you," Kaya insisted.

"Yes, but listen to them sing now. It is a praise song they have made for God." Both melody and words struck Kaya as different and strange. One man with a beautiful baritone voice sang the solo, the whole village joined in the chorus and the women's affirmation divided the praise into distinct parts. Together they all produced strange effects on Kaya as Chavush translated the words for him. His skin tingled and the hair on his neck rose.

Solo:

1. Come hear of Yesu Christ, Who gives a second life.
   He fought a mighty fight to set you free.
   Come seek the Yesu way, from sin and evil save.
   His wondrous life He gave to make you free.

All sang together:

Yesu lived in conflict over sin's great power.
Yesu rose to new life. He makes the victory ours.

Women sang:

He paid a price on Calvary. He saved us from our sin.
He gave us joy and gladness, showed us the way to win.

Solo:

2. Joy fills the Yesu road, We've shed the awful load,
   Of sins weight and control. He's set us free.
   He gives us power to stay. We guard the narrow way
   That keeps us every day, within His love.

Everyone joined to sing:

Yesu's mighty victory over Satan's sin,
Yesu won redemption; gave us the power to win.
He gave us the will to win, yes, opened the way right in.
He gives us power for victory, Love, peace and hope within.

They all added:

He does, with endless joy.

Laughter and happy sounds followed the end of the praise time, and food was served to the people. Chavush explained the nature of the tribe to Kaya as they sat eating their part of the feast.

"Mountain people, like the Dolgans, have a hard life," contended Chavush. "They live in poverty and fear, surrounded by stronger peoples, and are always being pushed. There is only one way to go, up. The higher up you go, the poorer and less productive the land. So, they build resentments against those who take their lush valleys. Their memories are eternal like their mountains. They never forget an injustice, that all the lush valleys were once theirs.

"When the surrounding people are weak or harsh, they rise against them and pay with vengeance. It matters little that the land is claimed by others. They have older memories. In war they will kill five invaders for each defender, and they know their land and strike where not expected. Strong in defense and savage in attack, any foreign occupation costs more than it produces.

"Only by generous treatment and reconciliation can this cycle be broken. Did they torture me because I'm Christian or because I'm Chipchak, the feared people? I hope it is for the first, but it was probably mixed. If I go back, God will have lost the opportunity to better their lives and have the knowledge of salvation. This spirit and knowledge will make the urgencies of this life less final. It gives people other options."

"You have decided to stay then?" Kaya concluded.

"It is Yesu's will for me," Chavush answered. But you need to get back to your father and the tribe. Search parties will be out looking for you. They may blame the Dolgans or other northern tribes for your disappearance. That will mean war and retaliation."

Kaya reluctantly agreed. He realized he had forgotten all about Fewsoon, Altom and Kutch. What stories would they have about the raid? Then, he chilled with the thought; would they be alive and free?

"*A-jee-lay yet*, hurry," Chavush advised him, and he did.

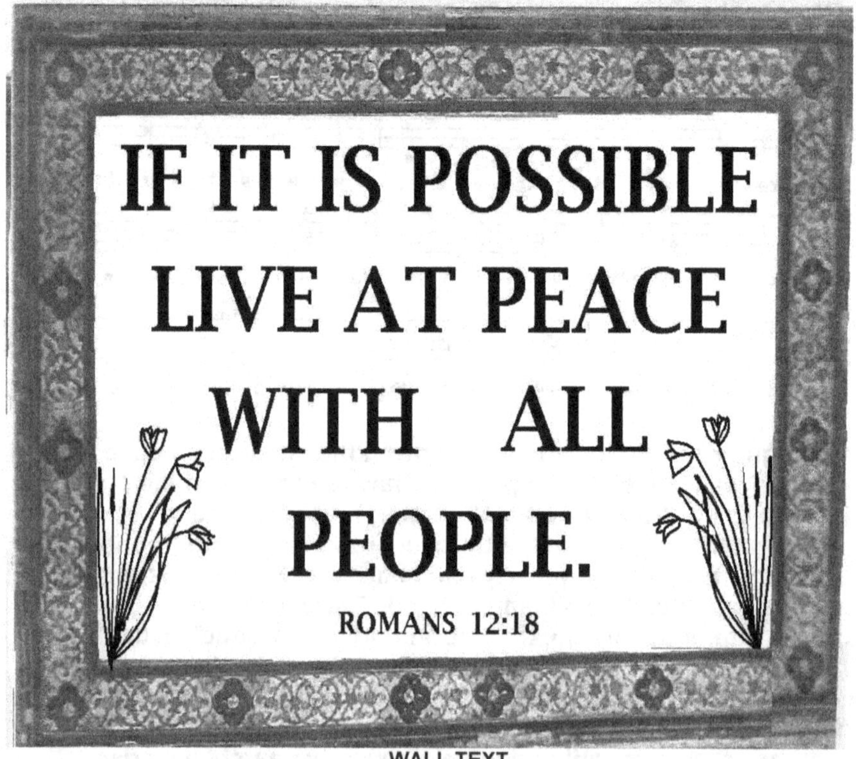

WALL TEXT

JUST IN TIME (Page 181)

PEOPLE, PLACES & PLOTS IN CHAPTER 17

Ahjit: a caravan master of Jomer's trade, with a dark past.
Er'tach: ten-year old son of Kan'su, an avid hunter.
Fewsoon': controls the baby corral, and work teams.
Kaya: returning to direct work with the band.
Kaplan: a Siberian Tiger, an avid poacher.
Kutch: works as chaplain and dispatcher of work teams.
Oz'kurt: a short, skinny hill-man, foraging others' herds.
Tez'lee: a stocky buddy of Ozkurt, traveling with him.
Yownja: a derivative of Fewsoon's baby name of 'clover flower.'

GLOSSARY HELP:

ah'blah: big sister; older sister; a term of respect.
al-dure'ma; it's not important; pay no attention; never mind.
bar'ish: peace; I mean no harm.
bear a bear'lick: togetherness. literally means oneness.
cooper-dah'ma: do not move; don't even wiggle.
cop-lawn-don day-eel': not from a tiger; never from a tiger.
dough-rue'der: it is true; that's right; it is the truth.
do'er: stop; halt.
e-yee': good; I agree; okay.
hep'see old-do'moo? are they all dead? Is everyone dead?
hair'suz-lar: they are thieves.
jan'um: dearest; my soul; beloved; family affection.
old-dure' on-lar: kill them; let them die.
Tartar'la ol'ma-sin: you are not a Tartar.
Yesu gel: God help me; come Jesus;
ye'tea-shin: help me; lend a hand.
yan-nun'dawn git: get away; go back; get off it.

AMBUSH

A small dirty-faced boy held the drawn bow aimed at Kaya's heart. "*Dure*, stop," he challenged. Kaya reined in and shouted "*Barish*, peace," and held his hands with the reins chest high. The boy couldn't miss at this close range. He had left the Dolgans in the mountains hours before. Alone, he had no hope of help from anyone as he rode home.

"*Tartar-la ol-ma-sin*, You aren't a Tartar, Kaya bey." The tone carried deep disappointment and chagrin. Slowly the bow descended, and the boy, with an angry gesture, put his arrow back in the sheath. Kaya let his breath out slowly. He had been careless to be ambushed so easily. He studied the boy carefully. He was about ten-years old but still small. He had his father's face.

"You are Ertach son of the Onbasha, Corporal Kansu. Where is your father and the troop?" Kaya allowed his gaze to sweep the terrain while his nose quivered to scent. The little valley seemed empty.

"Gone with Erkan to recover our stock and people. Our Khan has lost wife and daughter. My mother, too." His face clouded, but he raised his head proudly and took a deep breath; A ten-year old does not cry. "I hoped you were Tartar. I'm hunting game toward the northern mountains. Our people are hungry." He pointed to his mount tied to a bush at the far side of the meadow, near a freshly killed deer.

"Good hunting, you will start back now? How many in your party?" Kaya continued to scan for a trail through the mountains.

"We are four and ready to return; come with us. The camp is in need of every hand. We sent our best for revenge and are without rations at camp." He led the way.

"The Dolgan have given me many food packets as friends. It will help our people," Kaya explained. "We are fortunate that we have friends to help us in time of need."

> - - - - - - - >

Fewsoon or Yownja, as Kaya liked to call her now, had organized one communal kitchen with all the rations guarded in one of the remaining whole yurts. Groups were dispatched to hunt, round up the scattered stock, milk the mares and rebuild the yurts. Tiny children were set astride horses pulling the wooden cores that the wet wool and hair was wrapped around in layers. They were set to dragging the rolling bundles over bumpy or rocky ground to thicken the felt. Shelter must be set up now, before the worst of winter.

Kutch dispatched the hunters and those seeking scattered and straying stock; he had not been allowed to go with the warriors. He stayed in camp leading the songs and prayers for the success of the warriors and the survival of the camp. He had a way with words and a scholar's mind, so this work was what he liked to do.

Kaya assumed supervision of the work bands in camp or rode Altom with the wood or wool collectors and worked like any of them. He was the natural leader, young as he was, and all respected his words. Orders were immediately carried out, and the spirit of the tribe changed to optimism as steady progress was made in the reconstruction of yurts and improvement of the camp. The outriders sent in a steady supply of wild meat, to be dried or used and the strays enlarged the horse herd, which supplied milk, meat and transport.

The women in the kitchen with Bayan Chavush in charge, cooked large supplies of food, some of which was preserved and the rest eaten over the number of days it lasted. They dried fruit and fish for winter.

Maya had a baby corral set up to keep children that could not sit a horse (those who were under four, and over two-years-old that could leave their mothers). Women with babies worked with the child strapped to their backs. The pregnant women were helpers at the corral, while Maya took care of any injured in the line of duty.

Those from four to seven were tied on the horses' backs, and older children watched and supervised. They took their duties very seriously. They called it `*bear a bear lick*', togetherness. It was always a prime need for survival in the far north; sharing and united action were the only way to survive.

Kaya and a large group of woodcutters had gone to a woods on the edge of the south border. Beside the far north Horse Road, passing through the Kara Irtish River Valley and Lake skirting the southern edge of the Altai Mountains to the Yunggar Basin, stood this last luxuriant woods in an increasingly dry environment. A small stream ran in the woods near the road, and the crew picked trees of the right girth to make the arched roof supports for the new felt yurts being constructed.

Fewsoon had the girls gathering any broken or dry wood available in the underbrush. She found an old log about eight inches in diameter and called for help to dislodge it. Kaya, who usually managed to be somewhere near her, was immediately at her side. He rolled the two-yard-length trunk, first to one side then to the other with his feet, to disturb any dormant insects and started lifting from the small end.

"Wait," shrilled Fewsoon, "There's a hole here and a nest." Kaya waited, humming aimlessly, while she stooped and peered into a six-inch hole near the middle of the trunk and pushed her hand gingerly into the nest.

"Oh," she exclaimed, and started moving her hand from one side of the opening to the other, "Oh, look!" She pulled harder, up and out. She brought into view an old copper knife, green with age, but still strong and intact. The point was a different color and less corroded and had come out of the wood into which it had been driven. The handle was straight, but at the butt end was a life-like wolf head, growling, with lips curled up, showing two eye teeth of ivory. Two polished eyes of onyx stone shone dully in the light. She tested the blade with her fingers.

"Look, brother," she grinned triumphantly, "I have a new knife." She rushed over to the stream for some sand to scrub the blade and handle.

"*Ahblah*, big sister," he said, "it looks very old to me. The blade will be rotten; throw it away."

Busy polishing and cleaning the knife, she chose to ignore him. After all, she was almost three months older and deserved the title of respect. Besides, what did he know about a girl's personal knife.

Kaya moved the log up on one end and stood watching her. Then, he continued down the hill, pulling it up and letting it fall. It was about ten lengths from the clearing where the others were piling the lumber and firewood.

ARMED BOW & QUIVER

The children were talking excitedly and passing around an old Chipchak arrow, with dark bronze point and rotten bone and feathers still clinging to the stem.

"Where did you find that old war arrow?" Kaya inquired. "This was a battle field long ago, but it has been picked over for years."

"It's a secret," the larger boy replied hiding the arrow behind his back. "We found it; it's ours."

"From a secret place?" Kaya touched the smaller boy's head and shoulder where bits of earth and leaves had lodged. "Some small animal's den?"

"Big, not small..." the little one replied spontaneously, looking over his shoulder at the boulder-strewn hill. His friend pushed him and hissed, "*Soos*, quiet! It's a secret!" Kaya nodded solemnly and put his finger to his lips, "Our secret."

Back at the camp the lame smithy was able to help Fewsoon salvage the knife and bring back some of the old meteoric metal's original dark color, but it always bore a greenish tinge; the long-necked wolf looked old and mean.

> - - - - - - - >

The scattered herds were back on the meadows guarded by the children. Meat ponies and golden riding stock too, grazed on the grass and leaves of the brush. A crooning song, soft whistling or the sound of flute soothed the animals as they cropped and put on weight. The old traditional sounds were imitated now by those who had listened to their elders on similar occasions. A line would come from one mouth to be repeated or added to by another or whistling a reply. The herd was soothed, and the time passed until relief herders or sleep in the saddle arrived.

Come herder brave and defend your droves.
Wild beasts now lurk in all nearby groves.
(They hide in the woods!)
The tiger, glutton, wolf and bear,
(They seek you. They stalk for their food.)
(They hunt you.)
They hunger for all in your care.
(Sing quietly, keep alert.)
(Watch carefully. Stay awake.)
They will scatter them all everywhere.
(They would if they could.)
I stand on guard, all's safe you'll see.
I'll let no beast get the better of you and me.

At this point the starter would repeat the first two lines of the verse and sing, adding the last two lines:

NIGHT HERDERS
Come herd - er brave and de - fend your droves. Wild beasts now lurk in all near - by groves.
They hide in the woods. The ti - ger, glut - ton, wolf and bear. They seek you.
They stalk for their food. They hunt you. They hun - ger for all in your care.
Sing qui - et - ly. Keep a - lert. Watch care - ful - ly. Stay a - wake. They will scat-
- ter them all eve - ry - where. They would if they could. I stand on guard, all's safe you'll see.
I'll let no beast get the bet - ter of you and me
Chorus
Come herd - er brave and de - fend your droves. Wild beasts now lurk in all near - by groves.
I stand on guard, all's safe you'll see. I'll let no beast get the bet - ter of me.

Chorus: Come herder brave and defend your droves.
Wild beasts now lurk in all nearby groves.
I stand on guard; all's safe you'll see.
I'll let no beast get the better of me.

Then another would start a verse from the beginning:

Go tribesmen bold and survey your folds.
Sly beasts now stalk in meadows and holds.
(They hunt near the trails.)
The cunning, wily, strong and fierce,
(They scent you. They search for their food.)
(They watch you.)
They wait for a chance at your wares.
(Move silently; use your wit.)
(Hear everything; know your herd.)
They will panic and run everywhere.
(They won't if we're here.)
I guard the lot; all safe they'll be.
I'll let no beast scare them off from you and me!

Chorus:

Some would improvise other verses after the chorus.

> - - - - - - - >

Kaya was doing his turn on Altom when he felt a tremor pass through the herd. His head was on his chest, arms draped across his Altom's neck. He woke to feel the rush of the horses away from him and the scream of a pony near by. In the pre-dawn light he could faintly make out the large shape that clung to the horse's back.

Kaya's mount panicked too, running in the near-dark. The fleeing victim kicking and plunging had almost dislodged a growling tiger and dragged it into a collision with Kaya's golden Altom. Both horses fell in a tangle of legs and screams. The tiger growled, as he sought to transfer his hold on the nape of the neck to the throat of the squealing meat pony in order to suffocate his victim. The golden mount, scrambling to her feet, lashing out with hooves and teeth, managed to connect a kick on the tiger before plunging into a run.

"*Yesu gel. Yeti-shin*, God help me!" Kaya moaned, struggling to get to his knees. The tiger quickly got to its feet and limped to the side of the quivering pony. Kaya after searching his cummerbund for a weapon, started running his hands across the ground searching as he crawled toward the two animals. Then he straightened up clutching a short wooden club complete with root; dry and hard, but a clumsy weapon for such an opponent.

"*Yon nun dawn git*, get away from it." The boy growled, glaring into the tiger's face. An open-mouthed roar of defiance was his answer. They faced each other across the prone body of the victim who squealed anew as a great possessive paw was placed on its bleeding neck. Kaya lifted his club and with an ululating scream jumped near and slashed out with a connecting forehand drive that forced the beast, hissing spitefully, in pain, to retreat a pace. Kaya stood over the pony and with club raised again voiced the roar of a charging bear and swung a backhand blow at the top of the head. The tiger dodged and gathered its great muscles for a spring at this thief of its rightful prey. With a roar the body flexed and stretched upward and out to the boy who held the club ready.

The roar of the bear, tiger and ululating war cry clashed as the sound of running hoof beats drew near. The angry buzz of arrows punctured the tenseness. The dawn light fell across three bodies each moving feebly. A horse nickered; Altom returned. Two horsemen pulled up short.

"*Tanram, hep'see old do' moo*? My God, are they all dead?" One warrior dismounted with a leap while his companion held his bow pulled at ready. The young man approached the tiger carefully and poked its neck with his knife. A quiver ran through its body as the blade pierced between the vertebrae. Digging his heels in the grass the man pulled the heavy body off the other two.

He was heaving and out of breath when his friend joined him and moved the carcass to one side.

IT'S MINE, GO AWAY!

"Your arrows hit throat and shoulder; mine got its heart and stomach. Fast shooting, Tezlee, we'll have a skin and a story now." The taller, skinny man smiled at his short dark friend who pointed to the meat pony. "I'll cut its throat; it's too mauled to live." He drew his knife.

"*E-yee*, good, you get us some nice cuts of meat while I bury the boy. Did you ever see anything so brave? I thought he was going to bluff it away for an instant."

"*Cop-lawn-don de-eel*, not from a hungry tiger. That's why I broke cover first. I knew it would spring. The boy was brave, but foolish to get himself killed." Tezlee started to work on the pony. "If we had a bowl, we could collect the blood for sausage," he observed sadly. Behind them Altom nickered again.

"We missed the herd, but got some meat and a skin by good luck. The tiger had the same idea, but lost." He stared down at the limp body of Kaya. "A big strong boy, handsome too. The Chipchaks must be really down on their luck since the Tartar raid." He leaned over and grabbed an arm and leg and moved Kaya's heavy body. A deep groan resulted. Altom walked behind the small man and pushed him away with her head.

"*Coop-er-dah-ma*, don't move," the order came loudly in child's voice, and Kutch rode from a clump of bush with bow stretched and arrow aimed. "Ertach, come take their horses and bows. Fewsoon, come see to Kaya." As he spoke other armed children of various ages showed themselves running toward the men. The two men held out empty hands.

"*Do'er*, stop; you don't understand. I'm Ozkurt of the hill people, and this is Tez. We were traveling by night and saw this tiger stalking the herd. We arrived in time to kill the tiger. The boy was attacked by the beast, but we saved him. See, here are our arrows," he pointed.

"Why have you killed and butchered the pony? Why drag the one you saved like a carcass? Look at his head; it bears the marks of a blow." Kutch's voice was angry. "Did you raid the herd and the tiger interfere?"

"*Old-dure on-lar*, kill them," Ertach urged. "*Hair-suz-ler*, Thieves, We lost animals before to neighbors."

"The pony was mauled and dying. The boy was out cold. We were doing what we could. See the claw marks on them both?" Ozkurt pointed to claw marks on Kaya's hair line. At that moment Kaya groaned again and moved his head. Altom sniffed him.

"*Dough-rue-der*, he's right." Fewsoon interjected. "Down the weapons and help me get Kaya to camp; bring our guests for a meal. Perhaps they will work with us." There was a sigh of relief from the two guests as they took the steaks with them.

> - - - - - - - >

The Khan's war bands returned months later in triumph and despair. They had caught the horse herd and the golden horses were again in their power, but they had lost most of the female captives except for the children's band with the pregnant attendants; a group that from necessity had moved more slowly. Now the camp was filled with even more children, but young women were fewer. Kutch had lost mother and little sister. Most of the tribe had lost parts of the different families: wives, sisters, mothers, daughters and aunts. Women from 14 to 29 were noticeably missing.

The Khan looked older and worn. He had taken an arrow in the shoulder joint and another in the foot in the attack to reclaim the herd. Plump Maya became his nurse, and he ate the best Lady Chavush could provide, but he left the running of the camp to Kaya and Kutch. Brooding on his couch, Erkan grimly nursed internal and external wounds. He kept control of the diplomatic and commercial contacts of the tribe and inspected the merchandise and slaves offered by those who had heard of the disaster faced by the Lion Horse People.

Females were replaced in time, but the expense was great. Replacements were often unsatisfactory and of alien cultures and skills. Total effect on the camp was nearly disastrous. This and the loss of warriors made an age gap, almost a generation gap between those under 14 and the older adults. Tensions arose as those children, doing adult tasks successfully, expected adult treatment, respect and rewards.

All adults with saleable skills were sent to the city or caravans to procure goods or cash for the tribal needs. Feelers were sent to all the friends, relatives and neighbors that they were interested in trade for women or money and were open for any help or suggestions.

In this way, Fewsoon, happily found herself being sent, at the request of the merchant Jomer, to E'peck Kent to help with the sorting and bookkeeping of his thriving enterprises. Word was sent that Ahjit would meet Kaya and Fewsoon at the tribal southern post on the Horse Road, below the River Irtish. There, they camped in the enchanted woods where Fewsoon had found the knife. Here they awaited the foreman's coming. Kaya gathered wood around the hillside while Fewsoon prepared food. He returned with wood, but was covered with smudges of earth and leaves. He was humming happily as he laid the wood in place by the fire. He walked over to fondle Altom's nose and feed her bits of dried honeycomb from his pocket. Fewsoon looked daggers at him saying, "You took long enough. Were you hunting badgers and moles?"

"I was discovering a secret shared with two little friends." He looked at her teasingly. "Girls can't be allowed to know." She tossed her head in disdain.

"Look at you, Ahjit bay will see how careless you have become since you left his service." She pointed with chin and lip to the stream. "Wash now, or you'll get no supper." She watched as he turned his back on her, striped off his shirt, and washed his head and muscled shoulders with the water from the stream. She sat watching his broad back. He had grown this last year. She looked down at her breasts starting to press against her blouse. She was suddenly frightened by all the rapid changes in their lives this year. Frightened by the big change to the city. She looked longingly toward Kaya. She wished they were still children. She could kiss him and share her fear. Then he would comfort and tease her, make her feel confident in his bumbling, cheerful way. . She felt her heart melt at the thought of separation. An awful feeling of depression filled her. She gasped and shuddered, rose to run to his arms, but instead checked and stood defiantly staring at him unable to decide what to say or what to do.

As he approached he saw her proud pose, knew she was covering anxiety and proceeded to encourage her.

"You will like Ahjit bey. He will treat you like a daughter. His babies will be like your own corral here in camp. His wife is a city woman and can tell you about everyone in town. She will teach you how they cook, how to dress and how to act. The work is fun and the church is beautiful," he smiled encouragingly.

"Is it true that he is a Chipchak in disgrace, an exile from his band?" She shuddered, looked at him meltingly, tears near, but still with head erect. "Now, I will know the pain of exile and separation." Her breath came raggedly. She moved toward him.

"But not the disgrace, *janum*, my dearest. There is no humiliation in working for the benefit of the band in another place." He drew near, she clung to him, looking over his shoulder. She started to press nearer, but checked herself as a new sound came to her ears.

She whirled away and spoke even more harshly. "*Al-dure-ma*, Never mind! I hear the sound of horses; Ahjit bay is near. Go invite him to come for supper. It is ready now." Excitement swept all the bad feelings away, not to be recalled until some future, lonely night.

>------->

The caravan master sat carefully to one side where the fire did not illumine his face. He had come past the boundary of tribal land and the dangers it offered, but he had come to draw away what he considered their most precious treasure: Yownja, the child with flame for hair. A living remembrance of the woman who had called forth his love and sacrifice. His voice was cool almost brusque. He nursed the drinking bowl of tea and talked about the trips Kaya had missed and of the chaos in the Eastern Lands. He spoke of the growing power of Tedbir in business affairs. The city council was seeking special taxes against the commerce of Jomer. The specialties that he imported were being restricted and licensed for others to handle. Jomer was threatening to move his center elsewhere. Yownja's face bloomed with excitement as she listened.

Kaya spoke little, but listened carefully. He noticed that Ahjit Bey sat between them, and as they worked stayed between him and his sister. He thought he would sleep beyond the wood pile, and not in his accustomed place by her side. The father had quietly claimed his daughter at last.

The departure at dawn was restrained and short. She had petted Altom in a show of affection, but nothing more. The pair rode away and from the distance, Kaya heard their laughter. The taciturn caravan master was displaying his dry humor and good nature. He would win her regard, then her love as she became part of his family. Kaya wondered at the sense of loss, even dread, that filled him as he returned to the tribe for the winter. How would he fill his time?

TEDBIR BEY DEMANDS (Page 195)

PEOPLE, PLACES & PLOTS IN CHAPTER 18

Ah'jit: caravan master and founder of a large family.
Cha-vu'sh; family's oldest boy of ten, good hearted.
Day'day: an old traditionalist of much experience in war.
Er'kan bey: Khan of the Chipchaks, warring on Tartars.
Er'kan: Ahjit bey's seven-year old dreamer and inventor.
Er'tach: son of Kansu bey, impatient to be a warrior.
Few-soon': joins Jomer's enterprises under an old name.
Jo'mer: a rich merchant, helping friends of his heir.
Kan'su bey: a counselor for the Khan, father of Ertach.
Ka'ya: goes to war riding Altom, with Ozkurt as a friend.
Kutch: son of Ke'ke, is not allowed to go to war.
Mer'yen: oldest girl named for Ahjit bey's mother.
On'der: family's youngest child, somewhat spoiled.
Op'tal and Pesh: appear again entertaining in town.
Oz'kurt: a new friend. He is a brave hero to the people.
Shef'ta-lee: a city-girl married to Ah'jit bey.
Ted'bir: an unscrupulous city politician of E'peck Kent.
Tez'lee: a friend of Ozkurt and warrior joining the tribe.
Vash'tie: family's six-year old, a sturdy, quick helper.
Yown'ja: while with the family, Fewsoon uses her baby name.

GLOSSARY HELP:

abacus: a primitive calculator using beads on a wire frame.
ba-rock' ben'ny: leave me; leave me alone; get away.
boo'ran: buran; a blizzard wind whirling snow in great quantities.
hamom: public bath; providing steam, hot & cold water.
ha-mom'ja: any person who works in the public bath.
nee'shan: the engagement ceremony, with feast & gift.
nay'yo?: what's that? what's up? what happened?
nev'ruz: a festival for the spring equinox and new year.
oo'yan kalk: wake up, move; get up.
poor'ga: purga; brings a dry, Arctic-cold from the east, high wind.
Yeet: brave young man; sometimes exaggerated to a he-man or hero.

THE MUSICIANS

"Yownja *gel*, come now. It will be late soon," Sheftalee called. The *hamom*, public bath, was open for women only until 4 o'clock in the afternoon. Soon the crowds of tired, sweaty men would be coming to wash away the grime of the day. At the hour of four, the *hamamja*, the keeper's wife would run through the rooms to make sure all were out before the men were admitted. To exit, those leaving late had to run a gauntlet of gamy smelling men with leering faces and prying eyes. Most of the women would try to leave well before that time, for theirs would be the meals to prepare and the primping and sprucing up as the women dressed for the homecoming of the men.

It was deemed essential that the women look their best for the evening meal. Small children were cleaned and dressed in their best. After all, if a man was laboring all day to support a family, it was important that the ones who ate his bread showed him their best side for his efforts. A man's displeasure could be shown by late hours at the tea house before his return home or even his not coming. Enough families had been abandoned for women to know the cost of negligence and value of loving attention.

Yownja came to the door, her red hair in braids coiled on her head and properly covered by a small pill box hat. She loved the baths with both steam, hot and cold water.

"Here Mother Sheftalee, ready," she proclaimed in her hearty, natural way. She loved her little, bright-eyed companion, whose name meant kiss or, also, the golden fruit of the peach tree. She was a golden-skinned, black-haired beauty.

Outside, a drum played. The children were moving now, straight over to the source of music, the gypsies were there with their bear. The idle, the early and the men who liked to watch women leave, were there smoking water pipes, drinking tea and enjoying the antics of the bear and the children. Sheftalee hated being late; the men were a nuisance and the other distractions even worse. She loved to leave early, but moving Yownja was a problem. The musicians were singing now of a far land of beauty and wealth.

> If you seek for warmth and pleasure,
> Come, come to Hindustan.
> If you long for love and leisure,
> Come, come to Hindustan.
>
> There you'll find great treasure,
> All there in Hindustan.
> There's wisdom without measure,
> All there in Hindustan.
>
> Jewels, spices, fabrics, ooh,
> You will find your heart's dream:
> Cities, beaches, mountains, too!
> There you'll be content.

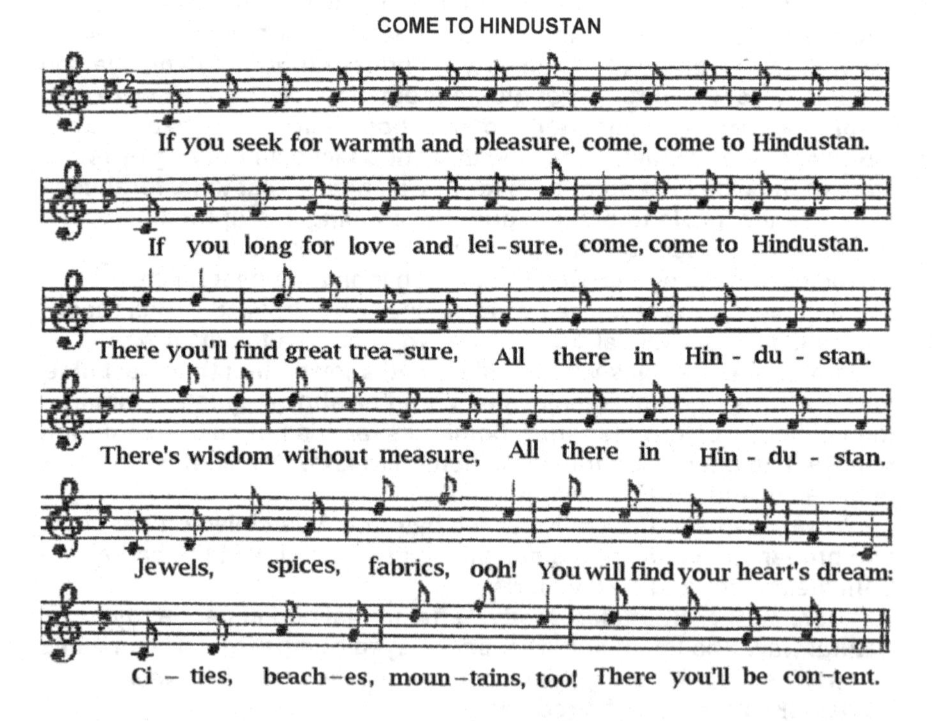

The children were shouting and so did Sheftalee. "Meryen, bring the others and come; we must hurry home." The sturdy twelve-year old grabbed a pair of hands and urged a four-year old boy and a girl of six toward their mother.

Resisting, the boy held out his hand, calling, toward the man who juggled five blocks with a borrowed apple balanced on his head. Pesh laughing, gathered in his blocks only dropping one and, forgetting, bent his head to retrieve it. The fruit dropped and rolled toward the bear, which rapidly moved from the dance to fall protectively over the apple and eat it.

"Mine," shrieked the child in shocked anger, freeing himself from Meryen. He plunged recklessly forward to rescue the apple. "Onder, stop." shouted the frightened girl. The bear master caught the boy before he could fling himself on the animal, which was now finishing the last bits. A sturdy ten-year-old boy moved forward. "I'll take him; he's my brother," he said. "Hush, you were generous to loan the man the apple; let the bear eat it. I'll get you one from the vendor over here." He moved to a stand.

"Chavush, bring him here; there are apples at home," called Sheftalee. "Meryen, bring Vashtie and come, no need to talk." She was flushed and embarrassed at the excitement caused by little Onder. Taking him from Chavush, she carried the screaming child homeward, trying to sooth his indignation with promises.

"He is very determined and strong; thank you for stopping him." Meryen said to the bear master. Fewsoon drew near to stare at the bear, intrigued.

"He means no harm, but like your Onder he is determined and strong," ventured the bear master. He turned to Fewsoon "You are not of the caravan master's family, but have been here over two years now; some say you are a tribal girl..."

"Chipchak from Khan Erkan's band," she announced proudly. "Your bear is tame; I have never seen one so close, though I have watched them in the woods." She held out a plum from a bag she carried. The bear ate it from her hand.

"You like bears then? It seems to be a trait among the Chipchaks. I remember a youth raised by bears." said Pesh, who had put his equipment in a bag and joined the group. At the sight of their young faces, he changed the subject.

"You lovely ladies are invited to a party tonight. Our great patron, Tedbir bey returns from a trip to the great Sassanians." Meryen tittered, looked down shyly.

"No, Mother wouldn't let us." Fewsoon ignored the interruption.

"My brother and breast mate is Kaya whom some call the bear, among other names," she said proudly. "We rode herd together and sang songs and asked riddles to pass the time."

The bear master's smile showed approval, "You sing, do you? Would you sing for us?"

"Listen to a riddle then, and make your guess."

My heart is in my home,
My home is in my yurt.
My yurt moves on wherever,
But my heart stays always home.
My friends share in my heart and home,
Where Yesu rules supreme.
Though you don't know where I will go,
You'll always be welcome there.

MY HOME

The bear master laughed appreciatively and even the bear seemed to approve. He sat up and clapped at the touch of the master's stick.

"Well done, you could join our troop any day."

"Did you know the riddle's answer?" she teased.

"If I were near the sea I'd say a crab or snail, but here I'd be more likely to say a turtle you know tortoise, the land kind. I suppose the Chipchaks would also fit."

"*Dough rue*, right, they all fit. Here's another:"

Although I fly away.
I'll not be gone to stay.
I'll smell the flowers where ever,
And I'll bring home some whatever.
My friends will sing and laugh with me,
For Yesu rules supreme.
Though you don't know where I will go,
You'll always be welcome there.

"A caravan or, ah... honey bees?" guessed the bear master.

"You could even say pigeons. Do you know we carry bee hives and dove cotes with us on our carts when we follow the grass?"

"I had no idea you could move them." Optal confessed.

"I miss Kaya and home sometimes, but my work here is interesting. I work for his patron, the merchant Jomer, at the emporium. I sort for quality and work as scribe," she finished.

"Where did you get such knowledge," Pesh interrupted with a look of astonishment. Meryen's face carried admiration.

Fewsoon laughed at Optal's startled face, only the bear seemed unimpressed. "Kutch, the Khan's son taught us. Kaya and I learned together when they returned from the Hermitage."

"It must have been very hard; some of the students take years at the schools," Pesh spoke reverently.

"They learn other things; I learned writing quicker than Kaya. Girls are better students than boys," she spoke confidently. "I'm teaching Meryen now; girls are smart."

"There are many things to learn at the party tonight; there's a land of dreams and feelings where you can travel at will," Pesh affirmed. "You forget all your troubles and frustrations with the magic substance."

"We have better things to do," Fewsoon concluded, and moved away.

"You know the Apostolos, and the believers here?" asked Optal. "You gather with them on their day?"

"Of course, we are always there," Meryen hastily interposed as they left.

"I too, will be there this year," he resolved.

> - - - - - - - >

The yurt was filled with eager men who were behaving in a boisterous way. They only drank tea, but were acting as if it were stronger. Ozkurt had just returned from a family visit to his hill people with Tezlee in tow, showing off hunting trophies.

Kansu bey, the corporal, had just returned from a trading venture from the Sayan mountains. He was bragging about the exploits of Ertach on a hunt for the snow leopard.

Kaya sat listening to both sets of men as the noise rose. He did not speak of his exploring to the north and west. He'd been beyond the confines of the pasture and woodlands. Between the Irtish and the Ob Rivers, there was a crescent of land, shaded by the high looming Altai Mountains. He had followed the contour of the Chipchak brotherhood's living space, rather than the river and heights recognized as borders of his father's jurisdiction. The people were spreading north and west between the rivers and even south and west over the Irtish River. Both banks of the rivers were now in Chipchak hands with their own local men taking in farther ranges of grazing lands for their horses. However, Tartar raids kept the Western frontiers in constant tension.

Kaya waited until all the sharing of news events had ended and comments made before he spoke up. When he spoke, the entire yurt quieted instantly.

"Bata Khan has increased his count of yurts at Tuzkul, Salt Lake this winter. Now that *Nevruz*, the equinox celebration of the southern people, draws near and the sun returns from the south, we may expect much raiding in the summer. Unless..." His pause produced the expected results. Ozkurt's smile and rapid reply gave answer.

"We strike a preventive blow before they are ready. We'll take them off guard; all their action has been in our land these last few years." Kaya's smile was sincere and appreciative. It was sometimes difficult to initiate action as the youngest member of the Khan's council, but if the sixteen-year-old boy could lead an older member to make the first move it became easier.

Kaya made a gesture to gain the attention of all in the yurt. "If we travel while the ground is frozen hard, strike and return as it thaws, we will have time to select the next attack spot rather than wait for them to surprise us; we take the initiative away from them."

Day'day frowned and objected. "The season of the buran and purga is no time to travel. The increase of the sun's heat fools the unwary and young to expect steady increase of warmth, but the cold freezes all such fools. The winter returns for a week or three days with winds that kill even the trees that explode when the new flow of juices freeze. Such plans are sure to fail."

The ring of faces nodded. They all expected the negative warnings from their prophet of doom; enthusiasm to succeed must survive wise precautions. They had all heard at night, during the artic cold, the popping noise of the trees like logs burning on a bonfire.

Onbasha's deep voice spoke up. "The Tartars think in the same way. They may even be without sentries because winter attacks come after the first freezes, before the cruel short days and the treacherous spring thaws. Day'day gives us the reason to consider this novel innovation. But how do we avoid the results of the storms?" All looked thoughtful and silent.

"The herder's cloak of heavy leather turns the wind and since the fleece is turned toward inside to hold in the warmth; it would seem good to use. But is it enough while the storm blows? A troop needs protection from the wind," said Kansu, the foreign corporal and paused. "The cloak is too short; only a yurt would give the shelter needed."

"If we could make the cloak longer, to c-cover the horse, its heat w-w-would rise to warm the rider," Kutch stuttered hesitantly, conscious of his youth.

Day'day sneered, "Make a tent of man and beast? What of the animals head and eyes? Will he move blind?" he laughed.

Kansu spoke carefully, nodding thoughtfully, "No one moves during the buran. You would have to have a yurt large enough for the horses and men. A circle of horses and the men and hay in the center."

"What of the fire? It can't be near the hay; horses must eat in the killing days of wind," Erkan replied. The problem of fire; the blessing and curse of men, held them in thoughtful silence.

"Braziers, located near the entrance would help, the horses and men produce heat. All would wear their cloaks." Ozkurt ventured thoughtfully.

"One squad, ten men in each Yurt. Four or five horses to carry the equipment. Two horses per man for fast travel." Erkan stated.

"C-Could you g-get 25 horses in a yurt?" asked Kutch, who was not a council member, yet sat with it.

"We don't protect all our herds during the purga. They are free to take refuge in the forest groves or find other windbreaks," Kansu retorted.

"It is in freedom that safety is found, but free of bit and hobble means animals lost and time to find them. You will run out of time," said Ozkurt smiling, "It means a slow deliberate attack, a major offensive with carts and yurts as if against entrenched foe, not a lightning raid and withdrawal."

"To destroy the Tartar's offensive power is to make us safe from all future raids. It would roll back the river frontier by opening the border to Chipchak bands," Kaya's voice held the conviction all wanted to hear. Heads nodded and voice levels rose as men

MOBILE RAPID ATTACK

discussed the particulars of winter warfare with near neighbors. No vote was needed; consensus had arrived.

➢ - - - - - - - >

It was a bright, cold winter day. The array was drawn up before the yurt of Erkan. There the Khan formally presented the yak tail standard to Kansu who was co-leader with Kaya. The battle standard had to be present with the animus: spirit of the tribe. A wolf head topped the tall standard. It rested in the center of the T with the double cross bars dangling two rows of yak tails that hung downward. After that presentation, Erkan called and Kaya came forward to bow before him. Erkan placed an ivory swan medallion, a copy of his own, over his head. Kaya read the sacred words that defined his future role in the tribe. The words, written around the ivory medallion, read: 'The leader decides when and where to descend, for the good of all, in order to feed his flock.' Erkan then administered the memorized oath, learned from the ancestors, and repeated without variation to each new generation of tribal and war leaders, who received the ancient signet.

"Go and be a warrior. Kill the enemy and soon exterminate them from the earth. Take all they possess and make it ours. Leave no sign of them or theirs. Let all be as if they never were. May the powers of the spirits and the earth be yours. Be strong, be brave and overcome." He frowned.

The boy smiled and composed his own reply. "Thank you my Khan. With your authority we will repossess our lands of ancient promise, and enforce peace with our neighbors so that they respect our rights. We will fight all who resist and grant peace and safety to all who will it. Victory is granted to those who obey Tanra. May our cause be always just before Him," Kaya finished smiling happily.

There was a long pregnant pause. The array, assembled from all Chipchak bands, had listened with the care of illiterate men who remember every word and accent. There was much to discuss over camp fires and meals in these two statements. Two world views of war had met, the poles were established. The contrasts were great.

Kutch lacked a year and, also, deeds that might have obtained for him an ivory swan carved from a fossil mammoth tusk, but he went forward and embraced his father. He was now apprenticed to Ozkurt to learn of war. He stammered a bit as he boldly said, "Father, I think we should ask Tanra's b-blessing on our efforts. Many things can go wrong. We need His full approval." Without waiting more than a nod as answer, Kutch lifted his voice and without pause or stutter spoke to all. "May the God of all the earth, who is sensitive to all the intents and actions of men, keep our hearts and minds on His truth and justice, that we may be doers of all that is acceptable and right in His sight. And may the grace and love of our Lord Yesu be with us to bring peace even though it be through war." He smiled beautifically, and it was obvious that the army had a chaplain.

After this the army rode away with packhorses loaded and men wearing long quilted coats to their ankles with sleeves that extended beyond the fingers. Like a southern people going to war, not as raiders out for a quick skirmish and retreat. This group, far from home, would have to stand and fight to protect their base supplies, but surprise would be on their side.

They were fortunate: the weather held nicely and there were only two moderate purgas while they traveled; The enemy was caught completely off guard and routed with little bloodshed. The yurt of Bata Khan was taken with his wives, children and some officials present. Bata Khan was himself with the retreating troops. The army held the ground, not bothering to retreat behind the Irtish River. The Chipchaks concluded a generous peace, Bata, his family restored intact, moved west to the Ishim River as center of his empire. Hakdale bey, not present for the fighting in the East, had acquired land on the Ural River in the mountains. The Chipchak lands had a quiet summer.

Kaya earned a reputation for his calm control and geniality. His golden horse, Altom, was noted for stamina and strength. Ozkurt, gained the name Yeet: hero in battle. Kutch, displayed bravery, piety and dislike of killing. Erkan's subordinate brotherhoods and bands moved out over the Irtish River westward to new grazing.

> - - - - - - - >

The giant form of Tedbir filled the entrance to the emporium. Imperiously, he spoke, his voice filling the room. He knew his authority and used it.

"Where is Jomer Bey? The council has demanded his presence. How dare he delay his appearance?" Fewsoon, dressed in work clothes, baggy pants of wool and on her head, braids, under the green, pill-box hat, answered his impatience with civility as cold as the winter outside.

"*Ney'yo*? What's that? Can't you wait till the man is ready. The messenger just arrived. He was in his work clothes. We are not so rich and foolish that we lounge all day dressed in our best, and drink with `yes' men, and clods lost in opium pipe-dreams. If you will stomp and rage, go outside and leave this place for honest buyers of good products." Several customers stopped to listen.

Tedbir, a man in his forties, looked at the young girl with astonishment. She was just coming into womanhood, but she spoke like a competent adult. Their angry eyes held. A sneer appeared on his face; no mere woman had ever bested him.

"You are the red-haired, saucy one they speak of. You are a shrew, but also, have enriched your master; a shrewd buyer of silk and wool cloth. I know about you. You even read!" he accused, contempt was in his voice. Disdain for all that did not fill the traditional female role of servant and sex object. The cold temperature seemed to drop in the building as several buyers hastily departed for safer grounds. She deliberately turned her back to lift a bolt of material to a shelf behind her.

"I've heard of you also. I suppose you don't read, Councilor bey. Men like you pay secretaries to do your work; factors and caravan masters to do your travels and all your purchases; cooks, servants and entertainers to provide for other needs. Like the rich fool in Yesu's story you are looking to build bigger storage places for your wealth, while you enjoy." She turned. "If you have some need of our stock, I'm free to serve you now," her eyebrows lifted.

The man made a snarling sound like a dog about to attack. His complexion had become a dark red-brown. Fewsoon moved her hand to the small wolf-handled knife she always carried. It was not much for so large and formidable a man, but she kept it razor sharp to use for cutting the cloth. Suddenly, she smiled as a sound came, a door behind her had shut. The man's eyes lifted to look behind her.

She spoke. "You have an escort for your trip to council, Jomer Bey. They know how to honor quality. Don't worry; I'll take care of everything: close up and do the day's accounts on the abacus, ready to look over when you return." Her eyes shone in genuine love and appreciation. "Perhaps you should take another man to insure your safe return when you finish."

> - - - - - - - >

The council finished long after dark fell. Jomer bey was glad he had his man for the torch-lit return to his house behind the dividing fence that separated his sheds and storage buildings from the city residences and stores. Walls kept the envious and inquisitive at a safe distance.

Jomer sighed. He had now as great a love for Yownja, as Ahjit insisted he call her, as he had for Kaya. He had kept her beyond the two years due for her apprenticeship. He sighed again. He had felt the anger of Tedbir all evening long. The problems with the council would no doubt continue.

He directed himself to the house of his caravan master. It was a happy home full of life and fun; good for the heart of a lonely old man. The seven-year old Erkan was playing outside still, until Chavush called him in. Yownja was helping serve the table, bulgur and beef, tonight. He had a standing invitation to join them, and he had dismissed his house servants for the day, when the summons had come.

Yownja was coming into a beautiful maturity, but she had the weakness of all tribal people. They did not know when to fear powerful men outside the tribe. Respectful words might have gotten her by, but he had heard the last exchange at the door. Tedbir did not forgive. She must be sent away, even as Kaya had. It would be very difficult to persuade Ahjit bey. How can one send away a daughter? Ahjit bey will claim the right to defend her and challenge evil – even take on the council. That feud, however, would end in violence, murder, and the loss of his own enterprise -- the inheritance and lives of them all. Everything would be lost: all he had worked for and wanted f or Kaya.

> - - - - - - - >

She returned home in a caravan in the early spring, after more than two years in E'peck Kent. Ahjit bey continued on the Silk Road going west after meeting Kaya and leaving Fewsoon with him at the Steppe Road juncture.

A late storm caught and scattered them on the southern edge of the tribal territory where Fewsoon's horse went lame in the haunted wood, so named for some murdered merchants whose ghosts were thought to be seen there. It was near the spot where she had found her knife. The purga blew the trees over in arches and made progress impossible so they stopped where they had to stop. No fire could be made, but they investigated the rocky rise by the stream covered in brush and small trees to take shelter as they gathered some firewood. Kaya set Altom free to seek shelter behind the hillocks, but the lame one could not walk, and they kept him close.

They lay behind the now prostrate horse trying to garner some warmth together, hugging. They felt the lame, trembling horse die and start to freeze. They were shivering uncontrollably and knew their time was close: exposed, they too, would freeze.

The sound of moans came into the woods with the wind. It was like the voice of the dead merchants and bandits that died in the haunted woods. They were always heard in storms and the moaning was near, almost above them.

Kaya suddenly left her and started crawling forward toward the rock face. A kind of animal trail existed under the brush, and he was blindly following the trail to the rock. Then, his whole body disappeared. Screaming she followed, calling him; pleading for him to wait. She would not die alone, she wanted Kaya.

She was conscious that the wind had stopped, but a moaning sound continued. She was still shivering uncontrollably, but the warmth increased as she crawled forward. It was dark, but warmer. Her feet were still outside the cave when her face touched Kaya's feet. She grabbed him convulsively and pulled herself to her knees. Then she used him to pull herself up to full height. Reaching her hand up, she did not feel the ceiling. Her voice was thin and shaking.

"Are we dead now? Is this the underworld of death and hell? I thought we would go to heaven." Old tribal legends and the new doctrines were confused in her mind. She clung to Kaya, shaking. He seemed in a stupor and was breathing slowly and only a few spasms of trembling passed his body. He started to slump over and her hand found that the cave had an incline to one side, a 45 degree angle; he had backed into it and was now face up on its surface. She knew he had occasionally been torpid in winter, but now he was hibernating.

"*Ou'yan, Kalk*, wake up, get up," She cried, pleading, "help me." She groaned and opened her coat and unbelted his and moved as close as clothes and stiff limbs would permit. From her food bag, she brought out bits of dried horse flesh, feeding it to them both. It revived them somewhat. She saw that a hole near them made the moaning sound with the wind. She pounded his chest and shoulders, trying to rouse him. She succeeded, but not in the way she had expected. Clinging closely to him she felt his body stiffen and a hardness rise in him and press against her, she felt a response in herself. They clung, bundled together all night sharing warmth. A search party from the village, coming the next day after the storm, found them safe.

> - - - - - - - >

She was never sure that he was awake enough to remember. She knew that she was no longer innocent, but still virgin. She was almost a wife, but not quite. Suddenly, she was urgently desirous of that relationship: a new role, a title and recognition as Kaya's wife – to be his own from that time. She would allow no other girl near him. She was jealous even of the old women. At home, Maya, now a widow after the victory over the Tartars, suffered constant criticism, anger and quarrelling.

"*Ba rock benny*, leave me alone." Fewsoon cried. "I know that. I'm grown now. I could have been married two years ago. You don't have to tell me everything and order me around! I could run my own yurt!"

Kaya suffered equally from her jealous demands for his attention, time and affection. She tried to exercise censorship of any dealings with other women. He bore these things with only an occasional growl. Maya, however, went to the Khan to make her complaints and request, and a special council meeting heard and approved. Preparations for *neeshan*, a community feast, were made. Gifts would be exchanged with promises that constituted an engagement and the serious work of accumulation of household goods and building a yurt for marriage could start. Everyone would help because they considered them betrothed. It was a relationship that could last several years and was as binding as marriage itself.

The council decided that Kaya was to ride Altom and take a large herd of prize horses to the east, for the emperor. They would bring a great profit at a time when the three kingdoms of China made war. They were invited to co-ordinate their venture with a huge caravan Jomer bey intended to send to the Kingdom of Wei. Kaya would return next year for a great wedding feast.

Fewsoon passionately refused to allow him to go without her, not for jealousy alone; she was loathe to miss the excitement of a caravan, and the travel experience. The herd would follow the chain of the Altai Mountains and cross the Gobi Desert to China.

The community became very busy in preparations for these exciting events. Plans were made, animals were separated into herds, and drovers selected. Everyone wanted to go. The Khan dispatched messengers and made agreements as to route and passage, for a fee, gaining permission of the tribes. Everybody was occupied with work and happy anticipation. Strangely enough, in all this planning for marriage, no one bothered to consult Kaya.

STAYING WARM

This book, developed as historical fiction, deals with these key questions:

How is a child affected by the events preceding its birth?

Can early environmental handicaps be overcome?

How does family tragedy affect the destiny of a child?

How do family crises shape character?

How does the practice of faith affect a child's life?

Will a stunted child find resources for a prosperous life?

Does music make a difference in childhood responses?

Does personal danger always hinder development?

THE GOLDEN STALLION SERIES:

You have read the first of three: A Child of Promise.

It is followed closely by: A Questing Stranger.

It concludes with: A Hero's Return.